THE WHITE LION

JAMES BARRETT GRUBBS

Paperback ISBN: 979-8-9893022-6-0

Ebook ISBN: 979-8-9893022-5-3

First Edition

For Michele Grubbs

ACKNOWLEDGMENTS

Written and edited by human beings.
Theodora Bryant, Authorshq.com, Developmental Editor

Special Acknowledgments
Ben Marble, Native American History
Karm Bains, Sikh History
Nicholas Sanchez, Pastor Steven Neal, and
Clarice Kirkland for their continued and invaluable advice and counsel

California is a little different.

—Pierre S. "Pete" du Pont, former Delaware governor

Only a Moment

Finished, never done, forgotten memory, passed on.
The *Susan Constant* seeds drift on,
The *White Lion* runs aground; hate drowns.
Hope lives, hides ashore, searching for compassion,
Love joins, time stops, victims atoned, twilight abounds.
A vast and tiny eternal warmth glows,
Prayers fulfilled; oppression emptied.
Prosperity unleashed,
Safe and free, anonymity to be.
It's up to me to succeed.
It's up to me.
Anonymity, at long last, it's up to me.
God, it's finally up to us.
Anonymity and prosperity be.

—James Barrett Grubs

1

December 2037

At 6:00 a.m., after a sleepless night, Tyler Leggett got in his car and drove to the crime scene. He needed a last look around the house before writing his report. He drove up the driveway and parked. Toys were strewn across the lawn, the front door was closed, and yellow police tape blocked the entrance.

He put on a pair of plastic shoe covers, pushed the tape aside, unlocked the door and forced himself to go inside. The entrance rug was covered in blood. He looked left. The hallway leading to the garage was drenched in blood.

He felt a chill. *If I'd been one second later*. He began to sweat, his chest tightened; he felt apprehension, something he'd rarely experienced. *I almost failed them.*

He walked down the short hallway to the home office. A smashed computer monitor lay on the floor, along with scattered office supplies. He looked around to see if there might be anything the police or his agents had missed. He went back to the front door. He wanted to unzip his chest and climb out of his body. He knew he was on the edge of a panic attack.

He stood outside the front door to catch his breath and calm down. It got worse. He relived the moment he shot the psychopathic drug dealer Gloria Gysin to save John Barber.

He looked up at the clear Nevada sky.

I can't do this anymore.

He turned, left the house and got into his car. He went to visit Megan Barber, at the Reno Renown Regional Trauma Center. Megan had survived Gloria Gysin's attack with only a concussion. She was grief-stricken over the likely loss of her husband, now a fugitive from the United States government. He was not wanted for murder, he was being hunted for protecting a discovery that, if told, could destroy humanity.

And, as FBI director, it was now Ty Leggett's job to arrest his best friend for stealing government secrets.

After the hospital visit, Ty drove his government-issued white Taurus to the Reno FBI headquarters. He parked in front of the one-story industrial building, glanced to see himself in the rearview mirror. His brown eyes were bloodshot. He looked every bit his seventy-two years. He got out of the car carrying his blue suit jacket and walked to the main entrance.

FBI Special Agent Doris was standing at the door, watching Ty approach. Doris was shocked by his appearance. She knew what had happened the previous night and how much he cared about the Barber family and the dead agent.

She opened the glass door as he approached. "Good morning, sir. White House Chief of Staff Berg, DOD Secretary Turner, and HHS Secretary Hallett are ready for your eleven-thirty virtual meeting."

"Okay," Ty said.

"Sir, are you okay? I can reschedule the meeting."

"No, I must do this. It comes with the job."

He followed her across the slate-tiled foyer past the vacant security counter, to the door. She swiped her ID card key and opened the door. They walked along the colorless hallway to his temporary office. He entered the room, and Doris closed the door behind him and returned to her office.

Ty stood behind the metal desk for a moment, facing the monitor, and smiled, a technique he used to maintain his composure. His cell phone vibrated in his coat pocket. He removed the black government-issued phone and read: Alabama Senator James Alexander Tubber has stage-four pancreatic cancer.

Ty put the cell phone on the desk and thought about the impact this news would have on the FBI. A member of the Judiciary Committee, Senator Tubber was a friend of the FBI.

Ty looked up at the ceiling and whispered, "What's next?"

He straightened his tie, put on his jacket, sat in the desk chair, and switched on the camera. He saw a group of three people facing him, sitting in the chief of staff's White House office.

"Good afternoon, lady and gentlemen," Ty said.

Chief of Staff Eric Berg said, "We're glad you're okay, Ty."

Ty nodded and said, "Thank you."

"I briefed the president about the deaths at the Barber home and the infiltration of the Genetic Answer facility; he wants a detailed report explaining Professor Gysin's charade and how she and her brother outmaneuvered the background check."

Eric glanced at DOD Secretary Jordan Turner.

"On the positive side," he continued, "this issue did not go public, and GA's anonymity was not violated. On a not-so-positive note, I received Doctor Barber's resignation at four this morning."

"People can only be pushed so far," Ty said.

"Will John stay until we find a replacement?" HHS Secretary Carol Hallett asked.

"No."

She glanced at Eric.

"I'll reach out to Doctor Royer and tell him Barber has resigned and ask him to manage until we select a replacement," Eric said.

"We'll need someone as soon as possible. GA is scheduled to test AI algorithms on the Syntopicon Q1 computing system with the XPLK-99 superconducting material. That test is critical to our gain of function genetic timeline. And that specific material, if it works, is key to reaching room-temperature superconductivity. We must keep Royer focused on that test, and not HR issues," Carol said.

Eric glanced at Secretary Turner. "Jordan and I have several candidates in mind. We'll present them to you and Ty early next week," Eric said.

Carol nodded her head.

"Ty, your preliminary report didn't detail why the Gysin twins attacked the Barber family," Carol asked.

"I haven't fully tied that up. It appears they were working for a German pharmaceutical company and learned that John had made a discovery that would make them very rich. Unfulfilled dreams of psychopaths," Ty said.

"How significant a discovery?" Carol asked.

"Life-altering," Ty answered.

"Is that information at GA?" Jordan asked.

"I don't believe so," Ty said.

"Where is Barber now?" Jordan asked.

"I don't know."

"Ty, you're not being very forthcoming. This is not a Congressional hearing," Eric said.

"It's something only John can answer; his discovery, if made public, could destroy civilization. He risked his family to protect us," Ty said.

"That's not his call," Jordan said.

"I know," Ty replied.

"What's your plan, Ty?" Carol asked.

"That's tricky. The discovery is in his head and right now he's exhausted and alone."

"You know what needs to be done," Jordan said.

"That'll destroy his family," Ty replied.

"The discovery already has," Jordan quipped.

Ty nodded slightly, saddened by the reality.

"Ty, we have no choice—you must find him now. If this goes more than a few days, the President will want to accuse him of killing a government co-worker and he'll use the media to—" Eric said.

"That's extreme," Ty interrupted.

"He'll come in to protect his family," Jordan said.

"His family did not kill the Gysins, he and I did," Ty said.

"Ty, what did he discover?" Carol asked.

"A cure for progeria," Ty said.

"He can control aging?" Carol asked, astonished.

"Yes."

"Wow," Carol whispered.

"He'll sell it," Jordan said in a harsh tone.

Ty stood. "I'll be in DC tomorrow; we can continue this discussion then."

He ended the call, picked up his jacket, and left the building.

He returned to the Trauma Center to say goodbye to Megan before catching his jet back to Washington, DC.

When he entered her room, Megan was lying down, staring out the window. She turned to face him and cried.

Ty sat at her side on the bed and held her hand.

"Dear Lord, the terror of last night," she sobbed.

"How will I live without him? I know he had to run; he

had to. God, everything was perfect. I love him so much." She began to sob. She squeezed Ty's hand. "Ty, you must promise me this will never happen to another family. No more secret labs, no more excuses to kill. The idea of assured mass destruction is insane. Please find a way to stop the madness."

2

Ty Leggett had clerked for Supreme Court Justice Thurgood Marshall in his last year of Georgetown School of Law. He and Justice Marshall became friends—both men loved bourbon and the law. Thurgood would often give Ty advice. His advice was consistent: "Have a plan, look the part, never show emotion, and keep both eyes on your friends."

"Looking the part" came easy for Ty; he loved exercise and nice clothes. The day Ty passed the bar exam; Justice Marshall sent him a simple note: *Join the FBI. Those boys need changing.*

Ty followed Thurgood's advice, joined the FBI and worked at the Bureau for forty-seven years, twenty of those as director. He was the first person of African descent to be appointed director, which gave him great pride.

After almost a year, the FBI's search for John Barber had produced no results. At every meeting with the President, he would ask Ty about the Barber investigation. The pressure on the FBI to find Barber was mounting; the President was losing patience.

On Monday, November 1, 2038, Ty was driving his E-150 Ford truck down Jackson Parkway, listening to Samara Little Joy on the radio. He had an 8:00 a.m. meeting with the President.

"Breaking news" interrupted the music: "President Ralph Rodda announced moments ago he was signing an Executive Order to direct the Department of Defense to create an AI robotic shield around Taiwan. President Rodda said: 'The United States needs this initiative to prevent the Chinese from invading Taiwan.'"

The radio returned to music.

Ty stopped at a light just across from Lafayette Park and glanced to his left at Andrew Jackson's statue and found himself startled to see two women hitting each other with sticks, clearly intent on hurting each other. One was naked.

"Damn, AI robotic shields protecting an island and women fighting just blocks from the White House. We're so screwed. And I can't do a damned thing to stop any of it."

The light turned green, and he drove on to the White House.

The President's frustration with the John Barber situation boiled over on that Monday's GA executive committee meeting. In attendance were the President, HHS Secretary Carol Hallett, DOD Secretary Jordan Turner, FBI Director Ty Leggett, and Chief of Staff Eric Burg.

Forty-five minutes into the meeting, without warning, President Rodda blew up at Ty. "It's been eleven months, and your department has failed to find Barber or uncover his genetic discovery." He leaned slightly forward, his eyes angry. "I'm starting to question your ability to lead the investigation, and I think you're sandbagging the effort. John Barber is a middle-aged scientist, not a Chinese superspy. Find him or turn the investigation over to someone who can," he said.

Ty showed no emotion and made no reply.

The President stared at Ty for several moments, hoping to provoke a response. When none came, Rodda abruptly said, "Meeting adjourned," stood, and left the Oval Office.

Silence.

As the other attendees left the room, Eric walked up to Ty. "Can you spare a moment and join me in my office?" he asked cordially.

"Sure," Ty said.

They entered Eric's office by the Oval Office side door. Eric sat behind his desk and gestured for Ty to sit as well, then opened his bottom desk drawer and removed a bottle of Jack Daniels and two short glasses. He poured a shot into each glass and handed one to Ty.

Eric was fifteen years younger, and both were obsessively detailed and liked a good stiff drink. They had met when Eric joined Ty as a founding member of the FBI's AI Cyber Security Committee. What separated them was Eric's obsession to protect Rodda from stupid self-inflicted wounds. Ty did not like President Rodda and had a case-file full of reasons.

Ty leaned back after taking his first sip of whiskey. His and Eric's cell phones vibrated with the text from *The Washington Post*: "US Senator Tubber dead of cancer." Ty showed no reaction and put his phone back into his coat pocket.

"You got the same text about Tubber?" Eric asked.

"Yes. Sad news; he was a good man."

"Yes, he was, and I'll bet the fight to replace him has already started. But that will come later," Eric said.

Both men took a sip and sat in silence for a moment.

"The President is getting very frustrated about Barber. He feels, as I do, you're not committed to finding him," Eric said.

"That's only half true. The only tactic I've not embraced is accusing John of murder. I have my best agents looking for him. Megan and the children are under twenty-four-hour surveillance, phones, Internet, social media, and the CCTC cameras are being monitored."

Eric smiled. "That's more your way of protecting her and the girls from kidnappers than finding him."

"Maybe, but we *are* looking for him."

Eric shot an understanding grin and took another sip.

"So, what's your plan?" Eric asked.

Ty considered his answer. "I've been here a long time.

The Bureau and following the law have been my sole focus. I have watched the law become co-opted by politics." He took a sip. "I once believed we were the good guys. Today, I'm not so sure. There is always a reason to bend the law, now we're in bed with the Chinese perfecting self-replicating micro-bots. AI creations are being used to manipulate Americans—" He took a sip. "And I can't stop any of them." He smiled. "My plan is to find John *and* protect his secret. At this moment, I don't know how to do either."

"You can't, too many know, and this will not end well. Not wanting to sound like a jerk, maybe it's time you let someone else oversee the manhunt. Step back and refocus your perspective."

"That's not the answer. I have another idea." He smiled, put his drink on the desk, and stood. "Would you schedule a private meeting between me and the President before Thanksgiving? I have some personal business to discuss with him."

"Sure. I'll see what I can do."

"Thanks for the drink and advice. You've always been a straight shooter and friend. Goodnight, Eric."

Ty left Eric's office and walked to his truck. He stopped before opening the door and thought, *I can do this.* He removed his cell phone from his coat pocket and called the Alabama governor.

The Tuesday morning before Thanksgiving, Ty drove his truck down Pennsylvania Avenue toward the White

House. He was running five minutes late for his 8:00 a.m. meeting with the President. He stopped at the rear White House security gate, rolled down the driver's window and smiled at the Secret Service agent as she approached.

Ty flashed his security pass. After a quick glance at the gold badge and blue-and-gold plastic ID, the agent aimed the silver biometric iris scanner at Ty's right eye and activated it. She checked the wand, backed away from the truck with a salute. The gate slowly lifted, and tire spikes sank into the ground.

He pressed the accelerator and drove along the narrow lane through the White House compound toward the back entrance and his parking spot. He opened the door and jumped out.

He moved with the energy of a much younger man. He walked across the fresh-cut grass toward the cobblestone walkway leading to the White House. He hopped over the small hedge that lined the path. The action reminded him of his college track-and-field days.

At 6'2", 190 pounds, with the chest of a gymnast, Ty Leggett looked flawless, as usual, in his custom-tailored dark-blue silk suit. His security badge clipped to his coat pocket bounced as he walked. He maneuvered through the maze of hallways and security posts leading to the Oval Office.

It's impossible to tell if it's day or night in the White House. At every hallway intersection a stoic Secret Service agent stood studying every move, with a hand readied for a fight or salute.

At the last checkpoint he smiled at the Secret Service agent as he passed through the metal detector.

"You look happy, Director Leggett," she said.

"Very," he replied with a broad smile.

Ty checked his Rolex as he reached the mahogany door that guarded the White House's inner sanctum. "I can make it," he whispered.

He opened the door to the Oval Office waiting room. Sitting at her desk was Mrs. Oland, the President's personal assistant. She had met Ty six years ago, while she worked for then-Senator Rodda. She enjoyed his "that's life" outlook on problems.

"Jesus, Ty. I admit you're earlier than normal. But it won't help; you're still late."

Ty quickly passed her desk and pulled the Ovel office door open to step into the most pressurized room in America. He felt relaxed and comfortable.

He looked across the room to see seventy-three-year-old Ralph Rodda sitting behind the handcrafted oak Resolute desk. Rodda had been President for three years and was comfortable in the job. He loved the gossip and the gamesmanship of politics. He enjoyed watching the fallout from his pronouncements. Radda knew how to play the press and use the Presidency to intimidate the media.

He dressed to flaunt his wealth. The silk, hand-tailored shirt, solid gold coin cufflinks, and his pride and joy, a loose-fitting gold Presidential Rolex completed the picture.

Rodda felt humbled every time he entered the Oval Office. He believed Franklin Roosevelt was America's greatest president. As a sign of respect, he wore his suit jacket while in the room.

Rodda glanced at his watch when Ty entered the room.

"You just can't help yourself," he said, shaking his head. "Considering Tubber's death, I'll cut you some slack. Eric told me about your feelings of us accusing Barber of murder; is that why you wanted to meet?"

"No, Mr. President," Ty replied.

Rodda pointed at the chair facing his desk. "Okay, then, please sit. Eric said you had some personal business to discuss. I hope it's not about ending the Barber pursuit. As far as I'm concerned—"

"No, it's not," Ty interrupted. "It's about me and a favor."

Pleasantly taken aback, Rodda put an excited expression on his face, thinking, *Ooh, this could be good,* he leaned back in his swivel chair, and said, "Okay, I'm your hound dog."

"Governor Murphy announced yesterday afternoon that he will select a successor to fill the remaining term of Senator Tubber's seat on Monday, November twenty-ninth. And he will announce the date for the special election sometime after that. Since Tubber passed with two years left on his term, a special election must be called this year. Murphy's appointment will serve in the Senate until the special election is concluded," Ty said.

Rodda's expression was intense; he could hardly wait for the punch line.

"I spoke to Governor Murphy last night and asked him to appoint me to fill that seat."

Rodda looked perplexed and shocked. "This a joke? Are you pulling a prank?"

"No—"

"Ty, that dog don't hunt. You have the best job in

America! Why would you leave to run for public office, and the US Senate, no less."

"I have my reasons."

"Ty, that seat is only good until the special election in 'thirty-nine and the regular election will follow a year later, and Alabama is a Republican state. This is crazy. What are you thinking? Does this have anything to do with the screw-up at GA?"

"No, not at all. Murphy said he'd appoint me if you asked him."

"Ty, son, Pete Murphy and I are hunting buddies. Why would I ask him to appoint you, a DC cop—" He caught himself. "No offense meant, to you or the US Senate?"

"Two reasons, Mr. President. Upon my appointment, I will pick up the crap on my desk and leave for Alabama. Every case file under my control will be destroyed, along with your hunting buddies'. Second, the new director will be your man, with a clean slate."

Rodda smiled but then his tone turned serious. "What in state address do you have?"

"I own my parents' Alabama house."

"Good. When do you plan to announce your departure from the FBI?"

"The day my appointment is publicly confirmed by the governor, and you, Mr. President."

"I'll see what I can do. Oh, what Party—Democrat, right?"

"Independent." Ty stood. "Thank you for your time, Mr. President," he said.

"Ty, please, just a moment. Having a Democrat President and a Republican governor appoint an Independent in Alabama is a terminal, self-inflicted wound."

Ty smiled. "Thank you again, Mr. President."

"Okay, as you will. I'll make the call."

After Ty left, Eric came into the room. "What did Ty want?"

"I always thought Leggett was smart. But the idiot wants to be appointed as the US Senator from Alabama."

"What?" Eric exclaimed, snapping the T sound.

"Yep, as an Independent, of all things."

Eric's eyebrows shot up. "This is nuts. He's too smart. He's got to have a plan. Why—?"

"He didn't say, and I'm going to make it happen."

"Mr. President, Alabama is a supermajority Republican state. Our party will come unglued if we're involved."

"Yes, and that's why I'm going to make sure everyone knows I support a black man for Alabama's United States Senate. This will be a win for us; Leggett will get his ass kicked in the special. Murphy could get burned, and maybe we pick up a Senate seat." He put a big smile on his face. "Perfect."

On December 1, 2038, Ty's appointment by the governor of Alabama to the United States Senate was official. He was now a member of the most exclusive club in the world.

Ty was the first Black man to be a United States Senator from Alabama.

On first day on the job, Ty felt uneasy as he drove his truck toward the United States Capitol Building. He had an 11:00 a.m. meeting with the Senate Majority Leader's chief of staff to learn the location of his legislative office, his committee assignments and protocol responsibilities.

He stopped at the side entrance to the underground Capitol parking garage; he had used this entrance for decades, yet this time it felt very different.

A Capitol police officer walked up to the Ford truck. "Good morning, Senator Leggett. ID please." Ty handed him his security pass. With that, the guard pressed the remote in his hand and the gate lifted.

Ty felt uncomfortable; in the past, he'd known where to park; now he had to look for his assigned spot. This day would be filled with firsts: finding his office in the Hart Building, meeting his legislative staff, attending committee assignments, and walking onto the Senate Chambers as a member of the United States Senate.

As an appointed senator he would start at the bottom. Washington, DC, and most critically, the Senate, was organized by seniority; not experience, wealth, intelligence, or fame, just time in the job. The longer one served in office, the more power and perks one received. Office location, its size, number of staff, committee assignments, and most importantly, committee chairmanships were all based on seniority.

At seventy-two, Ty would never chair a Congressional committee or, for that matter, have the best parking spot. As FBI Director, that once mattered. Only the President's

Chief of Staff had a better parking spot next to the White House.

Ty no longer cared about power or prestige, which was why he'd left the FBI. He was aiming much higher—he wanted to fulfill his promise to Megan. Hopefully, after he won the special election, that would come. For now, he had to learn how the place worked from the inside and win the Alabama special election.

Ty passed through the lift gate into the underground garage and followed the driveway to the valet parking area. A young woman approached the car. Ty rolled down the window and, as the attendant reached for the door handle, he said, "Please point me to my assigned spot. I'll park it."

With a puzzled look, she said, "Number one hundred. Are you sure you don't want me to park it?"

"Thank you, I got it," he said with a smile.

He found his spot, number 100, in the darkest corner of the garage. Before leaving the truck, he sat for a moment. *This is humbling: Number 100, and I'm old.... How do I foster hope and create change?* He smiled. *The crap on my desk.*

He opened the truck door and walked across the garage back to the main elevator. He rode to the second floor and the Senate Majority Leader's office. He walked down the over-polished slate-covered hallway to the ornate, dark-stained and perfectly varnished wooden doors enclosing the plush offices of the second most powerful person in Congress.

Ty pulled the heavy door open and walked into the room, as he had done many times. This time felt very different.

A young-looking intern glanced up at him and said, "Good morning, Senator Leggett. The Majority Leader's chief of staff was called into a meeting with Senator Billings and will not have time to see you today."

She picked up a manila folder and handed it to Ty, saying, "Enclosed are your committee assignments, Hart Building office location, times, and dates for your sexual harassment prevention classes." She paused and looked past Ty as someone entered the room, "Your legislative calendar and protocol assignments are also enclosed."

She smiled.

"As an Independent interim appointee, you will not be invited to Majority Caucus meetings. You should reach out to the Minority Party and see if you can attend their caucus meeting." She smiled. "The Majority leader asked me to welcome you and say he looks forward to seeing you this afternoon on the Senate floor. Good day, Senator Leggett."

He felt dismissed and insulted. He left the Capitol Building and walked across the street to the Hart Building, where he rode the elevator to the fifth floor to find his legislative office. He walked along the hallway reading the door numbers.

He reached his assigned room, turned the doorknob, and tried to push the door open. It would only move a few inches; he peeked in to see a box blocking the door. He pushed harder.

Once inside, he looked around the ten-by-ten-foot room packed with filled boxes. The only desk, near the back wall, was covered by folders and legislative books. He could barely see a young woman sitting behind the desk.

"Wow, are we coming or going?" he asked with a laugh.

The college age–looking women looked up with surprise and jumped to her feet. "Senator Leggett, y-you're here," she stammered.

Ty walked to her and offered her his hand. "Please call me Ty," he said.

"My name is Jannett Winter. I am your office manager. The chief of staff and the rest of the team are at the old office picking up boxes."

"Okay, that answered my question, we're moving in."

"Yes. Yesterday we received our new location and all but four of us were reassigned to another senator's office."

"Don't miss a beat, do they?"

"Normally things move very slowly," Jannett said.

"I'll check out my office. Please ask our chief of staff to schedule a staff meeting as soon as she's comfortable."

Ty stepped around several boxes and opened the door into his office and was surprised. "Wow, it's ready to go." He looked back at Jannett.

"Yes, we did it first. We wanted you to feel comfortable."

"That was very thoughtful."

An hour later, Ty's office intercom buzzed. "Senator, the chief of staff along with everyone else are here. If you're available, we can have a staff meeting," Jannett said.

Ty opened his office door to see four people standing before him. He smiled and approached them. "Hello," he said, shaking each person's hand.

"I'm Carol Mary, your chief of staff," the first person said.

"I'm Vickie Herd, your legislative assistant."

"I'm Jay Miller, your communications director."

After introductions, Ty looked at Jannett. "And you're the office boss," he said with a grin.

She giggled.

"This is going to be the quickest staff meeting in your lives. We only have a few weeks before the end of the legislative session, and because I'm an appointee, there is not much for us to accomplish."

He looked around the room.

"Thank you for setting up my office and making me feel welcome. I do. My short-term plan is to stay in DC through Christmas in the hope of facing next year's legislative session prepared. While I'm in DC, please schedule constituent and/ or lobbyist meetings. Also try to arrange a meeting with the majority leader. I want to talk about several legislative proposals. Lastly, I am very sorry for your loss of Senator Tubber. He was a great person. I hope you will accept my naiveté and lack of senatorial experience and guide me to a successful legislative career." He smiled. "I look forward to building our team into a family."

The Senate recessed for Christmas and Ty Leggett's brief tenure in the US Senate ended with little notice. Some of his colleagues liked Ty's affable and quiet personality. Others thought he acted like an arrogant cop and resented his appointment to the United States Senate.

That message was delivered loud and clear the third week of the January 2039 legislative session while Ty was on the Senate floor. At the end of the session, Ty walked up to his longtime friend, Senate Majority Whip Terry Joseph. "Terry, my staff is having a difficult time scheduling a meeting with Senator Timmons to discuss my legislative assignments. Is there a problem?"

"No. You're an Independent, interim appointment with no future. Go back to Alabama, win the special election, then Timmons and everyone around here will be your best friends."

Ty smiled and turned to leave.

"Ty, wait. Don't expect any help from your old friends in law enforcement or the DC consulting class. You're on your own. It's nothing personal; it's just how things work. The President screwed you by being so vocal, telling everyone how close the two of you worked and what a great friend you are. No one on my side trusts you. Go to Montgomery, reach out to State Senator Hugh Peterson—he's a good friend—and win the special election."

3
THE DEAL

February 2039

Seventy-four-year-old Alabama State Senator Jeffery Ullman strode down a long, over-polished, linoleum hallway. His clenched jaw and his weathered face radiated anger. His brown eyes narrowed as he reached the ornate entrance to State Senate Majority Leader James Jacobs's office.

Senator Jeffery Ullman looked every bit the cowboy, at 6'3", 175 pounds. He dressed in worn blue jeans, Western riding boots, oversized silver belt buckle and a felt Stetson hat. All he lacked to complete the image was a horse.

Jeffery had been in the legislature for twenty-five years and built a persona of a cowboy. The truth was he could not spell horse, no less ride one. He was born in Gadsden, Alabama, along the Coosa River. Silver-spoon rich, he had never worked a job in his life.

He grabbed the gold-plated door handle with his right hand and pulled, intending to rip the door off its hinges. To his surprise, the door hardly moved, and he almost knocked his forehead against it when his body jerked forward.

"Damn it," he growled through clenched teeth. He collected himself, grabbed the door handle with both hands, pulled hard and the door jerked open. He entered the reception area as the door slammed against the hallway wall, making a cracking sound.

The room was the size of a modest living room, and a rich blue, gold, and red rug covered the center of the marble floor. A nine-foot-long leather couch lined one wall, and two ten-foot-high, French doors faced Washington Avenue and the Liberty Bell replica.

Across from the entrance, behind the reception desk were two floor-to-ceiling, mahogany doors leading to the majority leader's office.

Senator Ullman glared at the young woman sitting at the 1920s English Tudor chestnut library desk, daring her to say a word.

He strutted past her toward the Majority Leader's office. He grabbed the brass doorknob with both hands, pulled the door open with a whooshing sound. Using his best cowboy swagger, he strutted into the room.

Sitting at his desk was fifty-year-old State Senator Jim Jacobs, a failed Northern Alabama fertilizer salesperson.

Jim Jacobs had been the upset winner in his race for the state senate two years earlier. He had just been selected President Pro Tempore.

Alabama followed the legislative protocol that the lieutenant governor was the President of the Senate, but the real power lay in the hands of the President Pro Tem.

At 6'2" with his boots on, he had the look of a wealthy

rancher, something he was not. He was married, with two high school students at home. He did not have a dime to call his own. It was his wife's wealth that kept everything going.

"You screwed me," Ullman hissed through clenched teeth as the door closed.

"That's not true, Senator, and I resent you barging into my office," Jim Jacobs said as he lifted his legs off the new, maple executive desk.

"I don't give a damn what you resent. You cut a deal and slit my throat," Jeffery yelled, standing within inches of the desk.

"You told me you had no intention of running for reelection."

"That's not true."

"Yes, it is. The courts screwed you, not me. You know Alabama lost population and with the redistricting we had to give up a seat. The courts ordered we create two Black Congressional districts."

"You're doing it a year early and you *chose* me to fuck."

"You told us you weren't going to run, and I needed a seat. That's the end of it; the governor has moved on."

"I haven't, and I want you to fix this right *now*. Get me my district back!" Jeffery yelled.

"No, I can't. It's over. We're dealing with Tyler Leggett's appointment to the US Senate. Murphy screwed all of us by that stupid appointment. We're meeting this afternoon, as a matter of fact, to strategize our options."

"I want my seat back and you damn well better find a way. I don't care one hoot about that Northern DC cop." His face growing redder by the moment. "I'm telling you right now, if you don't fix this, and in one quick hurry, I'll fuck you up," he said, shaking with rage.

Jim leaned forward in his chair, looked Jeffery straight in the eyes and asked in a cold, sarcastic tone, "With what?"

For a moment, the two men stared at each other. Jeffery, trembling, slammed his right fist on the table and stormed out.

With Ullman gone, Jim stood up from his high-back, leather chair and walked across the room to the leather couch that faced the French doors that opened out toward the Capitol gardens. He sat, leaned back, put his feet on the Marbella and Lyon coffee table. He picked up the gold-plated telephone and called Governor Pete Murphy's private line.

Sitting behind his Capitol desk, the governor picked up the phone. "Murphy."

"Jacobs here. May I come by your office this afternoon at two-thirty?"

Pete glanced at his desk calendar. "Yes. What's the topic?"

"Leggett."

"Okay."

"Thank you, Governor; see you then."

Jim returned the phone to its cradle, leaned back against the couch's cushions and pressed his head back against a silk throw pillow.

He crossed his legs, with his boot heels resting on top of the lacquered coffee table. He chanced a glance at his feet and noticed his right boot toe was scuffed. He sat up, put his right foot on his knee, spit on his index finger and rubbed the scuffmark. There was a gentle knock at the door.

"Yes," Jim called out.

The door opened and his political consultant and Chief of Staff Anne Spenser Gray walked in. The door gently closed behind her; she crossed the room with a smile while Jim rubbed his boot.

She sat on the edge of the coffee table, facing him, leaned forward with her elbows on her knees, and said in a whisper, "I heard Senator Ullman is a little pissed-off."

Jim paid no attention; he continued to frantically rub the toe of his boot.

She stared at him with a concerned look. "He's meeting at this moment with the minority leader. So, what happened?"

Thirty-five-year-old Anne Gray, 5'8", light-brown hair, and a figure most women pay for, had worked in politics for ten years. She possessed a strategic mind and was a trailblazer. Anne was the first woman to manage a statewide political campaign, when most women were overseeing fundraising events.

Anne was at the top of her game. She knew how to survive the political backbiting and make money in the off-campaign years. Her position as Jacobs's chief of staff was temporary, by design. "Familiarity breeds contempt," she would often say to friends and colleagues.

Anne also knew how to play men and her opponents. She had married into one of Alabama's wealthiest banking families and produced the first male heir. She did not need anyone or anything. Anne loved politics and her wide eyes showed it at every political meeting or function. The only thing she could not find was true love.

"So, tell me, what happened with Ullman?" she asked.

Finished with his boot, Jim put his foot down on the carpet and looked up. "Nothing I didn't expect. His act as an awe-gee-whiz cowboy is running thin, he's all hat and . . . bullshit."

Anne nodded. "So why is he meeting with Senator Roberts?"

"I'd bet he's trying to cut a deal to save his seat. He's a lame duck and will be a goner after the next general election."

Jim glanced toward his desk.

"Can you believe that senile bastard accused me of lying?" he said with a crooked smile. "Anyway, Dave, is done with reapportionment too; all he's thinking about is Leggett's appointment and how to handle that special election. Unless Ullman can figure out how to screw Leggett and the governor, Dave will slap the goat on the back and promise him bull."

"Leggett's run is important to us. My surveys show having a DC Independent running for U.S. Senate hurts Murphy. If we're smart, you could be the next governor, and Senate Majority Leader Simmons becomes irrelevant."

"Leggett can't win," Jim said as he gently touched her hand.

"Jim, we don't care if he does or not. We just want everyone in the state to follow that campaign and know Murphy is responsible," she said.

The side table telephone buzzed, surprising them and breaking the moment.

Jim hesitated, not wanting to answer, but he picked it up. "Yes, Linda, what is it?" he asked with a gruff voice.

"It's your wife, Senator. She says it's important."

Jim sighed.

Sitting behind his Wesley desk in the Alabama State Capitol Democrat Minority Leader, sixty-year-old, Senator David Roberts sat facing a panicked Jeffery Ullman.

State Senator Roberts entered politics twenty years earlier as an aide to the State Senator from Mobile. He won the seat when his boss retired.

Of Italian descent, with the personality to match, he was popular with his peers, unless you were a rival. His sharp mind and political gamesmanship kept the opposition on guard. David sat listening unemotionally to Ullman's rant.

"I've always played ball. You can't let this happen," Jeffery said.

"There's nothing I can do. We have a deal. The redistricting is set, and a year early, I might add. Your leadership negotiated with us for six months. I'm sorry, there's nothing I can do." He looked sympathetic. "Jacobs and Murphy make the rules, not me."

"We've been friends for thirty years; you've got to help. I don't want to go out like this, just disappear," Jeffery said, pleading.

"You should have thought about that before dumping eighty grand against Rosa. It's against tradition to go after a fellow senator—the Dean of the Senate—at that. The old guy didn't deserve to get beaten by a thirty-two-year-old missionary." Roberts stopped speaking for a moment to control his growing anger.

"To sneak up on him like they did was a lousy cheap shot. So, don't talk to me about fair. Rosa did more than anyone for public education and to be beaten by a know-nothing punk Mormon." Roberts leaned back and slowly shook his head in disgust.

"I had nothing to do with that campaign. I didn't give a dime," Jeffery said.

"And to find out that Hugh Peterson, your former Senate chairman was behind it, really pisses me off."

"Hold on. No one hates Peterson more than I do. He's a gun—"

"Forget it," Roberts interrupted, "I know all about Peterson and his PACs."

"Dave, he used his own campaign money and team. No one knew until after the election what he'd done. Rosa and I were seatmates. You know what a bastard Peterson is. For Christ's sake, he's a former Birch Society member."

"That doesn't change a thing. Someone's got to pay for violating the code. Anyway, we tried every deal possible to save your seat, but your leadership said no."

David turned his head and looked way. "Come to think of it, if you really want to stay in office, why don't you run against Leggett in the primary? You'd make a tremendous US Senator; I think you could beat him. He has no money or name ID."

"He's running as an Independent and automatically makes it into the special. I don't have the money or thirty-five percent statewide name ID to beat him. My only chance would be with the Republican Senate and governor backing me, and that's not going to happen."

David smiled, leaned back in his chair and said in a matter-of-fact tone, "So why not change parties?"

"What? Come on, Dave, I wouldn't stand a chance as a Democrat."

"I didn't say join us. Run as an Independent?" He stopped speaking, letting the thought sink in.

"Leave my party?" Jeffery whispered.

"If you agree to my terms, you'll have unlimited money and it'll just be basically you and Leggett in the special election—I guarantee it."

David leaned forward, and said in a soft, friendly voice, "Jeffery, this can work. You'd split Leggett's liberal votes and pick up most, if not all, your old Republican votes. There's no way Leggett can beat you." Roberts leaned back in his chair and waited.

Ullman pressed back in his chair. They sat in silence for what seemed like minutes.

Roberts looked disinterested; even though his heart was racing with excitement. *What a great poker hand*, Roberts thought. *This is perfect. Before the election, Ullman will vote with my caucus, we beat Leggett. And the cherry, I'll send a message to that pompous-ass president to stay out of Alabama politics.*

State Senate Democrat Minority Leader David Roberts had made a career of cutting the perfect win-win deals and he dreamed of the power of controlling Alabama.

Even though he was seventy-five pounds overweight, there was nothing lazy about his mind. Roberts was thrilled by the prospect of the deal. Roberts wanted to jump to his feet and scream, "Take the damn deal!" He truly believed Ullman running as an Independent would win against Leggett.

Ullman abruptly stood to leave. When he reached the door, he turned to face Roberts, who was still sitting, and said, "I've been a conservative for over sixty years. I don't know if I can leave her." That said, State Senator Jeffery Ullman turned and left the room.

Later that day, Alabama Republican State Senator Hugh Peterson was sitting in his senate office reading a committee hearing deposition when the intercom sounded. He answered it and heard, "US Senator Terry Joseph is on the Capitol line."

Hugh smiled; they were solid friends. Peterson picked up the black handheld telephone. "There must be a problem; you've been dumped as Majority Whip, or do we have a fishing date?"

"All is good, and we can't go fishing until early July."

"Too bad on the fishing. What's up?"

"The screw job is in on Leggett's run for the US Senate. The president and the majority leader just cut a deal to stay out and make it an all-Alabama affair. His start-up campaign money must come from us along with our special interest friends."

"Me? Hold on there, everything you've said sounds like

regular DC BS. So why call me? He's an Independent running in a Republican state for a federal office."

"Ty was a great FBI director, no games, no inside baseball or favorites. He put a massive dent in Washington corruption. Which is why the establishment's glad he's gone and they don't want him back," Terry said.

"Again, sounds like a *you* problem. I *did* like what he did against the Klan. It was about time. He should have run as a Rep; at least he'd have a chance."

"That boat has sailed."

"Sounds like a fatal, self-inflicted, wound."

"I'm not sure a Black Republican could win an Alabama statewide race," Terry said.

"A hell of a better chance than an Independent."

"Think about it: As an Independent, he splits everyone's vote and since Murphy appointed him, no Republican would dare run. The Dems will have a tough sell against a Black home-grown candidate," Terry said.

Peterson sighed. "It's too complicated."

"Hugh, he's our kind of person. He sends money to his ninety-year-old parents and visits them twice a year and has done so for over forty-five years. His only other family is an ex-wife who lives in Maryland, and she likes him."

"Well, he should have stayed with her," Hugh said with a laugh in his voice, "and the FBI."

"The country will be better off with him in the Senate."

"Again, why not a Republican?" Hugh asked.

"Come on, Hugh, there's only one Black Alabama Republican and he's in the lower house."

"How's he on guns?"

"You know the answer; like everyone in law enforcement, love/hate."

"NRA?"

"He pays dues and is a good shot."

"Come on, Terry. I can't help."

"He grew up dirt poor. Came to Washington with nothing, earned a scholarship to college and law school. He passed the bar on the first try, clerked for Marshall, and beat the Ivy mafia to head the FBI."

Terry paused.

"Helping him will be the best thing we've ever done. He's the ultimate underdog. Everyone around here will be against him. My bet is the local Dems will fight him. Our Party doesn't trust him because the president appointed him. It's him against the world."

Hugh sighed.

"He's the real deal. Someone you'd take fishing, have dinner and talk baseball with."

Silence.

"A DC Independent. Why the hell would I do this?"

"Because you've done it before."

Hugh sighed. "Does he hunt?"

"The truth, crooks and fish."

Silence.

"Helping him will be a mistake," Hugh whispered.

"Here's a little fact: The last high school desegregated was in Mississippi in twenty thirteen. You sit in a legislature that is obscenely segregated. There's never been an elected Black US Senator from Alabama. He's earned the right to be first. And us helping him is the right thing to do. Please talk to him."

Silence.

"All right. I'll meet him," he said.

Hugh Peterson was a former advertising executive, an avid game hunter and a nationally recognized conservative. He was gruff, strong-willed and hated by political elitists. He did not play games or compromise principle; he was honest.

A Senate colleague once accused Peterson of being unfaithful, and Peterson challenged the senator to a fist-fight. Peterson won, and the other Senator publicly apologized for the "misunderstanding."

When a lobbyist offered Peterson a bribe. He walked down to the Senate floor and announced what had just happened; the lobbyist was fired, and Peterson's honesty was never challenged again.

He would tell his staff and family, "A bribe was like a small fishhook caught in your skin and you could count on it being tugged when needed."

Peterson was in his mid-60s, 5'10", heavyset, and partially deaf from shooting too many ducks. His first and only true love was his wife and family.

His mission as a politician was to elect conservatives to public office who loved the outdoors. When he was first elected, he formed a political advertising company. Built a team of thirty-year-olds to manage his political action committees (PAC), run campaigns, and raise lots of money.

To quote a former Alabama governor, "In Alabama, you keep one eye on God and the other on Peterson."

He was a man they loved to hate.

4

On Thursday, February 14, 2039, Ty parked his car on the street and walked up the Alabama Capitol marble staircase to the main entrance and rode the elevator to the second floor. The elevator door opened and before him was the entrance to the governor's office. He crossed the polished hallway and walked into an ornate, twenty-by-twenty-foot reception area.

The room was busy with people milling about. There were two small groups of people crowded around the ten-foot-long, dark pine reception desk, trying to schedule an appointment with the governor.

After they left the room, Ty stepped up to the desk.

"Senator Leggett, what a pleasure," the middle-aged receptionist said. "The governor is expecting you. Please follow me."

The man stood and led Ty toward two ten-by-five-foot pine doors at the back of the reception room. He pushed a white button on the door handle and the door popped open.

A state trooper, wearing a flak jacket and sidearm, stepped out, blocking the doorway. "ID," she said in an intimidating tone.

Ty smiled, removed his wallet from his coat pocket, flipped it open and presented his driver's license.

"Please remove it from the wallet," she said.

Ty did and handed it to her.

She took the plastic driver's license and swiped it through a reader by the door. She handed it back. "Welcome to Alabama, Senator Leggett. Please proceed to the doors behind me and the governor's chief of staff will escort you to the governor's office."

Ty looked over at the doors and saw a middle-aged, gray-haired woman standing by the ten-foot-tall, mahogany doors.

"Welcome, Senator Leggett," she said. She started to pull the door open.

"May I get that?" Ty asked.

"Of course, if you'd like."

"Many people have opened doors for me. I like to return the favor."

Ty pulled the right-side door open. Once inside, she stopped and looked at him. "The governor will be right with you. Please make yourself comfortable." She turned and left the room, closing the door behind her.

Ty looked around the room, which felt cold and lacked personality. *This room must be ceremonial,* he thought. He glanced around the twenty-by-twenty-foot room. The plush crimson-and-white wall-to-wall carpet looked new, with the State Seal embossed in the center. He admired the two antique wooden chairs faced a cherry desk. Two ten-foot-high French doors draped by a red velvet curtain faced the north wall. *Wow, this is gaudy,* he thought.

The side door on the south wall opened, and Governor Peter Murphy appeared, smiling, presenting a warm welcome.

"Ty Leggett, Senator Ty Leggett, how wonderful of you to visit. I am so glad to personally meet you," he said almost running across the room. Ty reached out to shake hands, and Murphy placed his left hand on Ty's left elbow and gripped Ty's right hand.

Ty smiled and thought, *All the tricks with a strong handshake.*

"Please, come sit." He pointed at the chairs facing his desk.

Ty sat and instantly jumped to his feet. He knew the game: Power play. The front legs of the chair were cut an inch shorter than the back legs, forcing the occupant to lean forward. The seat was also extra soft. At 6'2", Ty would almost be at eye level with the desktop if he remained seated.

Murphy grinned when Ty stood. "Not too comfortable, is it? I've tried to fix it. Let's move to the sitting area." He pointed across the room.

Now it was Ty's turn to gain the advantage; he sat in the only chair that faced the couch. Without missing a beat, Murphy smiled. "Would you like a drink, Ty?" He pointed to the small wet bar to his left, which was lined with crystal glasses and half-empty whiskey bottles.

"No, thank you," Ty said.

Alabama Governor Pete Murphy was part of the Alabama Antebellum Club. At 66 years of age, he was still obsessed with politics. His ambition was to stay in public office for life. His goal was to take care of his friends and leave a legacy of developed infrastructure. At 5'10", thin, with a perpetual happy face, he was anything but intimidating. He was at his best making friends and remembering everything they said. He was decisive in a crisis and a good governor.

He was also greedy—which was why Ty had been appointed to the U.S. Senate: Ty knew the man's secrets and had kept a dossier full of his mistakes.

"Senator Leggett. Your visit is a little early. I haven't announced the special election dates, so the potential candidates have not registered." He studied Ty's face. "It's a long way home for someone who's made it good, and you made it good." He smiled. "What's your plan?" he asked.

"To win the seat."

"You understand a black person from Alabama has never won a US Senate seat, or for that matter, run before?"

"Yes, and no black person had ever been the director of the FBI." Ty smiled. "Before me."

"Well, I'm on the hook. What church do you attend?"

"That's open."

"Cute, but you're in Alabama, and people here really don't care what church, they just want to know you go. So, I'd pick one. The largest and most prominent is the Sixteenth Street Baptist Church in Birmingham." He smiled. "Where were you born?"

"Macon County."

"High school?"

That question had only one purpose: to discover if Ty's family had money. Public school versus private.

"Tuskegee Institute, class of 'eighty-three."

"That's impressive, a Fighting Frog. You must come from a great family."

"They are," Ty said.

"Do you have a campaign team?"

"No."

"Well, Senator Leggett, you have a lot of work ahead. An Independent running in a Republican state will be tough. The state legislature is fifty-three Republicans, thirty-five Dems. There are seven Congressional districts, all but one are Republican. There are less than a million blacks in a state of five million. Why are you an Independent?"

"I know I'm an underdog; it's not the first or the last time. I'm good with numbers, Governor. I'd lose in the Republican primary to a local politician, and I'd lose as a Democrat in the special election. As an Independent, I have an advantage over the club. I can do this," Ty said, relaxed and smiling.

"I like your thinking. Since this is your first time, I'll give you some campaign advice: Never respond to any attack; you don't want two headlines. Campaigns are all about organization, BS, and money. To win, you must have a lot of all three."

He raised an eyebrow to make the point.

"Speaking from experience, I can see you're not ready. It's the middle of February, and you'll need every extra day to compete. To help, I'll call the special election primary for June eighth, the special election to follow November eighth. That'll give you time to get your act straight." He rubbed his jaw, clearly thinking.

"Being the incumbent will help. Be careful, upsets happen; ask Roy Moore, he thought he had it in the bag in twenty seventeen. Nope." He smiled. "You'll need sixteen million dollars for the special election; the other side will spend fifty million. A good campaign team should overcome their spending and if your campaign strategy is correct, you'll win."

Murphy glanced at his gold Presidential Rolex. "Sorry, to say, we're out of time. I've got another meeting, as it turns out, to discuss your campaign with a couple members of the Democratic caucus. It seems they're still upset by your appointment."

He stood, as did Ty.

"Senator Leggett, if you need something specific, call. Normally, I'd join your meetings with the senate's President Pro Tem and his leadership team. Not this time. He's also a little pissed at me for your appointment. So, you get to go it alone." He put a broad smile on his face. "My daddy taught me long ago, don't stir cold shit, it stinks all over again. Good luck, Ty. It was a pleasure to meet you."

Ty left the room, thinking, *Man, I am such an underdog. But—I can do this.*

Ty left his meeting with the governor and walked down the marble staircase to the ground floor. He had an hour before his next meeting with Alabama's true power broker in the senate: President Pro Tempore James Jacobs.

Ty knew exactly where he had to go next. He left the Capitol Building and drove several minutes to the Legacy Barbershop. He parked in front of the storefront salon. The name of the shop was stenciled on the front window. Ty smiled at the sight, his father once cut hair and shined shoes to make extra money.

A throwback from another age, he thought as he stepped into the shop.

There were four new-looking barber chairs and matching hair-washing sinks lining the east wall. Mirrors covered the walls, along with Alabama sports memorabilia. Barber combs and haircutting supplies lined the small shelf running above the sinks. The room carried the gentle fragrance of talcum, Barbicide, and aftershave cologne.

I love that smell, Ty thought. "Hello," he said to a hunched-over, wiry man standing by an empty chair in the center of the room.

"Hello, Senator Leggett," he replied.

Ty was taken aback. "You know who I am?" he asked, surprised.

"Every brother knows you, and what you tryin' to do."

"May I sit, and we talk?"

"Sure, brother, but you still gonna get a trim."

Ty smiled. He knew this was the place to come if he wanted to learn what was really going on in the Capitol.

Ty took off his coat, loosened his tie, unbuttoned his dress shirt and sat.

"What's your name?" Ty asked.

"Darrel, sir."

"Please call me Ty."

Darrel smiled and nodded, rolled down Ty's shirt collar, and covered his shoulders and pants with a clean, white barber's cape. He wrapped Ty's neck with a thin, fresh cloth neck strap and clipped everything together with a sliver clasp.

"So, what have you heard about me and my appointment to the Senate?"

"You a good man. Like Thurgood, you trying to make things right. But the fix is in, nobody in this place wants you to win. Especially the suits, some of them want revenge for what the FBI did breaking that Northern Klan network and arresting their boss men."

"Everybody?"

"Not the regular brothers, of course, but the elected ones can't be trusted." He paused, looked around, the store was empty, he still lowered his voice. "That politics crap gets in the way. Like a preacher, they after money or fame."

Ty smiled and nodded slowly. "Who do you trust?"

Darrel laughed out loud. "You been in Washington too long. I don't even trust my wife." He laughed. "And we been married sixty years."

Ty laughed.

"There be one. Senator Peterson. He don't want people to know, but he comes by here, he's still a cracker. I asked for help once and he did and I'm not the only one. There's a brother, Jeremiah Damon, he's the only Black Republican in the whole damn place and he has FBI cred."

"He was in the Bureau?"

"No, got some special training. Protecting stuff."

"That's good to know."

Darrel unrolled Ty's collar and stepped back. "All done," he said.

Ty stood, "How much do I owe you?"

"On the house."

"That doesn't work for me. A man has got to make a living." Ty fixed his collar and put on his coat. Finished, he removed his wallet and handed Darrel a hundred-dollar bill. "You deserve a lot more," he said, thinking about his own father.

"Thank you Senator," Darrel said, with a humble bow.

"It was a pleasure, Darrel. Do you work outside the Capitol?"

"Yes, the airport on Wednesday mornings."

"Cutting hair?"

"No, shoeshine."

"That'll work. I'll see you soon. Thank you again," Ty said as he offered his right hand, and they shook hands.

Ty left the barbershop, drove back to the Capitol, parked, and walked to the rotunda. He glanced at his phone. *Next meeting could be tough,* he thought.

He walked to the marble staircase and climbed to the fifth floor, skipping a stair with each step. At the top, he again glanced at his phone and smiled. "On time," he whispered.

He walked down the empty slate hallway. Up ahead, he saw a ten-by-ten-foot mahogany-encased doorway at the end of the hallway. Above the opening, engraved in gold leaf into the marble facia, a header read: President Pro Tempore.

A young intern, sitting at the oversized desk in the center of the room, looked up as Leggett entered the room. "May I help you?" she asked.

Ty smiled as he made eye contact with the young lady. He wasn't surprised she didn't recognize him; this was his first time in the State Capitol Building, let alone the President Pro Tem's office.

"I'm Senator Ty Leggett," he said, with a pleasant smile. "I have a two-thirty meeting."

The young lady returned a delighted smile. "Oh! We've heard so much about you. Yes, yes, the senator is expecting you; just a moment." She picked up the telephone, called Anne Gray and said, "Senator Leggett is here."

While Leggett waited, several female staff members poked their heads up from behind their cubicles to get a look at the "Talk of Alabama."

Within moments, Anne Gray entered the room from Senator Jacobs's office. She was dressed in a tasteful, two-piece dark-blue Saint John's silk business suit. She walked directly to Leggett and greeted him with her standard straight arm handshake.

"It is exciting to finely meet our US Senator."

Ty smiled.

"Please follow me, the Pro Tem is expecting you." Anne glanced at her watch. "And you're right on time; that's rare around here."

"I hate being late," he said.

Anne agreed with a nod, and they walked to Senator

Jacobs's office. Anne knocked gently before she grabbed the doorknob on the heavy door.

"Please, allow me," Ty said.

With the door open, speaking in a formal voice, Anne said, "May I present United States Senator Tyler Leggett."

Ty laughed to himself, thinking, *My parents would love to hear those words.*

Looking up from his writing table, Jim Jacobs removed his glasses, stood up, and put on his best grin. "Absolutely; US Senator Ty Leggett is in the house."

Jim quickly moved away from his desk and with a skip, greeted Leggett with a pumping handshake and several pats on shoulder. "Welcome. Please come over to the couch and make yourself comfortable."

Ty hesitated for a moment while he looked around the large, plush office, thinking *This room is three times the size of my old FBI office.*

"Thank you for meeting me. This setting is very comfortable. Not many like this in DC, a fireplace, French doors and balcony opening onto the street below."

Jim smiled while pumping up his chest.

"The nights can get very long and cold." He pointed to the piles of papers on his desk. "The work never stops."

Ty glanced at Jim's desk, it was covered with legislative analysis booklets, government reports, and constituent letters.

"Someone has got to read the bills. Look here." He walked back to his desk. "We're not always small potatoes." He picked up a copy of a legislative bill. "See here, it took me an hour to convince the governor to sign it. Right there." Jim waved the thin, transparent paper booklet in the air. "Right there—" he repeated, pointing with his right index finger—"is the governor's signature. That bill is the structural guidelines for next year's reapportionment and it's a year early. All the negotiations are done, and we only lost one senate seat. Its passage will keep Alabama a Republican state for the next decade, if not longer."

He gloated for a moment.

"I know that doesn't mean anything to an Independent, but to us conservatives it's massive. All we do now is wait for the census data, align it through the Senate Redistricting Committee, put a bill on the Legislative Consent Calendar and boom, every Republican seat in the state is as safe as gold. The governor doesn't even have to sign it," Jim said, with a big grin.

Jim stepped closer to Ty and grabbed his right hand. "Congratulations on your appointment." He again patted Ty on the shoulder. "My wife and I have prayed for this day, and you deserve it; they're not many who can say they got a Democrat President and a Republican governor to appoint an Independent, small-town Alabama native to the US Senate." He smiled and winked. "You must be one hell of a negotiator."

"Thank you for the kind words," Ty said.

"Since this is your first run, you've got to understand elected office is a tough business, and friends must stick together. You'll need a family, if you know what I mean, and I hope to be your little brother. Your special election will by my top priority."

The two men stood smiling for a few seconds.

A little thick, Ty thought.

The Capitol telephone rang. Anne walked to the small side table next to the couch and answered.

"Yes, of course, show him in." Anne put the telephone down and said with a surprised look, "Majority Leader Simmons is here."

The main door to the room burst open as if hit by a tornado, and in walked, 5'9", 49-year-old State Senator John Simmons. He was rich and acted it. He had made millions of dollars in real estate development and won his senate seat two years ago, because "It was his destiny," he would say repeatedly.

John Simmons was "old family" rich and a wannabe player in state and local politics. Born in Birmingham at the University of Alabama Hospital, and raised in Mountain Brook, and he knew nothing about life outside the private clubs. He had a large following among Alabama's business leaders. It was for that reason he was elected majority leader, which was not what he wanted; he'd lost by one vote in becoming President Pro Tempore.

"It's official, the governor has signed the reapportionment bill; the press conference is in thirty minutes. Our seats are safe; not even Christ could defeat us," Simmons boasted.

His attention turned to Ty. John had not noticed Ty when he burst into the room. "You must be Senator Ty Leggett," he said, reaching out his right hand. "I'm Senator John Simmons. I'm the money guy." They shook hands. "We are going to be best friends." He grinned with his left hand firmly planted on Ty's shoulder.

Then John stepped away from Ty and said, "It's a free ride for all incumbents. That bill saved us millions of dollars in campaign money, and we owe it all to our President Pro Tem, good old Jim Jacobs," John said, bouncing on his toes.

"Let's celebrate; this calls for a drink," Jim said as he walked to the wall behind the couch and pushed on the mirrored cabinet, exposing a full wet bar. A row of spotlights turned on above the bar when the door was opened. The shelves were lined with crystal glasses.

A lead glass mirror covered the back wall, making the bar sparkle. Different brands of scotch, bourbon, vodka, and assorted mixes sat on the marble counter. There was also a wine refrigerator filled with bottles below the counter.

"What may I get you gentlemen and lady?" Jim asked.

Ty shook his head. "None for me, thank you, I've got another meeting and it's a long drive." Thinking: *These boys sure like to drink.*

"Sparkling water for me, heavy on the ice. I've got to go to a press conference and a fundraiser later," John said.

Jim and Anne laughed at the joke. Ty had no idea.

Jim read Ty's face, and said, "He's Mormon."

"Oh," Ty said, nodding.

"I'll have a sweet tea vodka," Anne said.

"How about a cold glass of water, Ty?" Jim asked.

"Sure, that would be nice."

Jim put all the drinks on a silver tray and passed them around. Then he put the now-empty tray back on the coffee table and held up a shot glass filled with bourbon. "A toast to Ty's campaign, and to reapportionment."

They clinked glasses and gulped them down.

"Which fundraising event are you going to?" Jim asked John.

"Let me look." Simmons reached into his shirt breast pocket and pulled out his digital calendar. He put on his reading glasses. "Nurses. I love supporting them," Simmons said with a grin. "Their upcoming legislation is raising us a lot of money."

"I'm scheduled for that, too," Jim said.

The Capitol telephone rang; Anne answered. She listened for a moment without speaking and hung up. "Your two o'clock appointment is still waiting; it's been over an hour, Senator. Should I tell her you're too busy?"

"Damn candidates. No, tell her I'll be right out. Gentlemen, I've got a meeting with the Mayor of Birmingham; you know she's got a ton of money and wants to run for the local senate seat next year." Jim turned to face John, and said, "She's a player. I'll send her over to your office, and you can handle that campaign."

"Okay, boss, that's my job," John said, taking a final sip.

Jim put his drink down on his desk. "Gentlemen, thank you for stopping by, and Ty, congratulations again on your appointment. As soon as the governor announces the special election dates, John and I will race to help. Gentlemen, if you don't mind, please use the side door. It leads directly into the hallway."

Anne picked up the glasses, put them back into the bar, and closed the cabinet. After Ty and John left the room, Jim sprayed a breath mint and walked out to greet the mayor.

"I am terribly sorry," Jim said, offering his hand, "to have kept you waiting for so long. The governor is upset with an upcoming vote on hydrocarbons, and he insisted on bending my ear. Please come into my office," he said, gushing the words with a beaming smile. She looked excited as they walked into his office.

"Welcome to my humble workspace, Madam Mayor. Please make yourself comfortable." He gestured toward the couch. "You know Anne Gray, I think? My chief of staff and political advisor?"

Anne and Linda shook hands. "You and Anne should become best friends. Anne is a political genius," Jim said.

"It would be wonderful to work with you," the mayor said, handing Anne a business card.

Anne's cell telephone beeped; she had a text so she turned away from Jim and the mayor. It read: State Senator Jeffery Ullman has called a press conference for nine a.m. Monday morning to announce he's registered as an Independent.

"I knew it," she whispered.

Ty left Jacobs's office and walked along the hallway to the grand staircase, to the ground floor, and left the State Capitol through a side exit.

It was a beautiful, crisp, sunny day; the sky was clear, and the gentle north breeze was not too cold. He followed the narrow path to North Union Street. He turned right toward the Alabama State House building.

He crossed the street and followed the sidewalk to the Washington Avenue restricted entrance for his 3:45 p.m. meeting with State Senator Hugh Peterson. Ty entered the building and was greeted by an Alabama state trooper.

"May I help you?" he asked.

"Yes. I have a meeting with Senator Peterson."

"Your ID, please." Ty handed him his DC driver's license. He turned to face a tablet-sized monitor and swiped Ty's card. "Yes, Senator, I see it here. Are you carrying a firearm?"

"No."

"Please empty your pockets and walk through the security station."

He did so and passed through the scanner without interruption. Finished, the trooper returned Ty's keys, car fob, and some loose change. "Senator Peterson's office is on the fifth floor, suite A. The elevator's straight ahead."

"Thank you," Ty said politely.

Ty looked around as he walked to the elevators. It was like every bureaucratic government building he'd ever been in: tired and dull.

He pushed the elevator call button, the door opened with a screech, and he rode it up to the fifth floor and stepped out into a cold, dirty linoleum hallway. The walls were undecorated and painted a grayish off-white.

He turned left out of the elevator and read the number signs on the wall as he walked, looking for suite A. *It feels like a prison*, he thought. He reached the door and turned the knob. The first thing he saw was a metal desk. Sitting behind it was a middle-aged woman. The black nameplate, with white lettering read: Ms. Lorane Heard.

She smiled. "Welcome, Senator Leggett. What a refreshing sight."

Ty grinned. "I don't know what you mean, but it sounds nice."

"You're the first, and it's about time. I'll tell the Senator you're here." She pressed the intercom. "Senator Leggett is here, sir."

"Send him in," came the reply.

The door to the right of Ms. Lorane's desk opened and standing, holding it, was Senator Hugh Peterson.

"A DC bureaucrat who don't hunt," he said, with a grin.

Ty laughed. "You forgot lawyer."

Peterson laughed. "Joseph said I'd like you. Please come in."

Wow, Ty thought, *what a difference power makes*.

The room was sparse. Everything looked used or hand-me-down. The only bit of personality in the room was a Remington sculpture of an Indian fighting a bison, sitting on the wooden coffee table facing his metal desk.

A seven-foot-tall white bookshelf stood across the room from the window. It was filled with hunting and political books; two books caught Ty's eye: *What Makes You Think We Read the Bills,* by H. L. Richardson, and the novel, *The Ninth Wave,* by Eugene Burdick

"'What Makes You Think We Read the Bills?'" Ty read aloud.

"Richardson, former California State Senator, was ahead of his time and set the national landscape with Gun Owners of America. What he wrote sadly applies today. I collect old hardback books."

I've heard of *The Ninth Wave,*" Ty said. "Someone mentioned it to me once."

"You surf?" Hugh asked.

Ty laughed. "No."

"It's a surfing story, a must-read. Burdick invented modern political campaign theory. It's the bible for every good candidate or consultant. Like Richardson, Burdick nailed it. You should read both books if you can find copies. Burdick was published in 1956—but wait a minute, they don't do any good sitting here; you can have them," Hugh said, removing both books from the bookshelf and handing them to Ty.

"Thank you, I enjoy reading," he said.

"Come, please sit," Hugh said, pointing at the chair facing the desk.

The desk was plain, and very used looking; it had a black government telephone, a computer monitor, and a photograph of a young woman on the right-side corner. Peterson sat behind the desk and Ty sat in the gray cloth chair facing him.

"Normally, I'd tell you how wonderful you are and how you're going to win. But you're not an idiot. Then I'd ask the BS question of the day: What's your proudest and most courageous moment?" He smiled. "I've heard some whoppers, near death, war, et cetera. The worst I've heard was 'keeping my sister from stealing my inheritance'—He lost, so all's well." Hugh shook his head and leaned back in his chair. "Well, Ty—may I call you 'Ty'?"

"Yes, please do."

"I have too much respect for what you've accomplished, Justice Marshall and running the FBI, so I'll get to the point. What the hell are you thinking, leaving the FBI and running as an Independent in Alabama?"

Ty smiled. "The best advice I ever got was to join the FBI and keep both eyes on my friends." He smiled. "I don't have friends."

Hugh laughed.

"Why leave and run? There comes a moment when one suddenly knows it's time to move on. That moment came for me last year sitting in a hospital room with my best friend's wife. And I'm glad I did. Thurgood felt it was the law that mattered; he even once said about Dr. King: 'He gives a nice speech.' I understood what he meant; it's the law that forces long-term change. Not judges, courts, or political mobs; it's Congress, and they aren't doing their job." He showed a small smile. "Senator—"

"Please, call me Hugh," Peterson interrupted.

"Okay. If you ask most Blacks, they'll tell you all the KKK did was take off sheets and put on ties."

"I believe that," Hugh stage-whispered.

"When I first joined the Bureau, every time I got rejected for something, I blamed it on being Black." Ty smiled to keep things light. "It wasn't true, but it's how I felt and how most Blacks feel. Even Colin Powell—we talked about it once. An example of silent, entrenched racism. 'Ty is coming over tonight; he's Black, you know.' That would not be said about any other group, and we hear it every day."

Peterson looked enthralled.

"The night before that White House call with the President's Chief of Staff, I watched two drug dealers die trying to steal medical secrets by torturing my friend's family.

"With AI married to quantum computing, the medical

discoveries will explode, and those rewards will overwhelm honesty and law enforcement. I knew that fateful night it was just the beginning of criminals realizing the real money was in those discoveries. Soon, only the naïve will have secrets, and each day power falls into smaller hands. Why sell street drugs when you can steal a patent, bribe a genius, or hack an AI data base. And now that people are being implanted with microprocessors, society is doomed. Only the law can stop that invasion."

Ty sadly shook his head. "Look at human relations. We don't enslave anymore, we marginalize, forcing people to shut up. Sapir-Whorf and Linguistic Determinism insist people's language determines their place in life. It's another form of fascism to rewrite history and force people to hide. I feel that's wrong. The bastards must talk so we know who and where they are." Ty leaned back.

"Hate must stay out front for everyone to see. Look what's being done to the Indigenous tribes; soon, using the word 'chief' will be racist. The first slaves were carried to America on a ship named *The White Lion*." Ty stopped speaking, feeling his emotions.

"Soon, that history and the use of the word *slave* will be racist," Ty said.

"I understand most of what you're saying, so why leave the Bureau and its national voice?"

"Political conformity has nurtured the FBI, and AI has become the omnipresent tool of political fascists, like Sapir-Whorf. Soon, very soon AI will stop being a tool and will make laws demanding conformity."

"All true," Hugh said.

"There isn't one person proposing federal legislation to

stop that. I'll forgo the soapbox to lead the club from the inside. If I'm lucky, I'll give courage to legislators to challenge the impossible and fight for the lone wolf."

Ty hesitated. "As for your BS question, my greatest moment of character?" He cocked his head, "My answer is: Defending my best friend against insanity and carrying that fight to DC." He stopped speaking, leaned back into the chair.

"Those're some good reasons. I know all about Orwell's fear of a police state and thought oppression," Hugh said, nodding.

Hugh's expression changed and became warm and friendly. "Okay, this is what I'll do. I'll get you some seed money and have my campaign team run your election. I don't give general election money, only primary, but I'll make an exception for you since you won't have a primary. That's it, the rest of the financing is up to you and your team."

He leaned forward in his chair. "My reputation is polarizing, so I won't publicly announce my support until you need the outdoor community."

He relaxed and leaned back.

"Some advice: Don't buy a white suit, do what your pollster says, and most importantly, it's all about Alabama sports."

He chuckled and stood, as did Ty, they shook hands.

As they walked out into the hallway, Hugh put his right hand on Ty's shoulder. "Joseph was right; you deserve to be first. Good luck."

Monday morning, February 25, Senator Hugh Peterson was sitting alone in his Washington Street State Capitol office, watching Senator Jeffery Ullman's 9:00 a.m. press conference on the Senate's live feed TV.

"It breaks my heart," Jeffery said in his best Southern accent, "to leave the Republican Party after thirty years in public office. It has been my life's work to steward the environment, lower crime, protect gun rights and the sanctity of life."

He looked down and wiped his eye.

"But the district I was elected to represent is gone, they have stolen it from us, and there is nothing I can do to stop that from happening. Our Party has been hijacked by Washington DC kingmakers and carpetbagging Northerners. I'm determined to fight those Northern powerbrokers to protect our most cherished Alabama values. Sadly, to do that, I must leave my party and become an Independent." He again looked down and wiped his eye with his finger.

"It breaks my heart to leave, but I have no choice. I can't stand by and let them win. I say no!" He pounded his right fist on the podium. "We are going to fight them. Therefore, I stand before you today to announce my candidacy for the upcoming United States Senate special election."

Hugh laughed out loud. "Thank God Jimmy Stewart is dead," he said to no one. He turned the live feed off, picked up his cell phone, and called his political consultant, Carlos Felix.

"Carlos here," he answered in a raspy, Mexican-accented voice from his Adams Avenue, Montgomery, office.

"Ullman announced he's changed parties and will run against Leggett in the special."

"No big deal."

"Yes, it is. Where is Leggett going to get sixteen million to beat Ullman? Have you called Abbott like I told you?"

"No. He's still pissed you made him take those photos of Roberts's wife using a state car."

"Damn it. Call him right now. He doesn't want *me* pissed at *him*." Hugh hung up.

Alabama Senate Democrat Minority Leader David Roberts was in his Capitol office, listening to Ullman's press conference. He turned off the pressroom intercom box and picked up his private desk phone and called Senate Minority Caucus Chair, Walter Hillyard.

"This is Hillyard," a male voice answered.

"This is Roberts. Ullman has just given us a shot at settling a score and picking up a US Senate seat."

"Yes, I heard the fool's speech. What do you want to do?"

"Let the dust settle until the governor announces the special election date," David said.

"This could backfire. Once he's elected, Ullman will never vote with the DNC delegation again," Walter said.

"Yes, he will, just enough to lose his base and the regularly scheduled election in two years. Leggett is the one I'm worried about. There's no telling what he'll do and unlike Ullman, he's smart."

"Do you think we could bring him over?"

"No. He would not have left the FBI without an agenda, and we're not part of it."

"What could he possibly want to do?"

"I have no idea, but he left Washington and the FBI to do it. We'll learn soon enough; campaigns expose secret agendas. His will be no different." David rubbed his lower lip. "In the meantime, get Ullman some seed money so he can make nice with his Republican constituents; switching parties could hurt him. Make sure that money is used to keep that wound closed. Contact Paul Anctil and have him oversee the pre-general lead-up and manage the special election. Tell Paul not to let Ullman spend a dime without my approval. Lastly, make sure they're no Democrats in the primary. I want it to be Ullman v. Leggett in the special. We get that, we win."

"David, why did Ullman become an Independent? Why not run as a Republican, for God's sake? The Reps own Alabama."

"Because he's pissed at being tossed aside, and he knows he'd never raise the money to defeat Leggett. With us he gets revenge and money."

"I understand; Okay, we'll put everything into that campaign," Walter said.

"Walter, we're not playing nice. I want to end the President's meddling in Alabama politics. Reach out to our state and DC money friends and shut off any potential Leggett donations. Also, put a team together to force the state central committees to keep candidates out of the primary. Also organize our Congressional delegation to shut off Leggett's national money." David thought a moment. "And coordinate with the Dem's National

Committee, the National party's major donors, and schedule a Hollywood visit to Alabama. I want to bury Leggett in money and press."

"Okay, I got it. How do we keep the governor out?" Walter asked.

"Don't worry about him. He'll stay out; he's a Republican and Leggett isn't. Anyway, there's always a deal." David hesitated, thinking.

"Changing gears, how's our fundraising going with the nurses and Indians' bills?"

"Great. We control the deciding votes to pass gambling and healthcare reform for the nurses. This is going to be a fun year. We'll raise lots of money, screw the governor, and send a message to that Georgia ass to keep his presidential nose out of Alabama."

"Yep, we can always use more money, but Walter, we must stay focused, the only thing that matters is defeating Leggett."

Sitting at his state Capitol Building office desk, Republican Majority Leader Senator John Simmons had just finished watching Ullman's live feed, about the same time Peterson was calling Carlos. He picked up his cell phone and called his political consultant, George Roka.

"Roka," he answered in his annoyed voice.

"Ullman's left the Party, and this could be good for us."

"How so? It means we just lost a vote," George said.

"That's for leadership, and it's settled for a year, and Ullman will vote with us on everything that matters."

"How do you plan on becoming Pro Tem with him gone?"

"That will come after the next state election, like I said, and that deciding vote will come from the mayor of Birmingham the day after you elect her to the Senate."

"Okay, so why are you calling me?"

"Because I want to help Leggett."

"Help him? He can't win. What are you thinking?" George asked in a voice filled with disgust.

"I think he can, and I want to be his number-one donor."

"This is crazy. He'll get help from DC national donors and conservative Alabama money."

"There's only one other person in Alabama who matters when it comes to money, and that's Peterson, and he's only interested in guns and electing right-wingers. The rest are fools and old men."

"How are you going to control a federal campaign? The Fed finance laws are different."

"As majority leader, I control all campaign funds, even the federal ones, and Leggett will come begging for money."

"What makes you think he'll need money? He's been in DC for a long time. I've heard he's got lots of friends."

"Not in the right places. He's out, and I've heard they don't want him back. He'll be lucky to raise a million in DC, and that's if Senator Joseph pulls strings. That leaves sixteen million reasons why he'll need me."

"What about Peterson in the special?"

"Peterson won't bail him out; it's against his philosophy. He believes if you can't raise enough money for the general, let alone a special, you'll make a weak legislator."

"That doesn't change anything. In a three-way race, Ullman and the Democrat split the votes, and Leggett sucks wind," George said.

"True, if the Democrat has money. I've heard Roberts is behind Ullman and the only potential Democrat is a hick named Horner and last year he called Peterson a fascist. That idiot won't raise a dime."

"Okay, for shit and giggles, let's say you're right, it's Leggett v. Ullman. How do you plan to control Leggett?"

"Money, money, and money. I control his money; I control the campaign."

"John, this is not worth the effort. Leggett can't win, period."

"Never underestimate a Black icon in Alabama and I'll tell you one time," John's tone had changed and become aggressive. "It's about federal contracts and Ullman will never come to me, Leggett will," John said, almost growling.

"Relax, John. I'm not your problem. How do you plan to direct Leggett's campaign?"

"I haven't got that far; it's all about who he hires."

5

MARCH — THE RACE IS ON

Monday morning, Ty was at his Lee Street, Montgomery, campaign headquarters. The storefront main room was empty. Ty had not hired staff, and there was only one metal desk, a folding card table, and two folding chairs, in the back office. Ty was sitting behind the desk reading *The Ninth Wave*.

Carlos Felix broke the silence as he entered the office for his 10:00 a.m. appointment. Carlos had worked in politics for ten years since leaving the Birmingham Police Department. Senator Peterson had hired him to manage his Law-and-Order Political Action Committee. The PAC focused on electing local judges and county sheriffs.

Carlos was not imposing at 5'10" and pudgy. His favorite line when teased about being fat was, "You don't have to be fast when you carry a thirty-eight."

Carlos was wearing dirty blue jeans, a wrinkled, white, long-sleeved Arrow shirt and black loafers. His wavy black hair was uncombed and in need of a haircut. His sloppy dress and bulging eyes belied a quick mind.

Most legislators thought he was crazy, but the smart ones knew he was the real deal when it came to managing campaigns.

Carlos had been married to Caroline for eighteen years, and they had ten children. Caroline was his opposite: a devout Catholic, petite, Irish, and loving. She also had a mischievous sense of humor.

Not seeing anyone, Carlos called out, "Senator Leggett?"

"I'm back here," Leggett answered from his back office.

Carlos stepped into the dirty room.

Ty stood.

"Senator Leggett, I'm Carlos Felix," he said, extending his right hand.

"Nice to meet you, Carlos. Senator Peterson speaks highly of your campaign skills."

Carlos rubbed his nose. "You must've spoken to him on one of his good days."

Ty laughed. "He's demanding—a quality I admire. Please sit," he said, motioning toward the metal chair facing the card table.

That same morning after a perfunctory roll-call attendance vote, John Simmons received a text message that read: "Confirmed Leggett in meeting with Carlos Felix."

Simmons left the Senate floor, returned to his Capitol office, and called Ty.

"Excuse me, Carlos, I've got to take this call."

"Should I leave?" Carlos asked.

"No."

"This is Senator Leggett."

"Good morning, Ty. This is John Simmons."

"Hello, John. What can I do for you?"

"Do you have time to meet this evening?"

"Yes, I have some time."

"May I come by your headquarters?" John asked

"How about six o'clock at the Renaissance, instead?"

"Sounds good. I want to go over some campaign details."

"I'm talking to Carlos about managing the campaign. Should I have him tag along?"

"No, that's not necessary. I want to keep our meeting casual."

"Okay, what are you thinking?"

"I've got to run. See you at six." Simmons hung up.

Ty leaned back. *That was odd,* he thought. He looked at Carlos.

"That was Senator Simmons, right?" Carlos asked.

"Yes."

"He's simple to work with if you remember that he's the smartest and richest guy in the room," Carlos said with a bitter smile.

"Carlos, I like you. We're going to get along just fine. Without building a watch, tell me how you see this campaign going."

"We raise sixteen million, you win."

"Perfect. How are we going to do that?"

"It's no big deal. With Peterson in our corner and a good team behind us, we can do it."

"Who's on the team?" Ty asked.

"I'll have to assemble it, but it starts with finance, Ed Abbott; Media, Gonzo Diaz; Advertising, Susie Diaz; Treasurer, Dave Tower; Mail, Tim Tracy; Social Media, Gary Hutchinson, and polling—"

"I've got that covered," Ty interrupted, "that will be Professor Val Price," Ty said.

"Val Price? You got him? He's the best in the country," Carlos said, rubbing his nose. "This could be a great campaign team."

Ty stood. "Sounds good. Assemble the team, draw up your contract, and let's get moving."

After the call to Leggett, Simmons leaned back in his chair, looked across the room, then made a cell phone call to Roka.

"What's up?" Roka answered.

"Just as I thought. Leggett is hiring Peterson's campaign team. I'd heard Leggett met with Peterson and he's interviewing Carlos. Our first step is to get Carlos out of the way until the start of the special election campaign."

"What! Leggett just hired the guy, now you want him to dump—"

"George, shut up and listen. I want you to manage Leggett's campaign until June."

George laughed.

"Leggett will never go for that? You're nuts; Carlos will tell Leggett he doesn't need to run a pre-special campaign."

"There is a reason I'm rich and you're not. I'll tell Leggett the pre-special election is the perfect opportunity to raise his statewide name Id. He will have no choice but to hire you. Your job real job will be to waste every dollar possible," John said.

"What?" Roka asked. "Waste money?"

"Yes, if Leggett's broke going into the special election, we've got him," John said.

"This is nuts. Waste money. Leggett will have a treasurer, and it'll probably be Dave Tower, who's not stupid. And if they use Ed Abbott, he's a jerk about expenses. On top of all that, how you going to get me in?"

"I'll promise Leggett eight million. That's half of a winning campaign budget—"

"Eight million, this is crazy," George interrupted.

"Shut up and listen," John said his voice sounding angry. I'll only give him the money if he agrees to have you run a pre–special election campaign."

"John, only a fool would spend money before the special election; as an Independent, Leggett automatically gets into the fall campaign. Carlos will raise hell if the campaign spends any money before June."

"I don't care about that stupid cop. Leggett will have no choice but to take my offer. This is worth billions in federal contracts to us. When Leggett wins in November and we're on the inside, that eight million will be pennies on the billions we get in contracts," John said, almost giggling at his genius.

"You're a little presumptuous. Ullman will have unlimited money and consultants," George said.

"That fool can't win. He'd find a way to screw up a wet dream and I'm banking on that."

"Why are you screwing me? Leggett or Carlos will eventually figure out what I've done and crucify my reputation," Roka said.

"You're taking one for me and you'll be so rich afterward, you'll never need to work again. Once inside, your job is to spend them into oblivion. It's all about cash on hand, and the July Federal Election Commission report. Your only job is to make sure Leggett is broke by that report." He grinned. "Then, I come to the rescue with eight million and Mr. Ty Cool Dude will be ours for life," John said, feeling euphoric by his genius.

"What about the remaining campaign budget of eight million?"

"I have faith in Mr. Ed Abbott, who I'm sure Leggett will hire."

An hour later, Simmons returned to the Senate Chambers for a quick roll-call vote. He loved walking into the most powerful legislative place in Alabama. The Senate Chambers were designed to radiate power and royalty. Only familiarity and arrogance shattered the awe.

A cushioned, gold-and-blue wall-to-wall carpet covered the chamber floor. Thirty-five wooden desks faced the legislative rostrum and staff gallery. Life-sized oil portraits of historic political leaders adorned the walls. The room was arranged in an oval, and each senator shared a six-foot-wide desk. On each side of the desk was a telescoping microphone.

Prestige was displayed by the location of one's seat location from the center front row to the rear of the room. The propriety in the room was always civil, enforced by strict etiquette and decorum rules.

The Senate cloakroom was a different story. Alcoholic beverages and finger food were served along with an occasional fistfight. Senator Peterson once punched a whiny, mealy-mouthed colleague for calling him a son of a bitch. After the altercation, the bloody-nosed legislator ran out into the Senate Chambers screaming, "Peterson hit me! Peterson hit me." Most felt it was about time the whiner got punched and Peterson was not censured.

Only serving senators were allowed onto the Senate floor. To make sure no one mistakenly stepped foot on that hollowed carpet, there is a three-inch-wide white line stitched into the carpet edge. It was forbidden to pass and the price for violating the white line was arrest. A reporter was once asked if she would like to cross over the line, and her instant reply was, "Why would I want to become a pain in the ass?"

There are four truisms in politics: It takes one year for moral corruption to void common sense; politicians are grade-B wannabe actors; money is power; and cash on hand is king. Senator John Simmons exemplified all those truisms; in his case, it only took six months to attain the first two.

Simmons walked onto the senate floor and headed

straight to Minority Leader David Roberts's desk, who was standing, talking to a colleague.

"Ullman for US Senate? Are you serious? Come on, David," John said, interrupting the conversation.

"Got to do something. Your party is having all the fun, and I think Jeffery has a good chance at winning." He smiled and glanced at the other senator. "Anyway, who would be dumb enough to support a DC carpetbagger in Alabama?"

"Me, and bum-hick Ullman, along with your party, will lose," John announced. His arrogance was palpable.

David smiled, thinking, *I'm going to enjoy kicking your ass.*

At thirty-two years old, Ed Abbott felt on top of the world. His business was growing, and he was gaining statewide recognition. The key to his success was his obsessive attention to details and creating a massive AI-generated donor database. It contained the names, addresses, emails, Instagram, LinkedIn, cell numbers, Facebook data, and X accounts to every major donor in Alabama, Mississippi, Georgia, Louisiana, Texas, California and Washington, DC. He also had the same information for the top 1,000 major political contributors in America, regardless of political party identification.

Ed had entered politics after graduating from Tulane University with an accounting degree and landed his first job as the Alabama Senate Republican Caucus Press Director. It was there he learned the art of mass media communication and respect for the State Capitol Press Corps and their fearless dedication to the news. It was also where he met Senator Hugh Peterson.

After leaving the press job, Ed worked for Senator Peterson for two years before he opened a political consulting business. It was in his first year in business that he'd garnered national credibility from elite donors when he successfully raised funds for the International Medical Corps, which transported doctors and nurses to the Middle East to help children maimed by war.

Ed Abbott came from a wealthy Madison, Alabama, family. He was naturally comfortable around wealth and never appeared impressed. He was, however, impressed by refined humility. Ed did very well with mature contributors because they enjoyed his sarcasm, loyalty, and little boy heart. He did especially well with tough, independent, successful women.

After the meeting with Ty, Carlos left the campaign headquarters and walked into the street, glanced at the police station at the end of the block, and felt a twinge of regret. As a nervous habit, he scratched his nose and thought, *I loved that job*. Then his thoughts turned to Ed Abbott. *How* do *I convince him to join the team? He works his hardest to rescue the underdog.*

He pushed the cell phone call button.

"Abbott here."

"We've got to talk."

"What's up?"

"Is it okay if I come by?"

"It's a Monday in March. I have nothing but time."

"Okay, I'm on my way."

Ten minutes later, Carlos walked up the stairwell to Ed Abbott's second-story, Commerce Street office. He entered the small reception area.

Not seeing anyone, Carlos called out, "You here, Abbott?"

"In here."

Carlos turned left and stepped into a large twenty-by-ten-foot room and saw Ed standing at the floor-to-ceiling French doors, looking at the river.

Ed smiled when he saw Carlos, returned to his desk, and sat. Carlos fell onto the leather couch that faced the desk.

"Where's Sabina?" Carlos asked.

"Do you really think she tells me?"

Sabina Thompson was Ed's only employee. She had worked with him for two years while attending Troy State University. A petite twenty-one-year-old, she had inherited her mother's strong personality, blonde hair, and natural beauty.

Carlos smiled, looking toward the windows. "Nice view," he said.

"I can't get enough. Everything in this part of town is ugly until you see the river. So, what brings you here?"

Carlos rubbed his nose.

Abbott leaned back in his high-backed executive chair. "What's so important that you drove across town to see me?"

"I need your help in Leggett's campaign."

"So," Ed said with a shrug of indifference.

"Peterson wants you to join us."

"Why would I do that? He demanded I take those stupid photos last year and yelled at me when I said no."

Carlos rubbed his nose.

"Senator Leggett needs your help. He doesn't have a clue about raising money, no less sixteen million."

"He's going to lose. Why should I care?"

"I'm not so sure, and Peterson feels the same; he gave him a hundred grand," Carlos said.

"What? Mr. Penny-tight-wallet gave Leggett a hundred K?" Ed asked.

"Yes, and I've talked to Leggett. He's not like anyone I've ever met. He cares, is honest, and isn't a game player."

"Shocking. An honest FBI agent. And I call BS. Like every politician, after a year, he'll turn into a jerk and be a disappointment."

"A little cynical, aren't you?"

"No, and I'm not having my heart ripped out again."

"So, you're going to work for Ullman, a seventy-five-year-old rancher who pretends he's a cowboy?"

"He's the last person I'd help. He'll get eaten alive in DC and embarrass Alabama."

"That would take some doing," Carlos said.

"What do you mean by that?" Ed asked, sounding a little defensive.

"Look around. We have a state Capitol that looks like a colorless, abandoned monument to the past."

"What happened with slavery and the Indian tribes was horrible," Ed admitted.

"Yes, it was, and George Wallace has been dead since

nineteen ninety-eight—forty-one years ago. The 'good ol' boy' control of jobs and money is over. International companies have located here, and highly educated young people *are* moving in, grabbing top-paying jobs. The days of graft and stupidity are over."

Carlos rubbed his nose. "We need to do something great, something that sends the message Alabama is looking forward, and in my opinion, it's about time. Young people want jobs and a decent place to raise their kids. When they graduate from Alabama and Auburn, we want them to stay, not run off to Austin or Miami."

"Maybe you should run. You sound like a politician," Ed said with a smirk.

"Come on, Ed, we need to elect Leggett. He feels that way."

"You think he can do that? Bring high-tech jobs here and put the hate for Alabama's past to rest?"

"The jobs, absolutely; maybe, a crack for the past hate. AI and robotics have changed everything, and we can join that future."

He rubbed his nose.

"I'm proud to live here. With a forward-thinking US Senator we can build on that, and I've got young kids—"

"That's an understatement," Ed interrupted.

"Ha ha, real funny. Ed, we need Leggett," Carlos said.

"No, I'm not doing this. He'll screw up or become a big shot."

"Ed, I need you," Carlos said.

"No, and sixteen million is a lot to raise. I understand from my DC friends there's no help coming from there," Ed replied.

"Ed, we can do this," Carlos said.

"No, this is insane. Where's he going to get sixteen million?"

"Peterson told me to speak to you."

"So, I don't work for him. Again, where's Leggett going to getting sixteen million."

"Ed, that's your job, and Peterson said don't piss him off."

"Screw him." He hesitated. "Did he really say that?" Ed asked, looking concerned.

"Forget Peterson, I've spent hours with Leggett, and I like him; he's real. Ed, you will never have a bigger underdog to rescue. He doesn't have a clue about being a candidate and he promised me, he'll do what we ask. And I believe him."

"That'll be a first. Where's he on the issues?"

"Pro-family and doesn't go to church much."

"You're kidding. And he wants to win in Alabama?"

"Yes."

"He's blackmailing you, isn't he?" Ed laughed.

"You know I carry a gun."

"You're a lousy shot."

"Not all the time."

Ed laughed. "So, what do you want me to do?"

"Join the campaign and get him sixteen million."

"Not possible. Normally, Washington helps, but those arrogant bastards who treat us like dirt, as I said, are out. Finding that much money is almost impossible. Conservatives won't jump in unless they're convinced he's real, and that takes time. The national lib machine will marginalize him, and their money will go to the chosen one, which appears to be Ullman."

Ed leaned back in his chair.

"That much money is not happening. I'm out."

"Ed, Leggett will be the biggest underdog of your life. Once you meet him, you'll understand why. He deserves a shot—come on, Ed, be part of something great."

Ed glanced out the windows.

"Who else is on the team?" Ed asked.

"Tim Tracy, direct and electronic mail, Gary Hutchinson, electronic outreach. Gonzo and Susie Diaz, traditional media, and Tower as treasurer. You know and respect everyone and they need money to do their jobs. Come on, Ed, join the team."

"Who's doing the polling?" Ed asked.

"Val Price."

"Price. I've heard of him. He's incredible. A DC guy and only does national campaigns. How'd you get him?"

"He's a friend of Leggett's."

"So, he's name-only, to give credibility to the campaign?"

"No, he's all in and said he'd be in Montgomery once a week and attend special meetings."

"He'll attend finance committee meetings?"

"Yes."

"Christ, Leggett's blackmailing everyone." Ed grinned and leaned back in his chair.

Ed looked again out the windows.

"Who"—Ed looked suspicious, "is actually onboard?"

Carlos rubbed his nose. "Me and Val."

"You're a piece of work," Ed said, slowly shaking his head.

Carlos shrugged, rubbed his nose again, and looked away.

"I'll have the team and everything in place by next week. Come on, Ed."

Ed turned his head and looked out the window. "If you get Tim, I'll do it. I want fifteen percent of the gross, no exceptions. I'm copied on all campaign expenses, and I'm reimbursed for all fundraising costs. The moment you sign Tim, I'll send a DocuSign contract. We can't screw around. We must start organizing now, before the end of March. May and June are the best fundraising months, next to September and October. We can't be late. It takes five weeks to get the money train running," Ed said.

"My next meeting is with Tim. Hopefully I'll have everyone onboard by early next week."

"When can I meet Leggett?" Ed asked.

"He'll be in town until Tuesday early afternoon."

"Set up a meeting at his campaign headquarters for tomorrow at eight a.m. If I like him, and you have Tim, I'll sign a contract." Ed hesitated. "He better not tell me his life's greatest moment of character was keeping the family inheritance."

Late Monday afternoon John Simmons returned to his Capitol office after a meeting with the governor to pick up his raincoat. While there he made a telephone call.

"Roka here."

"I'm on my way to meet Leggett at six. You got any updates?"

"Yes. I learned Peterson is going to give Leggett's campaign a hundred thousand in seed money, and Leggett met with Carlos Felix today. His campaign headquarters is a storefront on Lee Street next to the Knicker Knacker Market."

"Smart location; police station, public parking, and cheap food, all within walking distance," John said. He glanced at his new Diamond Dial Rolex watch: 5:45 p.m.

"I've got to go; I'll call you after."

He hung up and sent a text to his chauffeur: Pick me up in front of the Capitol.

John drove down Commerce, turned left on Tallapoosa and took a quick left into the Renaissance. The black CTX Cadillac passed the fountain and stopped facing the glass doors. John did not wait for the valet, he got out, left the door open, and strutted into the hotel.

Ty was sitting comfortably in the foyer reading the *Montgomery Advertiser* on his cell phone.

John approached, glanced at Ty's cell phone. "Senator Leggett," he said in this normally high-pitched voice.

Ty looked up. John was smiling.

"Thanks for meeting me on such short notice. I see you're reading the *Advertiser*. That's a good newspaper, the last print in Alabama; I'm a part owner. I read six news sites a day. Best way to keep up. How about we grab a drink?" John asked.

They walked to the lounge and sat in a booth. The server came to the table. "May I help you?" she asked.

"Yes, I'll have any Kentucky bourbon," Ty said.

"They have Clyde May's, get that," John said.

"You buying? May's is expensive."

"On me," John said.

"Okay, a Clyde May's neat," Ty said.

"A sweet tea," John said. "I understand you secured a campaign headquarters."

"Yes, great location near the police headquarters with lots of safe parking and food."

"How about a place to live? If not, they have long-term rooms here. It's where I stay while we're in session. I can talk to the manager."

"Thank you. I've got a place in Monroe."

"How about campaign staff?"

The drinks arrived; John took a sip of his tea, and Ty a sip of the bourbon.

"Only Carlos Felix. The rest are being hired now."

"Sounds like things are moving, which is good. I spoke to the governor this evening; he's going to announce the special election dates next week. He told me it's June seventh for the primary. The date that matters to you is November eighth for the special."

He smiled and took another sip.

"Which is why I wanted to meet with you tonight. We," he hesitated, "have a challenge; I checked with several members of my financial team after we spoke about Carlos being your campaign manager."

He took another sip.

"They don't have confidence in Carlos managing your campaign and are especially worried about his ability to raise money."

"Why?"

"Carlos is too close to Senator Peterson. Also, I spoke to Dennette Dakis yesterday; she oversees the National Republican Senatorial Committee. She said, since there are no Republicans running and you're an Independent, they're sitting out the special. That creates a large money hole, and you'll need sixteen million to win."

Ty smiled, thinking, *What's he after?*

"What's your point?" Ty asked.

"Carlos is not known to be a great fundraiser."

"He's not. Ed Abbott is." Ty leaned back, crossed his legs and took a sip.

"Oh, Ed and Peterson made up? Huh. He's good at raising conservative money. But sixteen million is a lot, even for him."

"Are you offering to help?" Ty asked.

"Yes. However, that help goes back to my friends' questions about Carlos. This being an extraordinary campaign: FBI director appointed to the US Senate for Alabama and trumpeted by a liberal Georgian Democratic president makes many suspicious." He stopped talking for a minute to study Ty's face.

Ty showed no reaction.

"I, for one, do not fall into that camp. But I must listen to them." He took another sip. "They feel it would be best if someone else managed the pre–special election buildup. Someone to organize the structure and build your statewide name ID. A person with decades of experience at positioning a campaign for a complicated special election."

What is his game? Ty thought again.

"Sounds like you have someone in mind."

John smiled. "George Roka's my political advisor; he's been in Alabama politics for over twenty years. He's the best, which is why we want him to handle your pre-election campaign."

"John, I have someone. Thank you for the suggestion. However—"

"Ty," John interrupted, "it's important to the governor you win. I've been authorized to offer you eight million in September for the special." He leaned back slightly, letting the amount of money sink in. "I should not say this," he focused on Ty's eyes, "to the governor and my team, Roka is the key to that money," he said in a fatherly voice. He leaned back in his chair and took another sip.

"That's a very generous offer. You don't leave me much room; that's half the special election budget."

"This isn't heavy-handed; you don't have to accept our offer. We only want what's best. If you want to go it alone, that's okay. Things can always change."

Ty smiled. *Stupid passive-aggressive tactic,* he thought.

"I'll give you my answer the day the governor publicly announces the election schedule," Ty said.

Simmons glanced at his Rolex and frowned. "It never ends. I've got to attend another meeting with the governor in twenty minutes."

He stood and waited for Ty to stand. "I'm sorry we can't chat more about this. I'll tell the governor we spoke, and please let me know as soon as possible about your decision. I want to lock Roka down and get things off and running." He reached out hand and shook Ty's hand. "Senator, this is going to work out perfectly."

He turned and walked toward the hotel entrance.

Ty watched him walk away and thought: *He's out to own me.*

Later that same evening, Carlos was at home watching television, and his cell phone rang. Ty's name appeared on the screen.

"Yes, Senator?"

"I met with Simmons this evening; he wants me to hire George Roka for the pre–special election campaign and he offered eight million in September if I did."

Silence.

"Wow, that's a lot of money. Until the November special?"

"Yes."

Carlos rubbed his nose. "That's strange. You're not running a primary campaign?"

"Neither are you."

Silence.

"Good move," Carlos said.

"A no-doubter," Ty replied.

"Okay. How much time do we have before you give Simmons your answer?"

"Next week, when the governor announces the primary and special election dates. I'll tell Simmons the day before that announcement."

"I'll form the team and get the contracts signed by Monday. This is great. We'll need that money."

Carlos called Ed. "Simmons offered Ty eight million for the special general election. So, we only need to raise half."

"That's crazy. Why would he do that?" Ed asked.

"I don't care why; maybe he wants to screw Ullman. I don't care."

"Something's not right. That amount of money is nuts. There's only one Black conservative in the state legislature and Simmons offers that much money to elect an Independent? Why? What's the quid pro quo?"

"Roka runs the pre-special campaign."

"Simmons's henchman? What's the real deal? What did Leggett offer to get that much local money?"

"He didn't offer a thing; this is all Simmons."

"Bull. This is as nuts as the governor appointing Leggett and the President endorsing it. There must be more to it. I smell FBI blackmail."

"Ed, who cares why? It's just for the pre-special."

"Not the special?"

"Yes."

"There's got to be more. At what price?"

"Me," Carlos said.

"You were forced to give up day-to-day for eight million?"

"Yes."

"You're not worth eight million," Ed said with a laugh.

"Very funny."

"Who runs the general election?"

"Me."

"This is not right. A godsend, but not normal. I knew we'd never raise sixteen million. Raising eight million will be hard. I'll bet Leggett has no Alabama fundraising base—

which worries me about the deal. Simmons could use our lack of money against us and pull the deal—Which is scary. And Roka is a jerk," Ed said.

"Yes, he is, and you will raise the money."

"When does it come in?"

"September."

"This is bullshit. Leggett must have something on everyone. I repeat, he gets a liberal President to sing his praises, a good-time governor to appoint him and Simmons to finance half the election. Something's not right. Simmons is buying us."

"I don't care."

"What's your plan if the deal with Simmons craters?" Ed asked.

"You get screwed."

6
THE TEAM

Ed Abbott's second-floor office overlooked the Gun Island Chute Riverfront Park. The location was perfect: three blocks from the Biscuits' baseball stadium and three blocks from the Renaissance Hotel. Most legislators conducted their campaign business at the hotel during the four-month legislative session.

His favorite dive bar, The Silos, was just a quick two-hundred-yard walk through the tunnel under the railroad tracks. The best restaurant in Montgomery, Central, was three blocks away on Coosa Street.

The view and location impressed clients. The office space was divided into four rooms: his office faced south, where he could watch the paddlewheel boats glide up and down the river. The middle office, a windowless, ten-by-twenty-foot room, was used as an AI call center, high-dollar solicitation station, and development room. The AI-Holographic-XP server was located against the west wall in an air-conditioned cabinet. It was linked to the cloud and every digital device in his office.

A casual visitor would assume Ed's office was primitive, and he relied on personality to manage campaign finances, a bad assumption. Ed knew political communication was led by hi-tech innovation and invention. His AI-holographic generating computer gave him that advantage and Sabina never stopped searching for products or ideas.

The balance of the room was filled with a used, four-drawer metal desk on the south wall, facing six metal fold-up chairs arranged around three card tables joined together in the center of the room, a stained console table against the east wall, covered with office supplies, and a Keurig coffeemaker and condiments finished the accoutrements.

The other two rooms were windowless ten-by-ten-foot boxes, which Ed leased out to visiting political consultants on a short-term basis. Most of the time the two back rooms were filled with Ikea file cabinets, extra card tables, chairs, and used campaign material.

Ed's 800-foot office was separated from the other offices by a wall with a doorway. A small ten-by-ten-foot carpeted reception area, which was where Sabina, his one employee, worked.

Her desk was a Victorian worktable, which contained the most expensive piece of equipment in the office: a revolutionary AI-Holographic Visualization cube with personal attendant, which Sabina named Handmaiden.

The machine was the size of a hockey puck, which only answered her voice, could display any venue in an authentic looking, real-time five-foot square 3D holographic image, complete with sounds and scents. It would arrange details, answer questions, and perform tasks with a simple command to Handmaiden.

One morning Ed passed Sabina working at her desk, and said, "How's my damn first house? And your desk is still a mess."

"Handmaiden, kill Ed," Sabina replied.

Ed's private office was nicely furnished with a handcrafted four-drawer Ford executive desk, and dark leather chair next to the windows that faced the river. Two comfortable cloth swivel chairs faced the desk, and a nine-foot leather couch was against the east wall. The wall behind the couch was decorated with three prints: a Calder, Salvador Dali, and a Miro. The east and west walls were covered with candid photographs of celebrities, Alabama politicians, and major national donors.

On his desk, he had a leather ink blotter mat his grandfather had used, pens, pencils, three, 20" voice-activated AI monitors, an iPad, four cell phones, each with a different number. During the day it was not unusual for Ed to have two different calls going at the same time. That would be on a normal day.

At the end of each day Ed would list his goals for the following day, and suggestions for Sabina. Monday evening, he wrote: Sabina, tomorrow I have a meeting with Senator Leggett at 7:45 a.m. I hope he does not try to blackmail us.

Tuesday morning at 7:45 a.m. Ed walked into the "Ty

Leggett for United States Senate" campaign headquarters, wearing his newest blue suit.

Seeing an empty and dirty room, he began thinking about his first campaign: *Nothing like starting at the bottom.*

He looked around, not seeing anyone or hearing anything. He called out, "Senator Leggett?"

"I'll be right out." A moment later, Ty walked into the room wearing a pressed, white silk shirt, gray slacks, and black loafers.

"Ed Abbott?"

"Yes, Senator," Ed replied.

"Thank you for meeting me," Ty said.

They shook hands.

Nice grip, Ed thought.

"Good handshake," Ty said.

Ed smiled.

"Please, come into my plush office so we can talk."

Ty sat in the second chair facing the desk and turned it to face Ed.

"Please take off your coat. I'm not too big on formality," Ty said.

Ed removed his coat and sat.

"That's better, not so formal." Ty leaned back into the chair and smiled. "Carlos and Senator Peterson have told me you're the best finance person in Alabama."

"Please call me Ed and that's high praise, coming from those two."

"Though we've just met, I've already made the decision to work with you, so the ball is in your court. Do you have any questions for me?"

"I pretty much know your background and Carlos filled me in regarding your legislative priorities. This being your first run for office, most candidates believe politics is just like they learned about in school and the truth is very different. Campaigns are all about money and unfortunately, the candidate," Ed paused, hoping to soften the next statement, "is the tool to raise that money."

"What do you mean?"

"I mean you will call everyone you've ever met and ask them for money,"

Silence.

Ty nodded and looked at Ed.

"Can you do that?" Ed asked.

"No."

Typical candidate, Ed thought. "Senator—"

"Please call me Ty."

"Okay. Ty, your address book is the only way we can start raising money. No one else knows you."

Silence.

Finally: "Ed, I don't have friends and the only people I know work in government, and they won't donate."

Ed sat back and nodded for a moment. "Senator—I mean, Ty, we need at least five hundred thousand between now and June first, and your friends are critical to making that goal."

"I guess you have a lot of work ahead," Ty said.

"Ty, I'm not an investment manager with clients who do what I say. It's all about you."

"Ed, if you need me to call or meet with anyone, I'm a yes ... as long as I don't know them." He smiled, thinking, *This boy's a little thick.*

Ed laughed. "Well, that should be easy since you don't know anyone."

"Exactly. Now we're getting somewhere."

Ed sighed. *No way this is going to work*, he thought. "What about the President or Governor, maybe they'll help?"

"No, those cards have already been played," Ty said.

Oh, Ed thought, *can't use blackmail twice*? "Well, we do have Peterson's seed money, maybe that will be enough to kick things off."

"I think you're getting the picture, Ed."

Yep, the man is a mule, Ed thought.

"My fee is—"

"Ed, whatever you want to charge is okay with me, since you're doing the heavy lifting. Just work it out with Carlos."

"I do have one more question; it's something I ask every candidate. It helps me understand their character and how to best work with them."

"Okay, ask away," Ty said.

"What event in your life, would you say was your proudest moment of character?"

"Inheritance," Ty said with a straight face.

Back in his office, that afternoon, Ed's cell buzzed. Ed looked at the screen and saw Tim Tracy's name.

"Are we going fishing?" Ed asked.

"I'm calling to say I just signed on to help Leggett."

"Good, I'm sending my contract now," Ed said.

"Fishing next weekend." Tim hung up.

Tim Tracy was like a second son to Senator Peterson and the president of Peterson's marketing company. They both loved to fish, hunt, and protect the Second Amendment. Tim was a gifted writer; having him on the team guaranteed a successful fundraising effort. Which was important; everyone who donated was a vote, and Tim was very good at getting votes.

Thursday afternoon, Ed was in his Commerce Street office, playing video games. His cell phone buzzed, but there was no name on the phone's screen.

"This is Abbott."

"Roka here." A gruff voice said, "Senator Simmons is hosting a reception at his home in Mountain Brook this Friday night to thank you and the others for working on Leggett's campaign. Be there by six."

He abruptly hung up.

"Are you kidding me? What a jerk. I don't want to go," Ed said to no one.

Like he did for every event, Ed arrived ten minutes early at Simmons's Birmingham home. He pulled up to the driveway on Old Leeds Road and parked on the street. He sat in his Honda Accord listening to WJOX FM catching up on Crimson Tide baseball. He glanced down the long driveway, thought: *Wow, nice place, on the golf course.* And, *What a waste of a Friday night.*

Tim Tracy drove up in his new silver Chevrolet Suburban EV LX, glanced at Ed and turned down the driveway. Ed followed and they drove along the tree-lined 1,000-feet-to-road circular driveway in front of the home. They parked in front of a 9,000-square-foot Mediterranean-style home.

Tim stepped out of the truck dressed in his usual cowboy boots, blue jeans, and plaid shirt. A lean 6'2", Tim was a man of very few words. Ed liked him and respected his talents. There was never any BS with Tim.

Ed got out of his car, and called out, "Tim, wait a moment; we'll go in together."

Tim nodded and stopped.

"How are you?" Ed asked as he put on his blue blazer.

"Rather be home, with the wife."

"I'll bet a buck there's not a beer in the house, but there will be a box of See's Candy on the table."

Tim smiled. "Too easy," he said.

They walked up to the front door and rang the doorbell.

The door opened, and they were greeted by an attractive, thirty-something woman. "Hello, welcome. My name is Julie Simmons."

"Tim Tracy."

"Ed Abbott."

They shook hands.

"I'm so happy to meet y'all. Please come in," she said with a Southern drawl.

Julie was the senator's third wife, in her mid-thirties,

thin, with blonde hair. She was dressed casually in a blue silk skirt with a white blouse.

The marble-covered, ten-by-ten-foot foyer felt cold and separated from the living room.

The twenty-by-fifteen-square-foot living room was decorated with a ten-foot-long beige cloth couch that faced the fireplace, four matching recliners with ottomans, glass-covered coffee table, and lamps.

Floor-to-ceiling French windows faced west, and opened out to a charmingly furnished, screened-in patio, Olympic-sized swimming pool, grass yard, and a forest of loblolly pine trees lining the golf course. The aroma of wood burning in the fireplace and just-baked cookies gave the home a feeling of family.

"There is punch and cookies on the kitchen table; please help yourself. John will be down in a moment. He's putting little PJ to bed."

The doorbell rang again, and Julie welcomed Carlos and Caroline Felix, and Gonzo and Susie Diaz into the house. They were followed quickly by the campaign treasurer, Dave Tower, and pollster, Val Price.

Most of Ty's campaign team had worked with each other for five years or more. Only Val was new to the group.

Tim and Ed went to the back of the living room closest to the executive kitchen and stopped at the dessert table. Ed nudged Tim and gestured at the opened box of See's Candy.

"Every Mormon has a vice," Ed whispered.

Ty entered the living room from a short hallway, just past the Roman arches. The hallway led to a private library, bathroom, and back stairwell. He was dressed in a blue blazer, white shirt, and gray slacks. His thick, black hair was cut short.

"Hello," he said as he walked to the center of the room to stand in the middle of the assembled group. He shook everyone's hand, saying, "Thank you very much for joining us tonight; I know it's a long drive from Montgomery."

He looked at Ed. "Where's Sabina?"

"She had a date with a Maxwell pilot."

Julie joined the group and said, "Please help yourself to some punch and cookies."

After five minutes of small talk, Senator Simmons entered the room with the flair of a movie star. "Welcome, welcome. You all know each other, so introduction won't be necessary, and this is Senator Leggett's party, not mine. Please take a seat and make yourself comfortable." He waited a few moments as everyone settled. "Senator, take it away."

"Thank you, John and Julie, for hosting tonight and opening your home to us. I'll keep this short."

"Since most of us have recently met, I feel it's important to give some background. I'm a lawyer by education and a law enforcement bureaucrat by profession. I'm divorced and single and, by choice, have no social life."

"Our number one goal is to win the upcoming election. In the Senate, I will work to build on Alabama's economic success. I will accelerate the recruitment of labor-intensive manufacturing and high-tech companies. I will work with Alabama and Auburn University to prepare students to live with AI robots."

He paused and looked at Val.

"My expertise is law enforcement, and that will also be a part of my focus. People must feel safe, and the bad guys must not. Politics is not in my wheelhouse, so I will make political mistakes and I'm hoping you will help me avoid the big ones."

He smiled and again looked at his audience.

"We are in for a very challenging campaign against Senator Ullman. I'm convinced with Ed, Tim, and Gary's fundraising skills, along with Carlos, Susie, and Val's creativity, we will have the resources and advertising to win. On that front, Senator Simmons has graciously offered significant financial support for the November election." Ty turned to look at Simmons. "Thank you very much, John."

He looked back at the group. "I'm convinced we will achieve our goal of raising sixteen million net."

Ed's eyes popped, and he thought, *Net? That's forty-five percent more*! He glanced at Tim, and mouthed, "Wow."

"I think most of you already know there will be one short-term addition to the campaign team. Mr. George Roka will oversee the pre-general primary—which we're not in—until June. He couldn't be here tonight due to a previous engagement. After the primary, Carlos will transition back into managing the special general election." Ty stopped speaking and looked at Carlos.

"There is one person here tonight who's new to Alabama. Please take the opportunity to introduce yourself to my old friend, Doctor Val Price." Ty glanced at Val. "Val is the nationally recognized premier campaign advisor. He will conduct our polling and manage our campaign strategy. To outline roles, Gonzo, along with Susie, will create, produce, and place all the traditional media advertising. Working with them will be Gary Huckabee who will produce the social media campaign. Dave Tower will handle the accounting, FEC reports, expenses, and payroll. Ed and Sabina will raise our money and assist Dave by overseeing the day-to-day expenses."

Ty smiled. "That's our team." He looked at Val. "A little background: I was born and raised in Alabama and fully understand its history, all of it. As you can see, there are only two black men on our campaign team. Val and I know that will be used against us. Barry Gordy, of Motown Records, got that criticism. I have chosen, like him, the best people for the job. Having said that, we will focus our message on the future, while acknowledging the past, hopefully to ensure that the history of slavery never fades. Thank you for joining the team and being part of something special. We are going to win."

The group stood and clapped enthusiastically. Simmons walked up to Ty and shook his hand, saying, "Nice job."

Julie picked up a plate of cookies and offered them as she walked around the room. The group stood and mingled.

Tim Tracy waited a few minutes, then slowly drifted to the front door and left. Ed caught sight of Tim's back heading out of the front door. *Sneaky guy,* he thought.

Caroline Felix was mischievous. At five feet tall and small-boned, she was the mother of nine children—which most people found surprising. Caroline walked up to Susie and whispered, "Ready?"

Susie looked at Caroline. "Are you sure?" she asked.

The only child of a Fairhope, Alabama, banking family, Susie had been married to Gonzo for ten years. She was beautiful, smart, and rich—and didn't give a damn who knew it. She loved politics and Gonzo with passion. Susie was the most genuine plastic person in politics, and very good at buying electronic advertising.

Caroline grabbed Susie's hand and they quickly walked halfway down the hall, where Caroline stopped. "You wait here. If Julie heads this way, call out. If she says anything we'll tell her I was using the bathroom."

Caroline quickly ran into the master bedroom. Susie counted the seconds. Suddenly Caroline reappeared from the bedroom, her breathing heavy, her face pink.

Someone must be in the room, Susie thought.

"Are we okay?" she asked.

"Yes," Caroline whispered.

"Did you find them?" Susie asked.

"No, the damn secret Mormon underwear wasn't in the dresser."

They laughed out loud and ran back downstairs.

The following Monday, Paul Snider was in his Birmingham ranch-style office. Owning the number one car dealership in America kept him busy. Having grown up in a Dallas County, Alabama, working-class family, Paul joined the Navy and participated in the Grenada invasion. After the Navy, he found a job selling cars at a Montgomery dealership.

Thirty years later, he owned six super dealerships. He believed in hard work, an open mind, and big-game hunting.

Paul had a gift for making people feel important. He was a workaholic; if he was not in Africa hunting, he would be in his office working or networking at a charity fundraiser.

Paul did not drink much, but when he did, he was fun; his friends would tag along to keep him on the rails until he was ready to be taken home.

Paul's office phone rang. "Hello."

"Paul, this is Senator Leggett."

"Hello, Senator Leggett. How are you?"

"Better than I deserve."

"That's not true. How can I help?" Paul asked.

"On Monday, April eleventh, I'm hosting a six-thirty p.m. private reception at Central Restaurant in the Wine Cellar. Would you please attend?"

"Monday? Won't you be in DC?"

"Normally, yes; however, it was the only day we could reserve the Wine Cellar."

"I understand. What's the ticket price?"

"None."

"Uh-oh, that sounds *expensive*."

"Yes, but I need something even more precious. Would you please serve as my campaign finance chairman?"

"Of course. It would be my honor."

"Dave Tower is our treasurer. I hope you know Dave?"

"Yes, fine fellow, and what Ullman's doing is out of line. I would welcome the opportunity to set him straight."

"Great. I'm calling to invite you to a meeting to discuss

my upcoming senate campaign and the sixteen million we need. I'm working with Ed Abbott—"

"I know Ed," Paul interrupted. "You could not have chosen a finer person, and you don't need to say anything more. I'll be there and look forward to kicking the hell out of Jeffery Ullman."

"Thanks, Paul." Ty hung up, feeling relieved. He looked across the desk at Ed.

"Not bad, only twenty more calls to go," Ed said.

Ty sighed.

An hour later, the last call was finished.

Ty asked, "Tell me more about the finance meeting; who from the team will speak?"

"Me, Gonzo, Carlos, and maybe Tim."

"Why not Val? Won't they want to hear from the pollster?"

"We'll introduce him, but no. If he gets asked a question, he'll answer it. Fully. I've watched all his interviews; he has a fatal flaw: He can't lie. I even tested him on the issue of blackmail."

Ty smiled and nodded. "Everything you've said is true. Val is dedicated to finding the truth, which is why he'll speak at the finance meeting."

7

APRIL

"I'm calling Simmons late this afternoon to finalize Roka and his eight-million-dollar pledge," Ty told Carlos on his cell phone.

"That should be an easy call."

"'*Should* is the operative word. But I have some concerns about cash flow. Dave told me this morning that we're eating into Peterson's hundred thousand. My concern is that Roka might cause waves if we're short of cash."

"Ty, November is seven months away. This money lull is standard for all campaigns. It takes time to get the money flowing. Remember, we're building a sixteen-million-dollar business from scratch. This is no big deal; Ed will raise the money."

"Okay, I'll trust you, and I'm not too good at trust."

Carlos laughed. "We'll be okay for the next thirty days. The finance committee will be working soon, and money from the May dinner will start rolling in. Structurally, everything is in place. After you talk with Simmons, I'll inform the team of Roka's start date."

"I'm uncomfortable being beholden to a game player."

"It's no big deal. After we win in November, it'll never happen again. By the way, aren't you scheduled with Val to discuss the benchmark survey?"

"We've been trading calls. I understand he's finished the opposition research; his goal was to be in the field as soon as possible. It might already be done. I think this is a waste of time and money, given I have zero name ID."

He's going rogue, Carlos thought.

"Yes, but Ullman's isn't, and your profile is not that good."

"What do you mean?" Ty asked.

"A Black, divorced FBI cop from DC who hardly goes to church, was endorsed by a liberal president and appointed by a good-time governor."

"The church part is not true. I've met with Pastor Leon at the Sixteenth Street Church in Birmingham."

"That's great, but you live in Montgomery."

That evening, Carlos received a text from Ty: George Roka is now officially overseeing the pre–special campaign.

Carlos called Gonzo Diaz.

"Hello," Gonzo answered.

"Roka will start tomorrow, making me the titular head of the campaign until June seventh."

"He'll do a good job; anyway, if a problem develops,

which I doubt, I've got two campaigns with the Senate Republicans and can go directly to Simmons if need be."

"Okay, please tell Susie. Ty is calling Val, and I'll handle Ed and David."

"This will kill Ed; he loves watching the money," Gonzo said with chuckle. "The only spending should be outdoor advertising and some October TV time."

"Ed is my next call."

"That could be fun; tell him Roka also controls fund-raising expenses." Gonzo laughed.

Carlos hung up, scratched his nose, and changed his mind. *I'm not calling him now.*

"David here."

"George Roka starts tomorrow. He'll oversee the campaign structure, non-fundraising expenses, and disbursements until June seventh."

"Ty agreed to this?" David asked.

"Yes."

"Okay, this should only affect the FEC reports. Have Roka message his social security and billing address. What's his fee?"

"Twenty thousand a month, and April was the first month."

Dave gasped. "Wow, forty grand. Leggett approved that?"

"He had no choice. Simmons."

"Does Ed know?"

"No."

"You're going to tell him. Oh my, that'll send him into space. Does Gonzo or anyone else know?"

"No, just you. Gonzo only knows Roka's been hired.

I'm calling Ed next, and Dave, no one else needs to know the fee. It's only for two months."

"That fee is more than I make for doing the accounting for the entire campaign," Dave snapped.

"Don't feel like a homeless cat. I'm completely out until June."

Silence.

"Please tell me what Ed has to say; that should be good."

"Very funny," Carlos said.

Carlos hung up and rubbed his nose and sighed. *I've got to do this face to face.* He left his office and drove downtown to see Ed.

Ed was in his office making fundraising calls when Carlos came in and sat on the leather couch.

"Thanks, Paul, that's perfect. I'll tell the Senator you'll MC the Central dinner. This is awesome; you're a great American."

Snider laughed.

Ed gave Carlos an inquiring look and mouthed, "What's up?" Back to the phone: "Yes, thanks very much, Paul. I'll talk to you later." Ed put the cell phone on the desk. "What's happened? What's wrong?"

"Roka takes over tomorrow. He's overseeing the campaign and I'm out 'til June."

Ed laughed. "There's something pleasing about hearing you're out. We knew it was coming and it doesn't affect me; so why are you here?"

"He'll control all day-to-day expenses."

"That better not include fundraising."

"It doesn't."

"What's the problem, then? Is Caroline pregnant and you need another godfather?" Ed laughed again.

"No, and I can't use you as godfather twice."

"All right then, what's up? Why are you here?"

"I shouldn't tell you this, but I know you'll find out." Carlos rubbed his nose. "Roka is being paid twenty a month, April's included."

Ed's jaw dropped, and his eyes popped bigger. He leaned back in his chair. He shouted, "Sabina, you hearing this?"

"Yes," she said with an angry tone.

"You're kidding. That's twice the going rate."

"It's no big deal—"

"Easy for you to say, Mr. Spender. You call Snider and tell him how much Roka's making?" Ed interrupted.

"It's only for two months."

"I don't care if it's—"

"We had no choice. Simmons used his eight million as leverage," Carlos interrupted.

"Carlos, we're running thirty grand a month, now it's fifty. That's eleven cocktail parties and two hundred calls. This is crazy. We're running out of money."

"There's something else," Carlos said.

"What?" Ed asked with an amused expression. "I've got to wash Simmons's car?"

"No. But I like the idea. Simmons wants See's Candy at the cocktail parties and on each table at the May dinner."

Ed laughed. "You're kidding?"

Carlos's face did not show any emotion.

"You're not kidding. Oh, my, God, you're not. Our expenses are going to kill us, and you know who's going to get blamed? Not you, me. This is nuts. This is going to kill all our net goals."

"Tower can account for those expenses."

"What does that mean? Just like he did when Leggett went to bum-hick Autauga County and bought a twenty-five-hundred-dollar lamb! A twenty-five-hundred-dollar lamb. Are you kidding me."

"He didn't want to look cheap. Ullman bought one."

"Two idiots, and we have a debt problem. Any more good news?"

"No."

"Tell your buddy Simmons, no candy until we have a surplus, and Mr. Candidate, no more sheep."

"Leggett is starting to hate you," Carlos said.

"Good. No more effing sheep."

The next morning Ty's cell phone buzzed while he was driving to a fundraising meeting in Birmingham. It was Val.

"What's up?" Ty asked.

"This a good time to talk?"

"Yes, I'm on my way to Birmingham and have an hour."

"Okay, the quick benchmark survey is done; what we

learned wasn't unexpected," he said in his soft, professional voice. "You're unknown—"

"Shocking," Ty interrupted.

"That's an advantage, a blank tablet. Your public record is good, it only contained a divorce, law enforcement speeches, interviews, and Congressional hearings. No peccadilloes, which, considering how buttoned up you are, was no surprise."

"I'm not that tight. I like bourbon and you know as well as I do, one mistake and they'd use it to toss my Black ass to the street."

"Not always. Some brothers survive stupid."

"Why take the chance?"

Silence.

"A lot has changed, anyway, back to the results, a majority of the voters don't care about color, all they want is someone who tells the truth and loves Alabama."

"How strong was the anti-black vote?" Ty asked.

"About five percent. Two percent would never vote for a Black, period. The other three percent said, if the person played Alabama sports they'd vote for him."

Ty laughed. "I ran track. We can get that three percent."

Val laughed. "You weren't that fast. To win, we must create a political persona of 'hometown hero returns,' which will take time and money."

"I am no hero—what about Ullman?"

"He is liked in his senate district, not known statewide. Changing parties hurts him, especially in his district, and his cowboy persona doesn't work with voters under forty."

"What's the attack on me?"

"Non-religious Northerner endorsed by a liberal Georgia president."

"What's your conclusion—do we have a chance?"

"The full survey will be on June twenty-eighth after we've spent some marketing money. Those numbers will guide our game plan. From what I've seen, we raise the money, don't screw up, and Ullman does something stupid, we have a shot."

"That's not inspiring," Ty said.

Ty, it's a long way to November and we need lots of money. Do that and we'll win."

Central is the nicest restaurant in Montgomery. Its location, combined with its signature ribeye steak, bar, and master chef separates it from all the others.

It is the gathering place for political celebrities visiting Montgomery. Its posh, rich atmosphere makes it the perfect location for an exclusive dinner or political meeting. The exclusive basement room, named the Wine Cellar, is reserved for national politicians, the Governor, US Senators, or celebrities.

It was the only choice for Ty's Monday, April 11, 6:30 p.m. campaign finance committee meeting. Twenty wealthy and prominent, self-made men and women filed into the restaurant and walked down the flight of stairs to the Cellar. The room was undecorated, its rich, oiled-teak décor, along with the wine wall and leather furniture broadcasting wealth. A long, dark-stained mahogany table, with twenty-two matching wooden chairs, filled the room.

Twenty blue-leather folders, with each person's name prominent on the front label, were at each seat. The folders contained the name, address, and cell numbers of each member of the finance committee, a draft campaign budget, and staff listing.

Each person was offered a drink of their choosing when he or she arrived. Delicate, handcrafted hors d'oeuvres were passed around by the restaurant staff. Senator Simmons was against having alcohol at the event; however, he had no choice but Ty and Ed insisted. After fifteen minutes of small talk, Ty went to the front of the room and stood facing the microphone and guests.

"Please be seated," he said. He waited while the room settled down. "Thank you very much for agreeing to support my campaign for United States Senate and joining us tonight. I promised Paul that this meeting will only last an hour, and I know for some, that will be sixty minutes too long."

The group laughed. Ty smiled as he looked around the room. "My future job as a United States Senator is to propose and vote for or against legislation and bring jobs to Alabama. Which I intend to do. But first we must get there. Which is why I've hired the best political consultants in Alabama, if not America."

He pointed at the team standing, to his right, against the side wall.

"It's important that each of you know how honored I am to have your support. Thank you.

"Senator Ullman feels differently; he has chosen to leave his conservative values and register as an Independent. We welcome the challenge."

People clapped and one person shouted out, "We'll show him."

Ty nodded and said, "Yes, we will. Senator Ullman's decision means the special general election will determine who wins the Senate seat. The campaign timing is as follows: The governor has called for a June seventh primary, and the general will be Tuesday, November eighth. We have one hundred fifty-four days to win this election.

"To most of you I'm only a voice on the telephone or an image on television. So, I'll take a moment to tell you about myself. I prefer to be called Ty, not Senator or Tyler. Please call me Ty. I love baseball and look forward to going to a couple Biscuit games. I am divorced, no children, and do not go to church much. I'm pro-family, open-minded, and a member of the NRA.

"When I told the President I'd decided to leave the FBI, his first question was, 'Are you nuts?'"

People laughed, as did Ty.

"He was right."

More laughter.

"I was born in Alabama, went to Tuskegee Institute, class of 'eighty-two, a Fighting Frog. Howard University for a political science degree, which was a challenge. I was more interested in girls," he twisted his lower lip slightly and put a wry smile on his face.

Laughter.

"Next came Georgetown Law School, the FBI, and now back here in Alabama. Yes, Alabama. The home of Rosa Parks, Helen Keller, and ironically, the first 911 call in America—what a surprise," he said with a sarcastic laugh.

Others joined in laughing.

"I fully understand the history of Alabama, all of it. My focus is on the future, while acknowledging the past, and the pain slavery and racism caused. As you can see, there is one other Black man here tonight, Doctor Val Price, who you haven't met yet. Val is my friend, and without peer, the best campaign strategist and pollster in America. He has one shortcoming: He cannot fudge the truth. Which makes him exceptional in politics. Lastly, I challenge everyone, please invite a person of color to join us, it will be hard, they will not want to go, you'll have to invite several times and push. This is how we overcome misunderstanding, and how we'll bring Alabama together as one great family."

Ty looked around the room and saw expressions of contemplation.

"While in law school, I clerked for Justice Thurgood Marshall. After I passed the bar, he sent me a simple note, it read: 'Go work at the FBIthose boys need changing.' I did and we made great strides in removing stereotypes and arresting thieves and evil thugs. Some thought they were the smartest person in the room." He smiled. "Now that really is true—at Englewood Federal Prison." Ty grinned and raised his eyebrows.

People laughed.

He looked around the room; everyone looked enthralled.

"My professional expertise is law enforcement. I have always believed that people must feel safe or nothing works. I've been told I'm too buttoned up, but that's not true; I like great bourbon and baseball." Ty smiled.

"After forty years with the Bureau, I've learned the bad guys never stop. I've seen enough hate and death to fill the ocean. I did all I could to make changes and I'm proud of my tenure."

He looked around the room.

"Now the boys in the US Senate need changing—why Independent? I've learned that independent legislators force both sides to play nice; they need that vote. Unfortunately, independence comes at a price. We're alone facing two Goliath forces. It's not the first time I've faced long odds. They will use every tactic to get us off course. Our campaign team will be criticized for not having enough people of color or we're Northern carpetbaggers. If that doesn't work, they'll just make shit up."

Surprise, loud laughter.

"Looking to the future, my plan is to build on Alabama's economic success. A two percent unemployment rate is terrific. My goal is to accelerate the recruitment of high-tech companies. And work with our universities and colleges to educate students so they stay in Alabama, raise families, and build a great Southern state."

Clapping.

"At the Bureau, my door was always open, and that will never change, please stop by, text, or call. We are a team. Again, thank you for joining this historic effort and being part of something special."

Some people stood and there was loud clapping.

Ty nodded, saying, "Thank you."

Lots of clapping.

"Before I introduce the campaign team, the governor gave me some advice. He said I'll need two things to win: A lot of money and BS and—"

"He would," Paul Snider interrupted.

Ty laughed.

"I've chosen the best people I could find. The men and women you will meet tonight are at the top of their fields, and I'm proud to have them on my team." Ty looked to his right and gestured towards Val, Carlos, Gonzo, Susie, Ed, Tim, and Sabina standing against the side wall.

"You all know Ed Abbott."

"There's the BS," someone shouted.

The room broke into loud laughter.

Ty also laughed and looked at Ed.

"Ed, along with Sabina, will coordinate all the campaign funds and manage the campaign expenses. Before we get to Ed, I have a special announcement: The Alabama Republican leadership, through Senator John Simmons, has committed to raising eight million for the general election."

Sounds of pleasant surprise and whispers drifted around the room, and people clapped. Ty gestured toward Simmons, who stood against the wall next to Sabina.

"Thank you, John," Ty said, clapping his hands.

More clapping.

"Ed, would you please come forward and say a few words. As few as possible."

There was laughter as Ed walked from the side of the room to the podium.

"Thank you, Senator. I will be brief."

"That's not possible," Paul said out loud.

Ed laughed and looked at Sabina. "Sabina, would you like to say anything?"

"No," she said, shaking her head.

"Okay then, the fundraising plan is contained in the blue folders, along with a copy of the Federal Election Campaign laws. No individual shall donate more than twenty-nine hundred dollars during the primary."

Ed looked around the room.

"We have forty-seven days before the general election kicks off. Since we are not on the primary ballot, our goal is to spend six hundred thousand between now and the primary buying TV ads and using social media. to lift Ty's statewide name ID.

"Our event fundraising plan between now and June seventh is simple. We will host eight small receptions and a fundraising dinner on May seventeenth, here at Central. Our goal is to raise fifteen thousand per reception and two hundred thousand at the dinner. Now, for the finance committee. Membership is limited to twenty-five. Each member is asked to donate the maximum amount of thirty-five hundred dollars, fill a table of ten at the Central event, and raise ten thousand dollars beyond that by June seventh. That's a total individual commitment of eighteen thousand five hundred dollars."

Ed looked around the room. "Any questions?"

No one did.

"Perfect. We'll email all the dates and timelines later tonight. Thank you."

Ed stepped away from the microphone and moved back to the far wall.

Ty stepped up to the podium. "Thank you, Ed." He

turned to look at Carlos and gestured to him to step forward. "Now, Mr. Felix is tasked with overseeing the special election campaign. Carlos is a retired Birmingham police officer, and he managed the Republican upset victory over Senator Rosa. Carlos, would you please say a few words?"

Carlos stepped awkwardly to the podium. He was dressed in a wrinkled black polyester suit. He looked uncomfortable. Regardless of how many times he spoke publicly, the Birmingham cop felt inferior.

"We will win in November. Mr. Ullman will have a tough time explaining his defection. The balance of my job is to ensure all the pieces of the campaign work well together." He stepped away from the podium and walked back to the wall.

Ty looked at Carlos for a moment. "Uh-huh. Well, thank you, Carlos. That kind of says it all," Ty said.

Paul laughed out loud.

"Now for Mr. Gonzo Diaz. Gonzo and Susie will create and develop the digital advertising campaign. They have a twenty-year career in political advertising and have consulted or done media for campaigns throughout the country. Gonzo, please say a few words," Ty said.

Gonzo was dressed in a dark, handmade, three-piece wool suit. Having spent many hours with the richest families in America, Gonzo was very comfortable speaking before money. Gonzo did not need to work but enjoyed the challenge of the political game.

"Good evening," he said with a hint of a Caribbean accent. "I will not get into specifics for tactical reasons. Our budget is designed to spend five and a half million on traditional media, four hundred thousand on direct mail, half a million on social media, and seven hundred thousand on billboards. All those numbers can change at a moment's notice; it all depends on how much Senator Ullman spends and how we're doing—"

"Excuse me, I have a question," Paul Snider interrupted, "you have not mentioned a Democrat opponent."

At this Carlos came forward. "I can answer that. Right now, sixty-two percent of Alabama votes Republican. That is why Senator Ullman did not become a Democrat. There is only one Democrat considering running; his name is Jack Horner, a self-employed truck driver with few financial resources and limited connections with the Democrat leadership . The registration is sixty-two percent Republican, thirty-two percent Democrat and roughly two- to three-percent Independent. This is a Republican state, and the election is between us and Senator Ullman."

"What if the Democrats go all in with Horner and split the vote?" Paul asked.

"That's a great question. If the Dems do that, we're guaranteed a win. Ullman needs every Democrat vote to win. If they back Horner, the Republicans will split between us and Ullman and we'll crush Ullman," Carlos answered and left the microphone.

Ty stepped forward. "And now for Doctor Val Price. Val is our truth doctor. He will tell us if our messaging is working, where, and by how much. He will also analyze our opponent's message. Our strategy will follow Val's survey questions and answers. In baseball, every team must have a closer, a pitcher who ices the game. Doctor Val Price is our closer. Val, would you please say a few words?"

Doctor Price approached the microphone dressed in a dark gray wool suit. When Val spoke, he commanded attention because he spoke softly and chose his words carefully. Val loved what he did for a living and radiated confidence and enthusiasm in trying to predict political action.

"Thank you, Ty. I also like baseball. Ladies and gentlemen, it is my pleasure and professional honor to be involved in this historic campaign. I have been in the public opinion business for over forty years, and I have one rule: The truth will set you free, and bias will lead you astray. We will not lose this campaign, and Ty Leggett will be reelected as Alabama US Senator."

"Wow, okay," Snider shouted out, "let's go help Ty."

8
COMPLICATED

Ed called Carlos. "Some good news. I just nailed down a Sikhs' fundraiser—which might raise enough to pay half of Roka's fricking fee."

"It'll be in Bessemer County, at Mr. Darsan Sing Bain's home, next Wednesday, at six p.m. The goal is twenty-five thousand and, most importantly, Sikh votes. Have Ty brush up on Alabama agriculture and Sikh history. Oh, you can tell Simmons they don't drink alcohol."

Ed laughed.

"You and Caroline should go, and drive Ty. This could be cool. This is my first time working with the Sikhs. I hear they're wonderful people and living the American dream."

"Okay, I'll ask Caroline. That's a long drive from Montgomery," Carlos said.

"It's not that bad. By the way, the money for the Central dinner is starting to trickle in and the cocktail parties are cash flowing. At this rate, we should have no debt and lots of money to meet our June seventh goal. That's if we stop spending."

The next Wednesday, Ed called Ty.

"Have you left for the Sikh event?"

"Yes, we are on our way," Ty said.

"Tell me about the Sikhs?" Ty asked.

"They're a religious people from the Punjab State of Northern India next to Pakistan. They migrated to Alabama beginning in the early 1950s. They're conservative, don't drink alcohol, have semi-arranged marriages, and are hard-working. I understand there are three things Sikhs care about: God, family, and money. I hear, they sometimes get a little confused if it's money or family." He laughed.

"The religion is five hundred years old and respects the universal truths found in all major faiths. They are farmers, professionals and entrepreneurs. They educate both sexes, treat one another as equals, regardless of social position. Something to keep in mind tonight; they don't keep secrets.

"No, keep going," Ty said.

"Darsan Sing Bains, our host, left the Punjab when he was eighteen and arrived in Yuba City, California. He was broke. He started out pruning fruit trees and working the orchards. He saved every penny, understood land value, and started to trade farmland. He met his future wife, a local girl, and on a napkin wrote how he was going to make her rich; had three children. Forty years later, he's the Sikh world leader and a billionaire."

"Ed. Great job. I look forward to meeting him," Ty said.

"I just arrived. See you in." He disconnected the call and drove down a gravel driveway toward a ranch house. The home had been carved out of a plum orchard. There was nothing special about the house; it was painted gray and could not be seen from Morgan Road. The only oddity was a two-story garage attached to the ranch home.

Ed parked in front of the house, went to the front door and knocked; no one answered. He rang the doorbell, no answer. He walked around the driveway looking for anyone; a boy who looked to be about ten years old walked out of the garage and approached Ed.

"Hello," he said.

"Hi. I'm Ed Abbott with Senator Leggett, and Mr. Bains is hosting a reception here tonight."

"My parents are working and not home."

"The reception starts in thirty minutes," Ed said, feeling a little panicked.

"Would you like to wait in the house?"

"Sure. What's your name?"

"Karm."

"Nice to meet you, Karm."

Ed followed the boy into the garage and saw a stairway leading above the garage.

"What's up there?" Ed asked, nodding toward the stairs.

"Our prayer room."

"That sounds cool," Ed said.

"Would you like to see it?"

"Sure."

They walked up the stairs and entered a 1,000-foot, almost-empty, carpeted room.

"Please take off your shoes," Karm said.

They removed their shoes. The walls were lined with ten life-sized colorful paintings of men dressed in traditional Indian clothing. The room had a gentle aroma of incense.

At the far end of the room was a two-by-three-foot four-poster bed. A silk shroud was draped around the bed. On the mattress was an ornate blanket and pillows. At the foot of the bed, a wooden stand supported a replica temple and a five-inch-thick book.

"May I go over there?" Ed pointed across the room.

"Yes."

Karm stayed near the doorway and watched Ed move around the room.

"Who are those people in the paintings?" Ed asked.

"Our gurus. You would call them prophets."

"And the bed, over there?"

"My father comes up here several times a day to pray. He puts the bible onto the small golden Palki temple stand in the morning, and each night he returns it to the bed."

"Why to bed?"

"Our bible is living; we even offer it ceremonial food and drink."

"Wow, this is cool." Ed studied the room for several minutes, then glanced at his phone: 6:10 p.m.

"We've got to go; Senator Leggett will be here any minute. Thank you very much, Karm, for showing me this beautiful room."

"You're the first. Most people don't ask."

They left the room and walked down the stairs, through a small office into the kitchen and from there into the living room. No one was home. Ed started to panic.

"I'll call my dad." Karm left the room.

Ed began to pace around the living room, thinking, *what do I do if no one shows?*

Karm came back into the room. "My parents are outside with Senator Leggett and another couple."

Ed quickly walked out the front door.

They were all standing in the driveway talking to Darsan and Santi Bains. Caroline was dressed in a light-blue business pants suit. Ty was wearing a blue suit with an American flag lapel pin. Carlos was dressed as usual, like a slob. The Bains were in dusty blue jeans, long-sleeved farm workwear. Darsan, like most Sikh men, had a beard, a silver bracelet, and a turban.

"Please, please, come in, come in," Santi said in her fast-speaking high-pitched voice.

The group moved into the house.

Ed followed behind, walking beside Caroline Felix. "I don't think there's any secret underwear here," he whispered.

Caroline laughed.

They entered the house.

"Please, please, sit," Santi said, pointing to a blue, ten-foot-long cloth couch, facing the stone fireplace.

Darsan and Santi left the room and disappeared down a hallway past the kitchen.

Ed looked at Ty, raised his eyebrows and shrugged his shoulders with a "I don't know what to do" look.

After about five minutes of silence the doorbell rang.

Karm opened the door, and twenty couples entered the home. All were Sikh farmers; the men were dressed in clean blue jeans, untucked pressed shirts, and each man had on a different color turban. The women were wearing colored, silk Salwar Kameez dresses. They all took off their shoes.

Ty stood and shook everyone's hand. "Hello, I am Senator Ty Leggett. It's a pleasure to meet you," he said to each person. The room came alive with conversation.

Finished, the room went silent; the guests stood facing Ty without making a sound. Darsan and Santi returned to the living room. They had changed. Darsan was wearing a dark business suit jacket, white shirt, gray slacks, and no shoes. Santi was in a pastel-colored silk Salwar Kameez dress, her feet bare.

Darsan took a seat in a large reclining chair that faced the couch, and Santi went into the kitchen. The men sat on the surrounding chairs and the women remained behind near the center of the room.

The room went silent.

Darsan stood and introduced each couple to Ty. After the introductions, Santi grabbed Caroline's hand. "Come with me, come with me," she said, with her fast cadence. All the women followed and moved away from the men toward the fireplace at the back of the room and sat.

After a long wait, which was becoming uncomfortable, Darsan, still standing, said, "Senator Leggett, thank you for coming to my home." He sat, as did the other men.

Ed looked at Ty and mouthed, "Say something."

Ty stood and walked toward the kitchen, turned and faced the assembled group. He said, "*Sat sri akal—*"

"*Sat siri akal*," the men quickly answered.

"I understand in Punjabi those words mean 'God is Truth,'" Ty said.

Darsan and the other men all smiled, and repeated in unison, "*Sat sri akal*."

"Thank you very much, Mr. Bains, for inviting me here tonight and supporting my campaign." He smiled and nodded. "My background is in law enforcement and not agriculture. I hope tonight is the beginning of my education in farming.

He paused and looked around the room.

"What you need to know about me is, I strongly support safety and family values. I'm not the type of person to grandstand or make a lot of noise. I will fight for what is important and do everything I can to bring high-paying jobs to Alabama. The right to worship unafraid is the foundation of being an American."

He looked around the room. There was no reaction to his words; all the men were staring at him.

Silence.

Darsan stood and looked at Ty. "Senator Leggett," he said in his deep, low-pitched mumbling voice, "thank you for coming to my home and we hope you will fight for farmers and our families." He turned away from Leggett and looked at the assembled men. "Senator Leggett is a good man." Darsan sat.

Santi, Caroline, and the other women returned to the front of the room.

Silence.

Karm came up to Ed and said, "You can go now."

Ed gestured to Ty. "Time to go."

Ty stood next to Caroline and Carlos.

"Thank you all for supporting my campaign," Ty said.

Ty, Caroline, Carlos, and Ed left the house and walked to Carlos's Explorer.

"I've been doing fundraising for a long time, and I've never seen anything like that. I have no idea what to do next," Ed whispered.

Ty took off his coat and turned to face Ed. "That *was* interesting, no food, no drinks, no checks. It took longer to get here than we were inside. What was the goal for this reception?"

"Twenty-five thousand. I'll go back in, see what I can learn."

Ty got in the back seat, Carlos drove, Caroline sat in the front passenger seat and they drove away.

Ed returned to the house. Everyone was in the living room, laughing and talking. Darsan was speaking in Punjabi.

Ed stood in the front foyer, not knowing what to do.

Karm approached him.

"You can leave. My father will negotiate, and you can come by tomorrow at noon to pick up the donations."

Feeling very confused, Ed said, "Please thank your father for me, and I'll see him tomorrow around noon. Will you be here?"

"No, just my father. If his car is not here, just go into the back office and wait. *Sat sri akal*," Karm said.

"Karm, before I leave, was the senator right? What those words mean?"

"It's a Sikh greeting. It means many things. My favorite is 'The truth will prevail.'"

"How cool. I learned a lot. Thank you, Karm; this was nice. Goodnight."

Ed got into his car and called Ty as he drove back to Montgomery.

"Well, how'd we do?" Ty asked.

"I have no clue. I'm to come back at noon tomorrow to pick up the money. Mr. Bains's reputation is stellar. I'm sure he's good for the donation."

"That was my kind of event. Short, sweet, and simple. I hope we see a lot more of Mr. Bains and his family. He's my kind of person. Hard-working and to the point," Ty said.

Carlos called Ed two days later. "I'm still not over it. That was the strangest event I've ever been to."

"It was different," Ed said.

"It took us longer to get there than the event lasted and talk about a bottom-line endorsement, 'He's a good man.' Wow, I wish my life was that simple."

"I wish fundraising was that simple. I picked up twenty-five thousand yesterday and there were no strings attached. I shook Mr. Bains's hand; he didn't say anything, and I left."

"Will they do something for Ullman?"

"No, I understand they don't cover their bets. They're not game players—at least, not Mr. Bains," Ed said.

"The timing is good. We now have enough money to get through May and can start paying off Peterson's loan. How's the Central event going?"

"The invitations are out; everything is set. Snider and the finance committee have their tickets, and thanks to the weekly cocktail parties, we have another hundred people selling tickets. At four tickets each, the event could explode."

"What's the goal?" Carlos asked.

"The Central holds four hundred; at five hundred per ticket, we could raise two hundred grand. The nonattending donations usually cover the cost of the dinner; we should net a hundred sixty thousand. And half of that money is in."

"Any PAC money?" Carlos asked.

"No. I've spoken to Terry Joseph's staff. They told me he's made some calls, but not to expect any help until late October," Ed said.

"That's no big deal. With what we're raising, we should get through August. Any complaints about Roka?"

"No idea. Haven't heard a word. He deals directly with Tower and the HQ staff. The only thing that's odd, I haven't seen any expense reports since he took over. Anyway, our net fundraising is on track. You know why?" Ed asked.

"Why?"

"No See's Candy."

Carlos hung up.

The next afternoon, Ed was in his office going over the finance plan when his cell phone vibrated. He quickly searched for it, pressing down on the pile of papers. He answered without glancing at the screen.

"This is Abbott."

"Tower here."

"Hey, Dave. Are you calling about the July FEC report?"

"No, we have a much bigger problem. The campaign is spending money as fast as it comes in."

"What?"

"Hillyard, the campaign office manager just called from the headquarters, and said six people just showed up and said they'd been hired. Ed, that's another eighteen thousand added to our monthly budget. We're going to run twenty thousand dollars over budget, and that doesn't include Roka's two-month fee."

"*What!* How can this happen? He's only been in charge for six weeks!"

"The campaign is buying enough supplies to last until next year. I just paid for a thousand pencils, pens, five hundred reams of paper, and five-thousand-yard signs."

Ed leaned back into his chair. "We're not running yet. We don't need yard signs, and nobody uses paper. This is crazy, why would anyone spend money like this?" Ed asked.

"It's not Hillyard or Leggett; this is coming from Roka, and Ed, we're almost broke. And haven't put a dime toward the special runoff election."

"Have you spoken to Carlos? He meets with Roka once a week."

"No."

"Call him."

"No."

"Come on, Dave, don't make me out to be the bad guy."

"No."

"Why?"

"I don't like you." Dave hung up.

Ed stood up, walked to the window, and looked at the Chute River. *Something's wrong. This can't be an accident,* he thought.

"Sabina," Ed hollered, "what's a guarantee about accidents in politics?"

"There is no such thing," she called from the other room.

Two hours later, Ed was calm enough to call Carlos.

"This is Carlos."

"What going on at headquarters? Tower just called and said we're running a thirty-thousand-dollar monthly deficit. He ran the numbers: After we repay Peterson's hundred grand, we won't have enough money to survive August. Carlos, we're in trouble. If you don't fix this, the July FEC report will kill us," Ed said.

"That's not possible. I meet with Roka weekly. He's experienced and hasn't said a word. Tower is jerking your chain."

"Tower's not the type of guy to joke around. This is a big deal. If the finance committee finds out or the July FEC report shows we're broke, we're screwed. We're one bad money headline from losing this campaign."

Ed paused.

"Ty can't say anything; Simmons would use this against him. Carlos, this issue could lead us into a trap."

"I can't do anything. I'm out until July. It took a lot of arguing to get Roka to grace me with weekly updates. Obviously, he's holding back," Carlos said.

"What do you talk about when you meet him, golf?"

"Not funny. All he tells me is money is coming in, and all's good. The rest is strategy and stuff."

Silence.

"This is crazy; it must be on purpose," Ed said.

"You're wrong. Why would Simmons put his guy in the campaign to sabotage us? You're wrong. Roka must have a reason."

"I don't care about the why, I just know we have a July FEC report and if we have a debt and no cash, we're done for. You've got to tell Leggett what's happening," Ed said.

"No, he'd freak out. We've got to keep him positive. We've got to take care of this," Carlos said.

"You're right; don't tell him."

Silence.

"I've got an idea," Ed said. "I'll call Tower and ask him to open a savings account and deposit fifty cents on every dollar we raise from now on."

"What about the weekly finance reports to Roka?"

"Dave can list the savings as expenses, and that should hold him off until June seventh," Ed paused. "Send Tower a text that you're onboard; he'll need backup if Ty asks whose idea this was."

"Ed, are you sure this is legal?" Carlos asked.

"Yes, as long as it's in the FEC report."

"This is dangerous. If Simmons or Jacobs find out, we'll never work again."

"So? Something is going on and we've got to protect Ty. Carlos, we must hold cash until we figure it out."

"This is dangerous," Carlos repeated.

"You remember what Wendy Borchardt did in the Reagan campaign?"

"No. That was in the nineteen-eighties."

"She hid a million dollars in the trunk of her car to keep it away from Reagan's idiot campaign manager. We're not the first to protect a candidate."

"This is a big deal," Carlos said.

Paul Snider was at his Montgomery Ford Lincoln dealership when he picked up his desk phone and called Ed.

Ed was at his desk making fundraising calls. "This is Abbott."

"It's Paul. I'm at the Montgomery store, and I have a bunch of checks for the Central fundraiser. What would you like me to do with them?"

"It's Wednesday. How about I come by and pick them up? Four-thirty all right at the dealership?" Ed asked.

"No, come by my home office."

Ed drove thirty minutes from his Commerce Street office to Snider's second home and private office. Paul spent most of his time working out of that building, and it was where he stored his hunting trophies.

Ed turned right into the driveway and pulled up to a 2,000-square foot, Frank Lloyd Wright–looking building.

At the front of the five-acre property was a gray building. It blended into the trees and bushes, to hide it from the road.

Ed parked and entered the building. He was greeted by a thin, middle-aged woman sitting at a long wooden desk. Papers covered her cluttered desk.

"Hello, Mr. Abbott. I'll tell Paul you're here."

Paul entered the reception room with a big grin, reached out his long, thin arm, and in his remarkable manner, pumped Abbot's hand like it had been years, and he truly missed seeing him.

"It's great to see you, please come in," he said.

Ed followed Paul down a short, carpeted hallway and turned left into a 1,000-square-foot comfortable living room-looking space.

There was a big desk at the back of the room, and behind the desk were two French doors leading to a patio and garden. Two deep leather chairs faced the desk, with a six-person conference table in the center of the room. A wood- burning fireplace was against the back wall, next to a crystal bar.

"What can I get you?" Paul asked.

"Jack, if you can."

Paul fixed two drinks. Abbott sat in the chair facing the conference table. Paul pulled a chair close to Abbott's and the two clinked glasses. He sat, leaned back, and took a sip of his bourbon.

"How's the campaign going?" he asked.

"Drama, lots of drama."

"Is Ty okay?"

"Yes, we're keeping him from the deep-dive BS."

Paul smiled. "How's the Central dinner coming along?"

"Thanks to you, the committee, and the cocktail fundraisers, we'll sell all four hundred tickets and raise the two hundred thousand."

"That's great. But you said there's drama?"

"Oh, it's nothing." Ed took another sip.

"Come on, tell me." Paul finished his own drink, set it on the table, leaned back into the chair. "What's the drama?"

Ed still feeling reluctant, "It seems Senator Simmons is playing money games against Ty. I won't know for sure until July."

"Okay, let's wait until then."

Ed smiled, finished his drink, and put it on the table.

Paul stood and reached out his hand and pumped Ed's hand.

"Thanks for coming by and picking up the checks. I'll see you in three weeks," Paul said.

Ed returned to his Commerce Street office. As he walked up the stairs, he glanced at his watch: 6:00 p.m.

Not bad, almost time to go eat, he thought. He cleaned his desk of that day's notes and finished writing his things-to-do list for tomorrow's tasks.

His cell phone rang.

"This is Abbott."

"You've got to come down to Silos; the place is a zoo.

The nurses are holding a reception to lobby the governor. Half the legislature is here."

Ed recognized Bill Saracino's voice. Bill ran one of Peterson's most successful PACs and was the cool intellect behind Peterson's conservative network.

"You're there now?" Ed asked.

"Yes."

"I'm on my way."

The Silos was a dive bar just blocks from the Renaissance Hotel; it was considered a Democrat hangout. However, there were times when both Parties' legislators and staff stopped by for drinks and to party.

Tonight was such an occasion. The Nursing Association had a landmark legislative proposal due for a final vote the next day in the senate, and the association was not going to lose that vote.

Hundreds of nurses had moved through the Capitol Building for weeks, lobbying legislators, staff, and virtually anyone who would listen. Campaign donations were flowing into the coffers of both parties, and it was all coming to a peak at Silos.

Silos Bar was owned by a retired lightweight boxer, and the clientele reflected him and the sport. Prostitutes, thieves, business leaders, community leaders, legislators and, on this occasion, anyone looking for a good time.

Ed walked through the underground tunnel to the infamous bar. Several lobbyists and a state representative were standing, talking, as he reached the gravel walkway.

He glanced around the outdoor seating area; it was packed with people and the conversations were loud, with lots of laughter. Ed didn't see anyone he recognized, so he walked up the single flight of wooden stairs toward the main bar to find Saracino.

Ed looked around the wood deck and thought, *I'm in another world. It's a feeding frenzy.*

The bar deck was twenty-feet-by-thirty-feet. A twenty-foot-long wooden bar was on the back wall, and stools faced the bar. Every seat was filled; the deck was packed.

Photographs of the owner in his boxing heyday, along with a set of used boxing gloves, a faded photograph of the Lynyrd Skynyrd band and Kid Rock hitting a golf ball, hung on the wall.

A cash register, sink, glasses, bottles of liquor and a beer tap filled the remaining front counter space.

Five six-person square wooden tables and chairs lined the railing that faced the lower seating area. Glasses and empty beer bottles covered the tables.

The lower seating area had two rows of Formica tables, surrounded by dirty plastic chairs. At the back of the seating area was a dance floor with a jukebox playing country western music. Tall cocktail tables and stools faced the dance floor; people stood around talking and watching the fun before them.

Ed looked out at the mass of people, and thought, *This is crazy.*

The bar was filled with tight dresses, low-cut silk blouses, and the regulars were soaking up the party; most were already feeling no pain. Loud laughter and talking, with the banging music made hearing difficult if not impossible.

Ed walked toward the bar and got a double-neat bourbon. Finished, he looked for Bill Saracino and, after a quick scan, found him sitting at one of the tables along the rail facing the dance floor. There was an open chair and Ed sat.

Sitting with Bill was Jesse Urban, the state treasurer, and without question the most influential and powerful politician in the state. He controlled the state's investment money and a lot of New York investment companies' job openings. He was considered the godfather of Alabama politics. Next to Jessie was his chief of staff, acting as a babysitter; it was a drinking night.

"Wow, what a scene," Ed screamed at Saracino.

Bill nodded.

Ed looked at Jessie, whom he did not know too well. "Hello, Mr. Treasurer."

Jessie did not reply directly. All he said was "No one cares, no one cares."

Ed smiled and glanced a knowing grin at the female chief of staff.

"Thank you for saving me a seat," Ed said to Bill.

"I didn't. The governor just left the table."

"Okay. Thanks, anyway. I've never seen anything like this. It's nuts."

"No one really cares," Jessie said again.

Ed finished his drink and left the table to fight his way to the bar for another bourbon. With a drink in hand, Ed spotted two lobbyists he knew and went over to talk.

"Hey, how are you guys tonight?" he asked.

"Having fun looking at who's here. It's a freak show," the shorter of the men said.

"This puts the Star Wars bar scene to shame," the taller man said.

"The governor just left, and Senator Ingles is in the

bathroom having his vote changed," the shorter lobbyist said.

"That's gross," Ed said, "he's married."

The two men laughed and looked at Ed, "You're so naive," the shorter man said.

"Ed, are you raising money for the Leggett campaign?" the taller man asked.

"Yes. Why?"

"You know Ullman cut a deal with Roberts to screw Leggett."

"How do you know that?" Ed asked.

"Several of us were called into a meeting last Tuesday with Roberts's chief of staff and given our marching orders. No money to Horner or any other Democrat, and if a conservative candidate asks, it's no. They want it Leggett versus Ullman."

Abbott looked surprised. "Wow."

"The entire leadership and all their friends are joining forces to defeat Leggett," the shorter lobbyist said.

"You can't blame them; Peterson broke all the rules. Rosa was an old man, and blindsiding him was terrible. You don't stand a chance; they'll cut off your money," the taller man said.

Ed smiled, finished his drink, and said, "Thanks for the heads-up." He returned to the bar and ordered another double.

With his drink in hand, he left the bar and looked for Saracino. Bill was sitting at the same table as before, but now there was a young woman sitting across from him. Saracino's facial expression was pure shock, and he was leaning back into his chair to the point of almost falling backward.

Ed sat next to the woman.

"This young lady," Bill said, "had some family photos she wished to share."

Ed looked at the twenty-something woman and smiled. She handed him one of the photographs. It was of her sitting on a bed dressed in fishnet stockings, high heels, and a leather halter top. Lying next to her was a red-leather riding crop.

Ed handed the photo back to her. "I don't think my friend is interested in a riding lesson."

The woman smiled, stood, and moved to another table.

Ed looked at Saracino.

"I didn't know what to do," Bill said.

"I just learned that Ullman cut a deal with the Dems, and they're united against Ty and so is the Republican leadership."

"The Dems are a determined bunch and have rules about fairness; Rada was not fair." Bill said. He stood up. "I've had too much excitement, it's almost midnight, and I'm going home."

Ed finished his drink and stood to leave, but with one last glance, he looked toward the tables along the dance floor and saw B. T. Rollins sitting by himself.

B. T. was an extraordinary personality. He had lost an arm and leg in Afghanistan, had a stainless-steel hook for hand and a prosthetic leg. He was a registered Republican and yet was very close to the Democrats. If there was a dirty job or agency that needed cleaning up, B. T. was the man for the job.

Ed joined B. T. "How are you, my Irish friend?" Ed asked.

"Alive," he said with a wry smile. "I suppose you heard that Ullman cut a deal."

"Yes, just now."

"Yep, and the governor is in on it."

Ed sighed and thought, *Shit, we're in trouble.*

A nondescript middle-aged man approached the table and leaned close to B. T. "Tom asked me to thank you for doing the favor."

B. T. nodded.

The man turned without another word and walked toward the tunnel exit.

Ed stared at B. T. for several seconds. "You lost your arm and leg, and you did that bastard a favor?"

"I do what I do."

"Come on. Hanoi Hilton. Remember."

"I do what I do," B. T. repeated, as he looked down at the table.

Ed, feeling sad, went home.

The next morning, Ed was in the Alabama statehouse building elevator on its way to the sixth floor, Senator Peterson's office. Before he reached the hallway, B. T. rounded the corner, and the two men's eyes met.

"Oh, it's Mr. Morality," B. T. said in his booming voice with a wide grin.

Ed laughed and returned the grin.

Ed opened the door to Peterson's office and asked Lorane, "Can I slip in to see him for a quick second?"

She pushed the intercom button. "Ed Abbott is here and wants to tell you something important. Can he come in?"

"Yes."

Ed opened the door to Peterson's office. He closed the door behind him and stood next to it. Peterson was sitting at his desk reading a legislative report and looked up at Ed.

"I just learned the Dems have joined with the governor to help Ullman, along with several Republican legislators."

Peterson smiled, leaned back slightly. "Sour grapes. They were not appointed, and the opportunity is lost. You know what a billion Chinese would say about that?"

"No."

"Phuq-um."

Ed sounded it out in his head, Fuck them.

"What should we do?"

"Keep raising money."

Ed thought about, Roka. *I can't tell him.*

"Ed, don't worry; they'll make a mistake."

Three weeks before the Central Restaurant fundraiser, Ed was at his office when he received a call from Paul Snider.

"Good morning, Paul; what's up?"

"Sorry to call so early. I hate waking people," Paul said.

"It's eight. I've been up for ten minutes."

Paul laughed.

"I need a favor. A friend of mine is running for the

State Senate in the twenty-eighth; his name is John Quad. He's an actor, mostly plays tough guys. Do you have time to talk to him today? Give him some advice and raise him a few bucks."

"Sure. I hope he's a Dem. That's a liberal seat and it's not up until next year," Ed said.

"Yes, he fits the bill," Paul said.

"Okay. What's his number?"

"He'll be in your office in five minutes," Paul said, laughing, and hung up.

Ed took a deep breath. "Sabina, we have a new client, and he'll be here any second."

"Mr. Quad is standing here, looking at me," she said.

Ed left his desk and walked out into the reception area, and standing next to Sabina's desk was a massive human being, at least 6'3" and maybe 350 pounds, with a scary, pockmarked face.

Ed offered his hand and John Quad gently offered his; Ed's right hand looked like a finger compared to John's. His grip was cold and soft.

Yuck, a dead fish, Ed thought as they shook hands.

"Pleasure to meet you, Mr. Quad. Please come into my office." Ed gestured with his right hand for John to go into the office. When John passed into the room, Ed mouthed to Sabina, "Join us."

She mouthed back, "NO."

Ed walked into his office. "Sabina will be joining us. She is an expert on the twenty-eighth."

"I hate you," Sabina whispered.

John sat on the couch with a loud cracking sound as air rushed from the leather cushions.

Ed smiled as he waited for Sabina; after what seemed like minutes, Sabina came into the room, turned one of Ed's desk chairs to face John and sat.

"Well, Mr. Quad, tell us about yourself and the campaign," Ed said.

"I spend most of my time in Hollywood working as a character actor in Western movies. I moved to Abbeville last year, and to fill time I got involved in local politics. It seemed easy compared to acting. So here I am," John said.

"Well, that's an interesting reason to run for the State Senate. How long have you known Paul?" Ed asked.

"About a year. I met him at a Team 100 meeting in DC. We both like to hunt and share a love of the outdoors."

"So, you're a member of Team 100. That's a powerful group, lots of money."

"No, I do not belong. I was asked to attend last year's meeting. Not too many gun owners in Hollywood."

Suddenly another massive man stepped into Ed's office. He was four or five inches shorter than John but just as scary-looking.

Silence.

"Sorry I'm late," he said, looking at John. He flopped

on the couch next to John, with a slapping sound. John popped up in the air about two feet and slowly lowered as the air screamed out of the cushions.

"This is my buddy, Tubby," John said.

Ed smiled and glanced at Sabina. Her expression was a mixture of surprise and suppressed laughter.

"Nice to meet you, Tubby. This is Sabina. She manages our state campaigns."

Sabina swung her head around and glared at Ed, her eyes wide with anger.

"John, a state senate campaign is expensive, about two million, and that's if there's no incumbent. Fortunately, the twenty-eighth is an open seat. What's your plan to raise the money between now and next year?" Ed asked.

"Paul said you'd handle that."

Ed laughed.

"He would. Unfortunately, that's not true. The bulk of your campaign money between now and then will come from friends and family. From what you've said, you don't know many people in Alabama. So, tell me about your connections in Hollywood."

"No money there and Tubby is my only friend, and he's broke."

"Perfect. Sabina, you got any ideas?"

"Mr. Quad, how much seed money will you put into the campaign?"

"A grand."

Oh my God, Ed thought. "John, this is impossible. How do you expect to win?"

"You and now Sabina."

Silence.

"Mr. Quad are you invited to next Thursday's Team 100 meeting?" she asked.

"Yes, Tubby and I are going to DC."

"John, this is very difficult. I think you have one shot at raising money this year. Here's what we'll do: For two thousand a month, paid on the first of every month. We will act as treasurer, file your FEC reports, and schedule press availabilities. You will also pay us a twenty percent commission and reimbursement of expenses. There's one caveat: This is only if you raise five hundred thousand at the Team 100 event. Sabina will go with you to DC and coordinate a reception to solicit donations."

Silence.

"Agreed. What about the money I raise?" John asked.

You've got to be kidding, Ed thought. "Family and friends, one hundred percent. Just provide us a list prior to your asking."

Silence.

"Agree?" Ed asked.

"Yes."

"Great, please text us all your contact information and we'll go from there," Ed said, standing.

They shook hands. John and Tubby left the office.

"You are so dead," Sabina said.

"This will be good for us; Team 100 is big money."

"I don't care. Those two giants—"

"Sabina, stop. Paul will host the reception and do the inviting. You'll get to spend two days in Washington sightseeing, and we can make extra money."

"How about *you* go with Two Tons of Fun if it's so easy."

"Thank you for doing this," Ed said.

"I hate you," she said.

The next day Ed left his office at 7:00 a.m. and walked to his private business mailbox. He passed his apartment at the Print Press Lofts and cut through the Alley Station walkway, which was two blocks from his office.

The route took him past Central. He loved the restaurant and spent a lot of time having lunch or drinks after work. The manager, Mario, was Ed's kind of person. He'd started as a busboy, moved to maître d', and ended up owning the restaurant.

Ed opened the brass door to the mailbox, and envelopes fell out.

"Wow, it's packed," he said to no one in particular.

Watching from the front counter, Lucy, the mail clerk said, "There's a lot more in the back room, Ed. We had to put the return envelopes into three boxes."

She left the counter and returned with three shoe-sized boxes, packed with return envelopes, and five packets of bad address envelopes rubber-banded together.

"Wow, that's impressive," Ed said, when she handed him the bundles. "Tuesday *is* usually the big mail day, but not this big. We only mailed a thousand reminder letters, everything else was electronic."

Ed bundled everything in his arms and left. He walked through the narrow alley to his Commerce Street office. The - was quiet; the small bars and restaurants were still closed. The only activity was across the street where a crew of men were power-washing the sidewalk after a busy evening.

Ed reached his building and walked up the narrow stairwell two flights to his office.

"Good morning, Sabina," Ed said.

Silence.

Ed walked into his office, sat at his desk and opened his

computer. Sabina entered and sat on the small bench that faced the river, opened the window and lit up a cigarette.

Ed looked up with a puzzled expression. Sabina did not smoke in the office.

"The bastard cheated on me. I just got a DM from some girl telling me."

Ed knew better than to say anything. He looked down at the box of envelopes on his side table, turned on his Apple computer and began depositing, scanning donors' names and correcting bad addresses.

An hour later, Ed looked over at Sabina. "Are you planning on working today?"

"No," she said with a red-eyed glare.

"Okay," he replied sheepishly, looked away and went back to work.

Just before lunch, Ed placed the pile of envelopes and checks on Sabina's desk to be filed for FEC backup.

"That's a lot of dead letters," she said.

"They're not dead letters. Most of those boxes are filled with return donation envelopes."

"That's a huge return."

"And the electronic pledges are off the charts."

"Maybe it's time I do a head count."

Ed went into his office and began making fundraising calls. After about a half hour, Sabina came into his office, holding her iPad. She sat in the chair that faced his desk, looking both happy and a little scared.

Ed felt uneasy, thinking something's not good.

"How many people does Central's patio and main restaurant hold?" she asked.

Relieved, Ed said, "Four hundred or so, why?"

Her brown eyes got big. "Ed, last week we had money for four hundred tickets. Today we got another one hundred reservations."

"Uh-oh, that can't be right," Ed said.

"Yes, five hundred, and the finance committee is still selling tickets."

"Oh, shit."

Ed picked up the telephone and called Mario.

"Central Restaurant, Mario speaking."

"Hey, Mario, this is Ed Abbott. We have a wonderful problem. We've sold five hundred tickets for the Leggett dinner."

"That's great. Where are you going to go?"

"Not funny."

"I'll make it work, but please don't add any more."

"That's a little out of my control."

"I'll make it work, don't worry. We'll need the final count by Friday."

Ed hung up and looked at Sabina. "This could get scary; we still have six days left for reservations and return RSVP mail. I hope Mario is a miracle worker."

On Friday morning, May 13, four days before the Central fundraiser, Sabina walked into Ed's office holding her AI pad. She sat in the chair facing his desk. "You ready for today's numbers and a total for Central to date?"

Silence.

Ed took a deep breath. "Okay, let's have it."

"The formal invitation got a regular three percent

return; electronic did a little better, but the reminder letter on both platforms got a seventy percent return overall."

"What?"

"Yep. Your little guilt letter worked. We've sold six hundred plus tickets and raised over three hundred thousand." She smiled, enjoying the panicked look on his face.

"Oh my," Ed said.

"Here are the totals: three hundred thousand for Central, Peterson's hundred thousand seed money, forty-eight thousand from the cocktail parties, and a hundred ninety-five thousand from the finance committee membership. Deducting expenses and our commission, the net to the campaign is two hundred seventy-seven thousand dollars," Sabina said.

"Oh my God, six hundred are coming Tuesday night. What are we going to do?" Ed asked. "Six hundred tickets! Oh God, we're too big for the restaurant. What are you going to do?"

"I won't go," Sabina said.

"Not funny. There's no way you're running away. We've got to tell Mario, and this is too important to handle on the phone; it's got to be done in person. Please create a draft seating chart, and we'll take it with us, and you can give him the head count."

"Wrong. I'm not going to tell him. This is yours, big boy."

Two hours later, Ed called Central Restaurant. "Mario, this is Ed. Can we stop by this afternoon? We've got the semifinal count and a draft seating chart."

"What's the count?" he asked.

"I'll tell you when we see each other."

"That does not sound good. Come on by in ten minutes."

"Okay. We'll be there."

Ed hung up.

"You are such a coward, and what's this 'we' stuff, cowboy?"

"The 'we' is us. Let's go," he said.

Ed and Sabina walked along the dirty sidewalk and crossed Tallapoosa Street, turned right, and followed it to the Alley Station entrance.

They passed along the red-and-green flowering Mexican creeper-covered stone wall and passed through the iron gates into Central's courtyard. The 1,000-square-foot patio was set for lunch; the centerpiece Italian fountain gently shot a stream of water into the air; the perfectly manicured flowering shade trees were just coming into bloom, and the pink flagstone added a wonderful hue to the white tablecloths.

"Man, this place is beautiful," Ed said.

They walked up to the hostess desk.

"My name is Ed Abbott. We have an appointment with Mario."

She picked up the telephone, spoke, listened, hung up. "He'll be right out, Mr. Abbott."

Mario entered the Alley patio from the restaurant's back door. He was wearing gray slacks, a blue blazer, red tie, and a white cotton dress shirt. At 5'6", thin, with naturally good looks he exuded hospitality.

He smiled when he spotted Ed and Sabina at the hostess stand. "You have that look on your face, Mr. Abbott," Mario said.

Ed turned and looked at Sabina.

Mario smiled. "How can I help?"

"Sabina has something to tell you."

Sabina glared at Ed.

Ed gave in. "It appears we've sold six hundred tickets."

"Ed, we can't sit that many and keep our quality."

"We can't move; it's too late."

"Wow." Mario looked around and pointed to the closed, black French patio doors on the east wall. "If we open that room and squeeze in another four tables ... but I am very worried about our quality and people getting served in a timely manner."

"That'll work. I knew you'd save Senator Leggett. Mario, you're a great American."

Mario laughed.

"Thank you. We've got to run," Ed said. He turned and quickly left the restaurant with Sabina following.

"You are such a coward," Sabina said, trying to catch up.

"I learned a long time ago, when things go your way, shut up and run."

Later that same afternoon, Carlos was sitting at his desk when his cell phone rang and he saw Roka's name on the screen.

"What's up?" Carlos asked.

"I've been around the block several times and can't believe you hired these people. Your accountant is a jerk, and your fundraiser is a thief. Where's all the money? I understand the Central event is working and I don't see a dime coming into the campaign."

"You're in charge. Call the treasurer or Ed directly."

"I've tried. Abbott's girl puts me off and Tower told me to look at the April FEC reports and that's BS. It's in the past. They'd be gone after June if I was consulting."

"At the rate you spend money—"

"Don't you tell me what to do," Roka barked. "The people you hired are worthless fools and I'm talking to Simmons. Now that Anne Gray is out—"

"What? Anne's gone?"

"Yes, today. Jacobs got tired of her controlling personality and put Simmons in charge of her campaigns. There're going to be major changes, and that twerp Abbott won't like it."

"Anne's out?" Carlos asked again in a whisper.

"Yes," Roka said, sounding gleeful.

"Who's replacing her?"

"Ellen Paddick, a real chief of staff and hard-nosed consultant. Your campaign, if you keep it, is about to get some needed oversight."

Carlos hung up, leaned back in his chair and rubbed his nose several times. "Man, he's a dick. I liked Anne. What happened? Her contract wasn't up." He leaned back. *What the hell does this mean?*

Just as Sabina, John and Tubby were about to walk into the main ballroom of the Washington, DC, Watergate Hotel to attend the national Team 100 meeting, John stopped and said, "Sabina, um, because I'm an actor, people expect me to act outgoing and energetic, you know, very confident, even outrageous. So if I kid you about your boobs—"

Sabina glared at him as she stepped closer. "You say one word about my boobs, you and Tubby over there"—she pointed to Tubby—"are fucking dead."

John looked down at the carpet and sheepishly walked into the ballroom.

Later that evening, after dinner with Paul, John, Tubby and three other Team 100 members, Sabina returned to her Watergate hotel room and called Ed.

"It's almost midnight your time. Things must have gone well. How'd you do?" Ed asked.

"Two Tons of Fun delivered my speech perfectly and we picked up five hundred thousand in pledges. Paul is happy and I can't wait to get home."

"Nice job."

"You owe me a bonus for hazard pay."

"Okay, why?"

"There were only twenty women in attendance, the others carried guns, and I was the only one under fifty. I had to fight off happy hands all evening."

"Sorry."

"No sorry! You owe me dinner, a new outfit, and an expensive body wash. I hate old men and next time, I'll have a gun."

Ed laughed.

9

Monday, morning May 16, Ed received a text from Carlos: We have a 9:00 a.m. meeting today with Senator Jacobs at the Capitol.

Ed replied: Tough, I'm swamped.

Carlos replied: We have no choice.

Ed glanced at the time: 8:50 a.m.

Ed grabbed his coat and tie, rushed to his car and raced to the Capitol. He parked in the 15-minute-only spot near the side entrance and ran up the Capitol steps. Once in the building, he glanced at the elevator. *Not enough time,* he thought. He raced up the stairs.

Carlos was standing by the elevators, waiting, when Ed saw him.

"Why the panic meeting?" Ed asked.

Carlos turned and faced Ed, "They say we're not cooperating."

"What? With whom and why do we care? We're running a federal campaign."

Carlos shrugged. "We live here," Carlos answered.

They walked along the third-floor hallway to Senator Jacobs's office. Two women in their thirties were standing at the mahogany doorway. Ed recognized Rose Gordy by her bright red hair and frumpy dress. He only knew her by reputation as a single-purpose fundraiser from Birmingham.

As Ed approached the two women, he put on his blue blazer and tightened his tie.

"Just get out of bed?" the woman standing next to Rose asked in a snarky tone.

Ed looked at her thinking, *That was rude.*

He and Carlos passed them as Carlos grabbed the ornate door handle and pulled the heavy door open and approached the reception desk. A moment later, Rose and the other woman quickly walked past them to Jacobs's office door and entered.

Carlos said to the receptionist, "Good morning. I'm Carlos Felix and this is Ed Abbott, and we have a nine o'clock appointment with Senator Jacobs."

"Senator Jacobs is not in; your meeting is with Ms. Paddick. Please make yourself comfortable, and I'll tell her you're here." After thirty minutes, the receptionist said, "You can go in now."

"Thank you," Carlos said.

Ed glanced at his wristwatch. "Made us wait thirty minutes. We should leave now before it gets worse," Ed said to Carlos.

In Jacobs's office, the snarky woman stood in front of Jacobs's desk while Rose was standing across the room, speaking into her cell phone.

"Sit here," the woman said, pointing at the two chairs facing the desk.

"I beg your pardon?" Ed asked.

Carlos showed no emotion.

Ed and Carlos did not sit.

"I am Ms. Paddick, Senator Jacobs's political advisor. Ms. Brown no longer works for the senator. You two have been summoned here because Senator Leggett's campaign is fraught with irregularities and possible fraud," she said.

"Excuse me. Have we met?" Carlos asked.

"No, and from what I've seen, we will not meet again."

"I'd be very careful, Ms. Paddick," Carlos said with a stern expression.

"Ms. Paddick, we are running a federal campaign. What's the purpose of this meeting?" Ed asked.

"You are the purpose, Mr. Abbott. Senator Jacobs and Senator Simmons are intimately involved, and they believe your fundraising expenses and fees border on stealing."

"What?" Ed said.

"Ms. Gordy is here at Senator Simmons's request to bring some sanity to Senator Leggett's campaign. She, contrary to you, is a professional fundraiser and we have instructed her to consult the Leggett campaign."

Stunned, Ed said, "Ms. Paddick, you're on very thin ice. I've had enough of your attitude. I do not work for you or Senator Jacobs. Again, I ask, what is the purpose of this meeting?"

"I've placed several calls to your office, and they have not been returned," Rose interjected.

"This is about returning calls?" Ed asked.

"Not just Ms. Gordy's calls. According to Mr. Roka, you treat him with the same contempt."

"You have wasted our time. I am an independent contractor and do not work for Mr. Roka or you, Ms. Paddick. Is there anything else you want to address?"

"Mr. Abbott, my job with Senator Simmons is to raise the eight million from the senator's friends to fund your special election campaign," Rose said.

"That is Senator Simmons's pledge, and we are not involved, Ms. Gordy. And I don't have time to help you fundraise," Ed said.

"You might have more time on your hands than you think," Paddick quipped.

Ed turned to look at Carlos with a "We're gone" expression.

"And you, Mr. Felix, are in significant jeopardy. The FEC has been contacted regarding Mr. Leggett's extraordinary spending."

Carlos smiled. "Ms. Paddick, this should not come as a surprise to you, but Mr. Roka has been managing the expenses, and if we hear one note from the FEC, you and Ms. Gordy will face legal consequences."

"You ready?" Ed asked.

Ed and Carlos turned to leave.

"Please stop. If you play ball, there is a bright future for all of us," Rose said.

Carlos looked at Paddick, ignoring Rose.

"Bad tactics, Ms. Paddick," he said.

Again, the two headed to the door.

"Try dressing at home, Mr. Abbott," Paddick said.

Ed could no longer take it; he turned to face her. "Ms.

Paddick." He paused, regaining his self-control. "You need to brush your teeth."

They left the office and walked down the hallway to the staircase. Ed stopped. "That was the most unpleasant ten minutes of my life. I want to go home and bathe."

"I'm very proud of you, Ed. You were the target. She wanted you to lose your cool."

"I almost did. Why was she after me?"

"To force Leggett to fire you."

"Why?"

"I'm not sure, but they're after control or sabotage."

"Why were you there?"

"To send the message that I'm next."

"That was a mistake about the FEC," Ed said.

"I'm not sure; it could be the sabotage."

"Simmons must be having trouble raising the eight million and they're looking for an out."

"I'm not sure," Carlos said.

"Why were you so quiet?" Ed asked.

"The intercom on the desk was open, and the cell phone across the room was on FaceTime."

"I didn't catch any of that."

"You're not a cop."

"What should we do?"

"Make the Central event a massive success and set up the finance committee for the special." Carlos stopped walking and put his right hand on Ed's left shoulder. "Ed, don't stop for a second. That's what they want you to do. They're looking for an opportunity to screw us."

"No problem. The Central event is already a smash, and I work best pissed off."

"Ed, I think we're a threat to their plans," Carlos said.

"What?"

"Arrogant losers, play games. This was just their first move. I'll tell Leggett. He needs to know how ugly Jacobs's new team is and that they're trying to own us."

"I miss Anne," Ed said.

On Tuesday afternoon, the day of the Central fundraising dinner, Ed's cell phones were vibrating around his desk. People were calling to request more tickets or to add seats to their table. Ed was busy going over his event check list.

"Sabina, where's Leggett's speech and opening remarks?" he called out.

"On his phone and iPad," she answered.

"Have you double-checked your double-check?" Ed called out.

"Ed, put a sock in it."

Sabina was at her desk adding the final detail to the 24-by-36-inch cardboard seating/table diagram.

Ed came up to her desk. "How's it coming?"

"I've divided the guest list into ten equal parts, all in alphabetical order by last name." She pointed at the chart. "Each table is listed by the table sponsor's name. All the attendees have been assigned a table and that information is on their name tag."

"That looks good," Ed said

"There are ten volunteers in the middle office assembling the six-hundred-ten name tags. We have ten iPads containing the alpha list, and table assignments ready to be taken to the event," she said.

"Perfect." Ed went back to his office.

His phone continued to buzz with request. Finished with his last call he glanced at his watch: 3:00 p.m.

A jolt of adrenaline flushed his face white.

"Sabina," he called out.

There was no reply.

He left his office and raced around the suite looking for her. He found her sitting in the very back office, smoking a cigarette.

"What are you doing?" he asked in a panic-filled voice.

"Two-Tons-of-Fun and his sidekick want to attend and eat."

"You're kidding. Tell them no food, they can attend the predinner and only if they wear ties."

"I already did."

"You only told me to jack me up?"

"Yep, now relax. Everything is done; we're ready." She took a deep drag and blew the smoke out of her mouth at Ed.

"Done? Are you nuts? Have you double-checked all the seating and name tags? Where are the ten volunteers to hand out the name tags and guide people to their table? Has the text gone out telling people where they're sitting. Has Leggett's memo been sent?" Ed rambled, speaking so fast that the words blurred together.

"Ed, stop it—we're done. The volunteers are in the bathroom changing, and they're hoping to watch you freak out."

"I hate you," Ed said.

Sabina glanced at her phone to check the time. "Go look at the middle office. I'll bet they've returned and are ready to go."

Ed went into the middle office. "Hello, hello, thank you all very much for volunteering for Senator Ty Leggett's first Alabama fundraising dinner."

The twenty-by-ten-foot room was filled by two seven-foot-long Formica tables with chairs. Crumpled paper and trash sat in piles around the room. Empty pizza boxes were stacked on top of an overflowing trashcan along the back wall.

Ten men and women, dressed in cocktail dresses and business suits, were watching Ed.

"I'm sure Sabina has already explained everything, but please keep in mind tonight's event is oversold; if you cannot find someone a seat, please take them to the basement Wine Cellar; Mario and his staff will serve them dinner. Remember to tell them Senator Leggett will come by, and the wine is on the house." He smiled. "When I taught fishing, there was only one rule." He looked around the room. "No one cries and that goes for tonight. Especially me."

They laughed.

Sabina came into the room.

"Lastly, please keep an eye out for trouble; we have security," Ed continued. "If you see something odd, do not address it, either get me or a security guard. You've got an SOS text button on your cell phone. Press it and the security people will be there within seconds." He thought for a moment. "The table hosts will be wearing special lapel pins." He held up a gold-and-blue stick pin that read:

LEGGETT. "If anyone comes to you wearing that lapel pin, please treat them better than Sabina treats me."

They laughed.

"Lastly, please arrive at the restaurant by four-thirty. The older folks will show up at least an hour early. Thank you for helping. Tonight's going to be crazy; your job ends once everyone is seated. Mario and his team will take over then. At that time, please grab yourself a drink and if possible, something to eat. This is going to be wild. Thank you again for helping Senator Leggett."

"Mr. Ed," a woman said.

"Yes."

"Sabina promised we'd get to see you freak out."

Ed and Sabina arrived at the alley entrance to Central Restaurant at 5:45 p.m. Sabina was dressed in a St. John red-and-gold evening dress. Ed was wearing a Tom James dark-blue silk suit, with a red-and-blue Italian tie.

The alley entrance was blocked off by two ten-foot-long tables covered with white tablecloths, name tags and campaign brochures. Ed stopped and studied the nametags, double-checking everything was perfect.

The alley itself was decorated with flowers, Ficus trees, and strings of tiny white lights, which gave the narrow alley a feeling of warmth. The area closest to Central's entrance was filled with round tables for ten. Each table was set perfectly for an elegant dinner. The water glasses were full and white porcelain China plates, coffee cups, butter plates, and silverware were preset. A full outdoor bar was stationed against the far wall. Ed glanced up to see the restaurant's two balconies were set for dinner.

We might pull this off, he thought.

After making sure all was perfect in the alley, Ed and Sabina walked to Coosa Street, Central's main entrance.

Mario and his Executive Chef, Jackson McGarry, were standing by the gray, painted doors, next to the "129 Coosa Street" monument sign.

"Good evening, Ed and Sabina; thank you for choosing Central," Mario said.

"I hope you feel that way in five hours," Ed replied.

"Ed, everything will be perfect. We got this," Mario said.

Ed looked at Jackson. "I hope you're wearing running shoes," he said.

"We're ready," Jackson said.

Ed took a deep breath.

"Oh, this should make you smile." She gestured to her left. "Here come Two-Tons-of-Fun, and they're wearing matching ties," Sabina noted.

"God, that's funny-looking, Frick and Frack. I hope they're not hungry," Ed said.

"Ed, stop it. I'll deal with them. Follow Jackson into the kitchen and wish the team doing the real work good luck and thank them," Sabina said.

"Okay, Jackson, let's go."

Ed walked through the ten-foot-high, double-wide gray doors, and was instantly taken-aback by how organized and different the main dining room looked. Everything that could be removed had been replaced by round tables of ten.

The center stone-faced bar was preset with crystal, the bar stools were gone, silver trays, preset with linen napkins, lined the bar. The main dining room was separated by a three-foot-wide serving station. Hors d'oeuvre trays were lined up and ready to have the final ingredients added.

"Wow, this is amazing," Ed said to Jackson.

"We take pride in our work," Jackson replied.

The kitchen staff were wearing formal, white chef's coats, beanie hats, aprons, and black closed-toe shoes.

They walked around the serving area into the kitchen. "Hello," Ed shouted. The kitchen staff stopped and looked at him and Jackson.

"My name is Ed Abbott and I'm with Senator Leggett. Before organized chaos controls the evening, thank you very much for your dedication to perfection."

The staff smiled.

"On behalf of the senator, thank you—thank you very much. Let's have a wonderful evening." The staff clapped and went back to work.

"Jackson, this is going to work," Ed said as he left the kitchen and walked out into the alley.

He felt a sudden rush of panic.

"Oh my God, people are already arriving," Ed said under his breath.

Sabina, seeing the look on his face, walked up to him. "Want to run away and hide?" she asked with a grin. "Go greet people and have fun," she said.

Thirty minutes later, the restaurant and alley were chaotic, people were everywhere, looking for their tables or lining up at the bar.

Caroline Felix came running up to Ed. "There seems to be a problem at Mr. Matsu's table."

Ed shot a quick look toward Matsu's table; it was empty except for two people and something about them looked very odd. Mr. Matsu, the largest private nursery owner in Birmingham, and a very formal person, was sitting perfectly straight in his chair, his shoulders pulled back as far as possible, his neck stiff, and he was staring straight ahead.

Ed recognized the woman sitting at the table. "Oh, God," he said. He raced to the table. "Hello, Mr. Matsu, can I be of assistance?"

Matsu did not utter a sound, move his head or eyes, he did not have to, his face was displaying stone-cold terror.

Ed looked at the woman next to Matsu. "Hello, it's nice to meet you again. I think you're sitting at the wrong table; may I help you find your host?"

The young woman looked at Ed, after a moment she picked up her personal photographs from the table and stood. "My host is Mr. BT Rollins."

BT doesn't have a table, Ed thought.

"Perfect," he said. "Please take my arm and I'll lead you to Mr. Rollins."

She placed her right arm through Ed's left, and Ed moved them to the front entrance.

Ed, feeling panicky, began to walk fast, but suddenly her fingernails dug into his arm.

"Slow down," she growled through clenched teeth.

Sabina was watching, along with Caroline Felix.

"That looks fun. I hope it doesn't end well," Sabina said.

"Should we grab security?" Caroline asked.

"No, he's almost to the front door."

Ed and the young women left the building.

"May I walk you to the valet?" he asked.

"Yes," she said, releasing her death grip on his arm.

They walked to the valet stand, and Ed looked at the twenty-year-old-looking attendant. "This charming young lady has a car with you. I'll leave her in your good hands."

Ed smiled and did all he could not to run back into the restaurant. He joined Sabina at the name tag table. "That was close," he said.

"You're such a simp," she said.

Suddenly a woman dressed in a formal Tom James white gown, wearing a LEGGETT pin, approached.

"Hello, my name is Mrs. Glenda Snider, Paul's sister-in-law, and there seems to be a mistake with our table."

"No problem, my assistant Ms. Perfect, will help you," Ed said.

Sabina gave Ed a *really?* look, then looked up the table number on her iPad and glanced around the room.

"It's over there." She pointed. "I'll walk you over."

"Thank you. However, the people sitting at that table are not my guests and they will not move." Suddenly all eleven of Mrs. Snider's guests were standing around her.

Sudden panic.

Sabina checked the seating chart; looked at Ed and whispered, "Nothing."

Ed quickly twisted his neck to survey the room and spotted an empty table in the center near the bar. "There it is," he said, pointing.

Without hesitation, Mrs. Snider and her group hurried to the table and sat themselves down.

Ed looked at Sabina, "Shit."

There were sudden sounds of excitement and whispering voices coming from the Coosa Street entrance. They turned to watch Senator Ty Leggett walk into the room and stand by the doorway. He was dressed in a custom-tailored, dark-blue, narrow gold-pinstriped suit with a red tie and jet-black polished classic Oxford shoes.

Ed greeted him. "Good evening, Senator. I hope you're prepared for this."

"Yes, I think so. I've read your memos, all of them." He smiled. "And memorized the important names. Still, I'm glad everyone is wearing a name tag, and I'm sure Sabina will bail me out."

Ty looked around the room. "Brother, this place is packed. Nice job, Ed. Not as much fun as Mr. Bains's home, but we can't have everything." he laughed. "Where do I start?"

"We've had to change things up, no photo lineup. Everything will be at the tables and candid. The formal photographer will follow you around. It's crazy." Ed looked around the room. "We're in survival mode. Sabina will walk you through the restaurant, please keep in mind, everyone wants to touch you and say something. You aren't eating, so take your time; the plan is out the window." Ed smiled. "When you and Sabina finish, just go straight to the dais and start talking."

"Ed, I got this."

Sabina joined Ty, looking excited.

"Sabina, let's have fun," Ty said with a grin.

The rest of the event had no drama.

After dinner and the desserts were being served, Ty had finished walking through the restaurant and speaking at every table. He returned to the main dining room and walked up to Paul's table. Paul quickly stood and Ty put his right hand on Paul's shoulder.

"Paul, I got this. It's eight-thirty. I'll introduce myself. We're winging it." Ty smiled.

Paul grinned as he glanced across the room at Ed coming towards them carrying the microphone.

"You got it. Seeing Ed race around has made my week," he said with a laugh.

Ed arrived at the table and handed the mic to Paul who handed it to Ty.

"What—" Ed said.

"Didn't you get the memo," Ty interrupted, as he turned and walked to the front entrance.

Paul laughed and sat; Ed stood looking at Ty.

"Hello, hello!" Ty waited for several minutes for the noise and voices to quiet down.

"My friends, what a great evening. Thank you, every one of you for attending this small, intimate gathering." He laughed, and many of the guests laughed and smiled along with him.

"Nothing like this is successful or even possible without the help of volunteers and many friends. This event would not have been possible without Paul Snider and his tremendous finance committee and friends."

People clapped.

"Paul, would you and your team please stand and take a bow?" The finance committee members stood to loud applause.

"Thank you, Paul, and every member of our team. Thank you very much for working so hard and making tonight extraordinary."

Ty looked around the room as Paul and the others sat.

"I left DC to come home, to remind myself of what life would be like when the dog dies and friends come over." People laughed.

"Every day I'm here, I begin to feel like a human being. Not a DC soldier. We have great plans to build a job-strong, family-strong, safe Alabama."

People clapped.

"Our families face a changing America, a country that is being pushed in directions none of us recognize. The sins of the past are past, it's time to forgive, remember, move forward and embrace the future."

People clapped.

"I want everyone who lives or visits Alabama to feel safe. Especially our children and the weakest among us. No fear. No fear of being hurt, harassed or forgotten. Let DC, San Francisco and Portland retain that honor."

People clapped.

"It's time to embrace the future, convert Montgomery into a city filled with hope and a state exploding with opportunity."

People clapped.

"We must help those who have very little and guide them to prosperity. It's time to celebrate what Alabama has become. It's time to celebrate the future and educate our college students beyond the Ivy League."

People clapped.

One person shouted out, "About damn time." Laughter could be heard around the room.

Ty smiled and nodded yes.

"Tonight is our introduction to Alabama and putting Washington, DC, on notice, we are coming, and we're ready to lead."

Loud clapping and cheers.

"DC talks a big game and does nothing. I am not going to that swamp to move chairs or play liars poker."

Paul laughed out loud.

"I'm working to demand respect for Alabama. To hell with the status quo of New York and the East Coast establishment. To hell with crime, and to hell with poverty."

People cheered.

"The morning sun symbolizes our future. Alabama embraces diversity, welcomes uniqueness and our future is limitless."

More cheering.

Ty took a breath and looked around the room.

"Let others hold onto the past. Let others wallow in hate to build power or get elected. By us standing together, nothing will stop us. I promise we'll never stop."

Ty's eyes watered and his voice became soft.

"Thank you for joining the first step of our campaign for United States Senate."

Clapping and cheering.

Paul jumped up from his table and rushed up to Ty.

They shook hands, other people joined in, and the evening slowly ended.

When most of the guests were gone, Ed walked around the restaurant, looking for Mario, who he found saying good-night to a couple at the alley entrance.

"Mario, thank you very much for this wonderful evening. You were right; it was perfect." Mario smiled. "Is it okay if I offer Jackson and his kitchen team a beer?" Ed asked.

"Of course, Mr. Abbott. They would welcome it."

Ed carried a large silver bucket of ice, filled with bottles of beer, into the kitchen. The room he entered was not the one he'd first seen that evening: It was a disaster; dirty dishes filled every space. The staff was covered in stains, their uniforms were unbuttoned and sweat dotted their foreheads. It was hot, and they looked exhausted.

"Thank you. Thank you, Mr. Jackson McCarry and team. Magnificent evening. Thank you. I have Mario's permission to offer you all an ice-cold beer."

Ed passed the ice bucket around the room and shared a beer with the staff.

With the restaurant closed and the alley empty, Ed walked past the parking lot on his way home. The parking attendant was sitting in the ticket booth listening to the Dodgers baseball game.

"You about to go home?" Ed asked.

"Almost. Did Sabina tell you what happened?"

"No, what happened?"

"After you left, that crazy bitch attacked me, screaming and trying to scratch my face, and the bitch refused to pay. So, I didn't return her car keys. I had to lock the shed to keep her away and call the cops.

Ed looked stunned. "I'm so sorry, I'm so sorry. You okay?"

"Yeah, the cops made her pay for the valet and they watched her drive away."

Ed just stood there thinking, *Oh my God, her fingernails.*

Later that night, Ty called Ed at home.

"Senator? Everything okay?" Ed asked.

"Ed, nice job. Tonight was wonderful, probably the nicest event I've ever attended. A great welcome to Montgomery and all thanks to you and Sabina's hard work. Thank you."

"My pleasure, Senator."

"See you tomorrow, goodnight."

At 8:00 a.m. the next morning, Ed and Sabina were cleaning up the office and calculating the final money haul when one of Ed's cell phones buzzed.

Sabina picked it up off his desk. "You can't wait 'til nine?"

"Good morning, Sabina."

"Good morning, Carlos. The total is three hundred twenty-five thousand and it's already deposited."

"Net?"

"We only talk net. If you knew how much we raised, you'd ask Ed to godfather another kid."

"Who else knows that number?"

"Tower, Leggett and Snider."

"Is Ed nearby? Please put me on speaker."

"You're on, Carlos," she said putting the phone on Ed's desk.

"Ed, I hope you're right about Simmons. Roka texted me last night. He heard the Central event was a huge success and wants to know by Thursday the amount raised and when it will be deposited. And he accused me of not being straight with him about the accounting."

"Who cares what he wants? Guess what showed up at Ty's headquarters yesterday afternoon."

Silence.

"Think COGS South."

"The yard signs company?"

"Yes. Fifty thousand unassembled, laminated yard signs are sitting at headquarters. Along with door hangers, flyers, and other crap no one uses anymore. All of it collecting dust."

"Roka's being preemptive," Carlos said.

"Bullshit, I can't believe you're not seeing what's happening. This is no accident. After what we experienced in Jacobs's office with Paddick—hold on," Ed said. He picked up his iPad from the desk and opened the campaign report.

"Tower called me at six this morning saying Roka has

maxed the two campaign credit cards and just emailed him two-month-old vendors' invoices," he said.

Ed changed to the expense icon. "I'll read the list of crap Roka has done: The digital printing company has not been paid in a month; we owe them for a thousand iPads, the production of E-voter maps, and E-precinct maps. The GOTV campaign organization team was paid for April, May and June. Why? We're not running in April, May and June."

Ed took a breath.

"And they have not been reserved, for when we need them, in the general election. Which means we're going to be in a bidding war with Ullman, who has unlimited money."

Ed looked up at Sabina.

"The Apple web developers were paid for April through June. Again why. Why now?"

He looked at Sabina again.

"The same for Facebook and the other advertising channels."

Ed tossed the iPad back on the desk.

"Carlos, this is no accident. The primary is twenty days away. Roka is spending like we're losing. None of the money he's spending will help us win in November. He's just spending to spend. I'm convinced this is all part of a plan," Ed said with conviction.

"What do you want me to do? I can't say anything, I don't want another ugly meeting with Paddick. I'm sure Roka's doing what he thinks is right," Carlos said.

Ed felt frustrated. "Oh my God, Carlos." He took a breath, calming himself. "Nothing in politics happens by accident and this is no accident. We're being set up, and I know it. I'll bet we don't know half of what he's spent. You hired Hillyard to manage the headquarters and oversee the volunteer operation, right?"

"Yes," Carlos said.

"Call and ask him to do an inventory of office supplies and campaign materials, then see if they're any invoices or W-2s in the drop box. Let's see exactly what Roka's done," Ed told him.

"I don't want to know. This is bad. We've got that July fifteenth FEC report in front of us. It can't look bad, we can't let Simmons, Snider or anyone know we're running a crap campaign and out of money," Carlos said.

Ed looked at Sabina and mouthed, "He doesn't get it." Back to the phone: "Carlos, what makes you think Simmons doesn't know? You don't think Roka's briefing him daily? Christ, this is part of their plan to own or kill us."

Silence.

"We must know the extent of the damage. Please text Tower, ask him to pull together our debt, cash on hand, and monthly overhead numbers, and especially how much is in the savings account. Tell him it's coming from Leggett, and you need it by tomorrow morning. As soon as we see those numbers, I'll rework the fundraising plan, which is going to be hard; after July fifth, fundraising falls off a cliff until September," Ed said.

Ed glanced at the electronic calendar on his monitor. "Simmons's money is not scheduled to start until September, and we must hoard cash until the July FEC report is filed. That gives us fifty days to overcome Roka's spending. We've already raised a ton, so I'll bet by June eighth, we will have raised seven hundred and sixty-two thousand. Only God knows how much cash will be left by the time Roka leaves."

Silence.

"Carlos, please trust me, we're being set up. We've got to put as much as we can into savings. And it's time to tell Leggett everything. Especially how much is in the savings account."

"What if he thinks you're wrong?"

"Me! You mean us, Dick Tracy, and he'll get it."

"Man, this is dangerous," Carlos said.

"So is being stupid. Please get back to me as soon as you tell Ty. Talk to you later." Ed hung up and looked at Sabina.

She put a concerned look on her face. "Ed, you can't let anyone on the finance committee know about this. They'd blame you and turn on Leggett."

Ed took a deep breath and nodded yes.

Friday afternoon, Ty called Dave Tower. "Yes, Senator, how can I help?"

"Have the numbers changed since we spoke last night?" Ty asked.

"No. I think we stopped the bleeding. The inventory is completed, and all the invoices and W2s are with me."

"We're still at three hundred thousand spent?" Ty asked.

"Yes."

"Okay, how much is in the checking and savings?"

"Fifty in the checking and a hundred-fifty in savings."

"Does Roka or Simmons have any knowledge of the savings account?"

"No, only the checking. They've got to believe we're cash poor, with a sizable debt."

"If Ed's right about Roka's intent, the savings will save us. If he's wrong, it's his problem and we'll have a lot of cash on hand. Simmons will praise Roka for his genius, hate Ed and give us the eight million," Ty said.

"Ed called this morning and he thinks we can raise another hundred-sixty thousand in the next two weeks from the finance committee and miscellaneous donations. Which completes his seven hundred-sixty thousand pre-special budget."

"What about June and July?"

"He told me, fifty from receptions, and a hundred-fifty from major donors."

"How confident was he?"

"Scared shitless."

"Good, that means he'll make it. We're still dangerously low on what we should have. Damn FEC report," Ty said.

Silence.

"Keep Roka in the dark, tell him we're broke. From now on, put every dime, minus expenses, into savings. If Roka asks where the money is or what's going on, blame everything on Ed."

"I love that," Dave said with a laugh.

10
THE SPECIAL ELECTION PRIMARY

Tuesday, June 7, 2039

Special Election Primary*:
    Democrat: Jack Horner: 220,223 votes
    Republican: Uncontested

Special Election Date: Tuesday, November 8, 2039
    Tyler Leggett: (Incumbent-Independent)
    Jeffery Ullman: (Independent)
    Jack Horner: (Democrat)

On the Thursday morning after the primary, Ty was at headquarters when Carlos called.

"Yes, Carlos?" Ty answered.

"Have you left for Fairhope?"

"No, not for another fifteen minutes."

"Good. Josh Washington is on his way to go with you."

"Carlos, I do not need a driver. Stop it."

"Ty, you can't be alone. Too many dirty tricks."

"What does that mean?"

"It means on the campaign trail you act like you're in DC. You stay away from hotel room meetings, bars, and single women. You don't move without Josh by your side."

"Carlos, I'm aware of what to avoid. I've been buttoned up my whole life. As for women, I have an ex-wife."

"This is not up for debate, Ty. Trust my campaign experience."

Ty took a deep breath. "Tell me about Josh."

"He's a retired police detective from Birmingham. He has a master's degree in political science and won the International Defense Pistol Association competition three years in a row."

"Okay, he's smart and can shoot."

"Not that you care, but he played football at Southern University. He'll be at HQ in five."

"Well, it's a long drive to Fairhope; he better not be a talker."

"He's a man of few words. Also, he'll have your new campaign iPad with the bio of Timmy Wayne and everyone else you're scheduled to meet with today."

Ty's cell phone rang while driving to Fairhope. "This is Ty," he said without looking at the phone screen.

"Ty, this is Senator Simmons; I hope this is not a bad time."

"No. Josh and I are driving to a fundraiser at Fairhope Yacht Club. What's up?"

"That's a beautiful part of the state. Thirty feet above the Gulf, can't flood. I have a home next to the club. Wish I was with you—the reason I called, now that Roka is done and the special is running, I've scheduled a meeting with my finance team to outline the details for our donation. Can you meet us at the Renaissance Hotel tomorrow evening at six forty-five? It shouldn't take too long. Just some quick questions about campaign finances, that kind of stuff."

"Sure, should I bring our treasurer, Dave Tower, or Paul Snider?"

"Naw, that won't be necessary. Hey, I've got to go. See you tomorrow evening. Have a great event."

Ty thought, *A meeting to discuss money. That's interesting.*

Eight hours later, just returning to Montgomery from Fairhope, Ty called Carlos.

"This is Carlos."

"I got a call from Simmons; he wants me to meet him and his money guys tomorrow evening at the Montgomery Renaissance to discuss money."

"No big deal. Is Dave going?"

"Not invited."

"Ed?"

"No."

"Oh."

"That's what I think. Patch Ed into this call," Ty said.

"What's up?" Ed asked.

"Ty is on the line."

"Everything okay in Fairhope?"

"Yes, it went well; we picked up twenty thousand. There's something else. Simmons called and wants to meet tomorrow evening at six forty-five to discuss money."

"You want me there?" Ed asked.

"No. It's a me-only show."

Silence.

"If you two are right, and Simmons was building a trap or trying to get out of his commitment, we'll hear the punchline tomorrow night. Ed, I need to know exactly what you and Dave believe our FEC report will show and how much free cash we have," Ty asked.

"I'll have those numbers to you by five tomorrow night," Ed said.

"And Ed, this is a lose-lose," Ty said.

"How's that?"

"If you're right, Simmons will hunt you down; if you're wrong, Carlos will." Ty laughed.

"I'm good with that."

Ty put the phone on the car dash and looked out the window, thinking, *How do I win this campaign?*

They stopped at a red light.

"You don't see that every day," Josh said.

Ty looked out the driver side window and two young boys playing cowboys and Indians.

"Yeah, I can't believe they even know what an Indian is," Ty said.

"Yep, all but forgotten. It wasn't that way when I worked my first cop job in Gallup, New Mexico. The

Navajo tribe was close, and the weekends were busy with drinking and gambling at the Fire Rock Casino."

Ty watched the two boys chase each other.

"They got a raw deal in Alabama, just like us. Sad," Ty whispered.

Ty left his campaign headquarters on Friday at 6:30 p.m., and Josh drove him to the Renaissance Hotel for his meeting with Simmons. Josh parked his truck next to the hotel and saw Dave Tower standing at the entrance.

"Dave. What brings you here?"

"Ed asked."

Ty sighed. "That's a little too much; I am a big boy and truly, to imitate Carlos, this is no big deal. Go home and tell Ed to stop trying to protect me. I've got this."

Ty watched Dave walk away. He smiled and went to the hotel registration counter.

"I'm Senator Leggett and I'm here for a meeting with Senator Simmons."

"Yes, Senator, they are in Senator Simmons's suite, on the top floor. The elevators are on your left. Here is your pass to activate the elevator."

Ty turned to leave, then stopped. "By the way, do you know when Senator Simmons and his guests arrived?"

She glanced at her monitor. "At five, sir."

"Thank you." *A meeting before the meeting,* he thought.

He rode the elevator to the penthouse. The elevator door opened into Simmons's suite.

That's convenient, he thought.

There was a partition facing the elevator door. Ty turned right and walked alongside the woven grass cloth wallpaper. An Egyptian rug covered the floor, and there was a silver wall table with miniature crystal ornaments and Swarovski figurines. Ty snickered and thought, *He used table tents to show off the crystal's name. He's such small potatoes.*

Ty stepped into the main room.

"Senator Leggett, great to see you. Thank you very much for joining us on such short notice," Simmons said, getting to his feet from the couch.

There were three other men in the room, all wearing summer coats and gray slacks. The sitting room faced the Gun Island Chute River. It was beautiful; the wall-to-wall carpet was a soft white plush, with a gold-inlayed abstract mosaic. To the right side, a light-gray Italian couch, and a four-by-four-foot hand-hued driftwood cocktail table was in the center. A bronze cast statue of Fredrick Remington's *The Rattlesnake* rested on the center of the table, with a printed paper name plate. It read: 1 of 10.

Ty smiled at the sight of the statue. *Perfect,* he thought.

Along the south wall was a crystal wet bar stocked with natural soft drinks and eclectic bottles of water.

"May I offer you something to drink, Ty?" John asked.

"I'm fine," Ty said.

"Introductions: This is Sam Huston, Robert Price, and Harry Drake. They are your team."

The men smiled and each shook Ty's hand on introduction.

"These men, along with six others, have pledged to

raise your eight million. We could not be more excited by the prospect of you serving in the United States Senate." John gently gripped Ty's left shoulder with his right hand.

"Please sit, everyone. Ty, you sit here," He pointed at the one oversized chair that faced the three couches.

The group sat.

Ty sank into the overstuffed chair. He stood up. "That would kill my back," he said, moving to the couch to sit next to John. *Nice try, boys,* he thought.

John smiled. "That's my favorite chair. Sorry about your back. So, let's get to it: We just have a few campaign questions and a little gossip. Harry was in DC last week on business and he heard that Ullman was meeting with the DNC for funding. Have you heard that?" John asked.

"Yes, that's true."

"Does that give you concern?"

"None. Money will not be Jeffery's problem; *he'll* be his biggest issue."

John leaned back and nodded. "So, you're not worried about Washington funding his campaign?"

"No, we've planned on him spending fifty million and having Hollywood celebrities running around Alabama calling us racist or whatever cliché his political consultant tells them to use."

"Good, good," John said, and looked at the other men.

Harry Drake spoke up. "Senator Leggett, I have one concern I hope you can address. We know it will take about sixteen million net to win your campaign and with our donation, you'll need an additional eight million, right?"

"Yes," Ty said.

"That could prove difficult, don't you think? My understanding is DC money is out and you're on your own."

Ty smiled, looking relaxed. "DC support will come when I don't need it. Senator Joseph is leading our Washington effort and he's very capable. I'm not worried about DC or our out-of-state donations."

"That is comforting," Drake said.

"Not being nitpicky, but George Roka and Ms. Paddick have complained about your management team. Especially Ed Abbott and your treasurer," Simmons said.

"Having run a massive government agency, personalities and professional disagreements will sometimes affect perspective. I am very comfortable with my campaign team."

"That is all true; I've seen it myself," John said.

"I had lunch with Ms. Paddick last week and her perspective was not personalities, but financial, debt to be precise—" Robert Price said.

"Now boys, that's not fair," John interrupted. "We're all friends here." He smiled and tapped Ty on his left leg, as he looked at the other men.

"Ty, we have some inside scoop. Ms. Paddick works for the Senate as well as being Senator Jacobs's chief of staff and she has expressed concerns about Mr. Abbott and his —her words— 'outrageous fundraising costs.' According to her, the Central dinner, though well attended, netted very little money, and ..." He looked at Leggett.

Ty showed only cool reserve.

Simmons looked a little bewildered by Ty's lack of emotion. "George Roka had the same concerns about your treasurer. Information was disjointed, and he said you did not have the cash on hand to meet the bare minimum for voter ID and outreach. Worse, in his opinion there was not enough cash to fund the campaign through the summer. Those two issues worry us."

Ty looked politely interested, while John looked suitably concerned.

After a moment, John continued, "Our eight million investment, along with your commitment, is the bare minimum needed to win that seat." He leaned forward and took a sip of water. "The worst thing we could do is dump good money down a black hole. This is not personal, it's business. Right, boys?" He looked again at the men sitting on the couch, and they nodded dutifully.

"Ty, we're all in this together to make Alabama a world-class state." John smiled, looking relaxed. "Every concern we have is just food for thought. We all know that the marketing campaign does not begin until after Labor Day. But we must get there. I know firsthand, fundraising is impossible in July and August. We're worried you don't have enough to get there. I'm not saying we're pulling out; we just need you to give us assurances or maybe make changes," John said as he looked at the Rattlesnake statue on the table.

Ty thought, *He thinks he's got me.*

"I love the law," Ty said. "It's where facts matter, and perception evaporates." He smiled. "John, gentlemen, thank you for your continued commitment to my campaign. It's rewarding and I look forward to November."

Ty looked at the perplexed faces staring back at him. "Facts: We will have a million in our savings account, and we can cash-flow the campaign until late September without touching the principal. Ed Abbott has designed a fundraising plan to reach our eight-million commitment. Lastly, I am very happy with my team; they are doing an outstanding job." He smiled.

Silence.

Late that Friday night, Ed received a text: Don't go to the Capitol for a while. You were right. Simmons and Roka hate you. Thank you. Ty

---

On Saturday morning, Ed was at his Commerce Street office, feeling good about himself. He was singing along to his playlist as he organized his desk and office.

Sabina walked into his private office. "Pretty chipper today, are we? Things must have gone well last night."

"I am a genius," he said.

"Oh, you were right about Roka's plan or could it be the hour of begging Senator Peterson to get us another four hundred thousand?" She smiled. "That does make you special. Because you are Ed Abbott."

"Debbie Downer, always Debbie Downer. I was right, that's all that matters."

"You mean lucky, Mr. Perfect. We have a million in the bank; we owe Peterson five hundred K and the FEC report is due July fifteenth."

"You could suck the joy out of Disneyland," Ed said.

His cell buzzed. He picked it up and looked at the screen: Carlos.

"I should take this," Ed said.

Sabina muted the music.

"Have you spoken to Ty this morning?" Carlos asked.

"Text last night," Ed said.

"I'm disappointed. I was looking forward to hunting you down."

"Very funny. May I put you on speaker? Sabina is here."

"Sure. How are you going to construct the FEC report and keep Simmons onboard?" Carlos asked.

"It's a little early for that; we're still in June." Ed looked at Sabina. "Anyway, the July FEC report will look a lot better than April's, which was easy since we started with nothing." Ed flipped on his desktop to open a draft FEC document he created. "By July fifteenth, we'll show nine hundred thousand cash on hand. We raised almost a million five. Dave is holding all invoices until after the July report to hold cash."

"What about Peterson's five hundred K?"

"The hundred K seed money from his twenty federal PACs has been repaid—"

"Why now?" Carlos asked.

"He's cheap."

Sabina laughed.

"The four hundred K is not a loan and came from eighty different federal PACs."

"What about Roka's expenses?"

"They'll be listed as prepayments for voter outreach and his outrageous salary will be shown as a consulting fee.

Everything Ty told Simmons last night was true. We haven't seen the totals from the direct mail and social media efforts, which I understand did well, so we could show more cash."

"Not bad," Carlos said.

"What, 'not bad'? You're a jerk," Ed said.

"Okay, I'll give you pretty good, and Sabina is great."

"True," Ed said, looking at Sabina.

"From what you've seen, do you think we can meet our eight million goal?" Carlos asked.

"Always, more pressure," Sabina said, looking at Ed.

"That depends on success outside Alabama. I know we can triple what we've done so far in state." He thought for a moment, "The rest will be very hard to find. Which makes Simmons's money critical."

"That's a non-answer answer," Carlos said.

"I know; best I can do, though. I'll fill in the blanks this weekend. We've got to go."

"Ed, before you hang up, should I tell Gonzo to cut his budget five million?"

"Now it's passive-aggressive pressure," Sabina said.

"No, passive-aggressive would be telling you Ullman went to DC last Friday and met with the NSCC team."

Ed sighed; Sabina glared at the phone.

"As for Ullman going to the National Senatorial Campaign Committee, it's a non-issue," Ed said.

"Actually, that helps us. They'll see what we know, that Ullman is a doofus," Sabina interrupted.

"That's true. Good job, Ed and Sabina. I look forward to your updated plan." Carlos hung up.

Sabina looked at Ed, as she sat in the cloth chair facing

his desk. "I don't know how you survive the pressure. Each day we're hit with: 'What's next?' and 'How much did you bring in?' 'We're going to lose, blah, blah, blah,' and all they do is spend and bullshit."

"He's just doing his job and they're right: If we fail, Ty loses."

"He's still a jerk."

Ed sighed again and looked at Sabina. "We're five million short," he whispered. He clicked the Leggett icon on his desktop computer. "I've done the math for the three million in-state we must raise. We have one hundred forty-eight days before October twenty-first. That's sixteen thousand eight hundred and ninety-one dollars per day. Figuring twenty percent fundraising cost and our commission, we should net one point six million from small events, high-dollar mail, and major donors without too much trouble."

Sabina laughed. "Come on, that leaves us one point four million short. Where is the rest coming from?"

"The remaining Alabama money must come from our website, social media, crowdsource, and small events—"

"More parties. That's not happening," she interrupted. "We need something bigger, a five hundred K reception. There must be one celebrity who will host Leggett. We can find someone—"

"Who wants to destroy their career?" Ed interrupted.

"Look who's Debbie Downer now. We've got to try. If we find one nationally known celebrity to host a party at their home, we can promote it nationally and raffle ten tickets and raise a million digitally."

"Maybe you're right. Who knows how many people

Leggett can blackmail," he said with a laugh. "Maybe the president. He's in DC three days a week, voting, and meeting lobbyists and constituents—"

"Not funny, forget it," she interrupted.

"Shit, come on, there must be an idea that works. We need five million. I'll call Tim."

"Tracy here."

"Tim, we've run the numbers, we're five million short. How much can you increase—"

Click, the phone went dead.

"Man of few words," Sabina said and laughed. "What if we double the finance committee membership to fifty?" she asked.

"That's too much work and dilutes the cachet of membership."

"Okay, Mr. Loserville. I've got it—*this* is what we're going to do. If Simmons can use greed to raise eight million here—

"Greed. Where did you get that?"

"You've said it yourself; Simmons wants to own Ty. Why? There can only be one reason, money and good old boy, federal contracts. If that loser Simmons has figured it out, I'll bet there are others. We need five billionaires: They're greedy and smart. That's a billionaire per state, five states, each person raising us a million or one billionaire at five million."

Ed stared at her. "What's gotten into you? You're on fire."

"I don't want to lose," she said.

"Okay five states, each raising a million, led by one whale in each state," he said speaking to himself.

"First, let's pick the most likely states, then the whale. The most likely are Texas, Florida, California, New York, and Georgia."

"Maybe Senator Joseph can introduce us to someone, or—" Ed put a grin on his face—"Ty can use blackmail."

"Stop it, this is too important. I'll go over the billionaires I met at the Team 100 meeting and match states. We have no choice. This must work; there's nothing in your plan if Simmons bails," she said.

"Yes, there is: We're screwed."

That Monday afternoon, Ed was at his office making fundraising calls and one of his cell phones buzzed: Shirley Knot.

Ed smiled. He liked everything about Shirley, her dark hair, deep-brown, sleepy eyes, and slow Southern style. At 5'8" with the willowy figure of a track-and-field athlete, she was a self-made success story.

They'd first met shortly after she'd arrived from Louisiana and was working as a bartender at the Alley Bar. She'd moved to Montgomery without friends or connections. After ten years of saving every penny and living in a studio apartment, she founded an online cosmetic company and bought her first home in Capitol Heights. The last time Ed saw her, she told him, "For the first time in my life, I can afford to go out to dinner."

Ed's only disappointment was she refused to date him.

"Hi, Shirley, what's up?"

"Can you meet me tonight for a drink at Central?"

"Sure, what time?"

"Six."

Ed left his office and walked up Commerce Street to Tallapoosa and cut through the Alley to the back door of Central Restaurant. The main bar was almost empty, not surprising for a Tuesday night.

Shirley was sitting at the middle table against the wall facing the bar; a five-foot-wide dark oil printing of a Victorian woman hung behind her on the wall.

Shirley was dressed in a dark tropical-wool pantsuit, a white silk blouse. A glass of ice water was on the table before her.

Ed smiled when he saw her. "You want a drink?" he asked.

"No," she said with a serious expression.

"Well, if you don't mind, I had a lousy day. I need one."

Ed walked up to the hand-carved bar and ordered a double Jack Daniels, neat. He took a sip and returned to Shirley.

"You had a bad day?" she asked.

"The worst. Just inside baseball. Not worth talking about. What's up?" he asked, taking another sip.

"I'm sorry about your day. What I'm about to say won't make it much better." She took a sip of water.

"Several months ago, I was on a date and the guy did not take it too well when I said no to him spending the night. Several hours later he climbed through the living room window, crept into my bedroom and raped me."

"Good God," Ed exclaimed. He put his drink down, leaned back, and searched her eyes for emotion.

"The next morning, I called the police, and he was

arrested. The trial starts this Friday, and I'm very uncomfortable. The prosecutor assigned to the case is not trying to convict the bastard. Yesterday he suggested it was my fault." She maintained a stoic demeanor, not taking her eyes off Ed's face.

"He hurt me, Ed, and he'll hurt another girl." She glanced around the room, her eyes started to water. "I don't know what to do. I need help."

"I can't believe this," Ed said.

"Ed, I'm from New Orleans' East Ward. This happens all the time. No one cares, and men like that walk until they kill some poor girl." She wiped her cheek with her hand, "I don't have the money to hire an attorney."

"This isn't fair. A prosecutor is supposed to care. I don't know what I can do, but I'll try. What's the staff attorney's name?"

"Robert Dull," she answered.

"And the creep's name?"

"Robert Anderson."

Ed took a sip of his drink.

"Are you okay?"

"Yes."

"'You once told me that all men are pigs," Ed said.

"Yes. My mother preached that. She said it was in their nature and couldn't help themselves. I still don't believe it."

Ed called Montgomery District Attorney Herb Jackson on Tuesday morning and asked for a meeting. Jackson had just won his reelection, and Ed had supported his campaign with a $4,000 donation.

On Thursday at eleven a.m., Ed, dressed in his finest blue suit, left his office and walked the five blocks to South Lawrence Street Montgomery County Administration Building, an ugly, dated-looking reddish slate-and-glass two-story building.

Ed walked around the metal railing guarding the entrance, opened the glass door, and stepped into a dirty foyer with two metal detectors just steps into the room.

"Empty your pockets and pass through," the armed security guard said rudely.

Ed placed his keys and wallet into the plastic dish and passed through the box. Finished, he picked up his property.

"Where are you going?" the guard asked.

"Mr. Jackson's office."

"Elevators are straight ahead, second floor, turn right, and go through the wooden doors."

Ed pushed the elevator call button and listened to creaking metal scratching sounds. The doors opened; Ed felt uncomfortable in elevators, especially ones where the doors took too long to open or close.

He stepped in, pushed the close button several times and waited. The doors closed and the elevator, after several seconds, lifted and stopped at the second floor; the doors did not open. Ed pushed the open button several times, beginning to feel uneasy.

Thankfully, the doors opened, he turned right and followed the linoleum hallway toward a wooden door at the end of the hallway. He glanced at the State Seal as he pulled the heavy door open, to discover a plain ten-by-ten-foot reception area.

A uniformed police officer was sitting behind a four-foot-high wooden counter desk. The room was austere; two cloth chairs, a couch, and a bare cocktail table filled the space. The new gray carpet gave off a toxic odor. Law enforcement plaques and photographs of former district attorneys lined the wall to the right of the reception counter.

Ed smiled when he saw a photograph of United States Senator Tyler Leggett, on the wall to the left of the doorway.

"My name is Ed Abbott, and I have an appointment with Mr. Jackson."

"May I see your identification and are you carrying any weapons?" she asked.

Ed, under his breath, sniggered. "No, I don't carry a gun or own one, for that matter."

He handed his driver's license to the police officer. She entered his license number into the computer facing her. She smiled and handed the license back. "Please make yourself comfortable, Mr. Abbott. I'll tell Mr. Jackson you're here."

After five minutes, the door next to the governor's photograph opened and a professionally dressed, tall young woman appeared, holding the door open.

"Mr. Abbott, the district attorney can see you now."

Ed followed her down a short, carpeted hallway, lined with hundreds of candid photographs of celebrities, national politicians, and photos of Mr. Jackson at major sporting events, car races, concerts and dinners.

At the end of the hall was an open office space. Ed entered and saw District Attorney Herb Jackson standing before his desk. He was dressed in a tailored, dark business suit. He reached out his hand; they shook.

"How can I help you, Mr. Abbott?" he asked in a friendly voice. He gestured toward the five-foot-round table to Abbott's right. "Please sit." Herb pulled a chair away from the table and turned it to face Ed, sat, and said, "It's a pleasure to meet you; what's on your mind?"

Ed liked Jackson immediately; his reputation was of a fun-loving and honest person, and it came across.

"Thank you for meeting with me, this is very kind. I'll be quick, the assailant of a friend of mine has a rape case trial starting this Friday. I don't know what really happened, but I do know she's very concerned that the prosecutor doesn't seem interested in convicting the bastard. Would you please put your best prosecutor on the case?"

Jackson smiled, looking relieved that was all Ed needed. "I'll see what I can do, Mr. Abbott. What's your friend's name, and who was assigned to her case?"

"Shirley Knot and the lawyer is Robert Dull."

"The perp's name?"

"Robert Anderson."

Herb smiled and started to stand.

"Thank you," Ed said.

"My pleasure."

They shook hands.

Ed left Herb's office and took the stairs down.

Ed was in his Commerce Street office Friday evening writing a fundraising letter when one of his cell phones buzzed. He picked it up without looking at the screen.

"This is Abbott."

"Thank you."

He recognized the voice.

"This morning, I was sitting in the courtroom gallery waiting for Mr. Dull and in walked a man carrying an armful of binders and papers. He dropped the stack on the table, and turned to me, and said, 'Yesterday, I was very busy. Today you're my sole focus. My name is Ross Relles,' and he shook my hand. Thank you, Ed," she said, her voice breaking with emotion.

11
JULY

Executive Summary: Tyler Leggett
2039 Alabama US Senate Campaign
Survey Conducted by Val Price,
Meta Research Corporation, Washington, DC
June 28–30
Sample size, 2,500 respondents
Fifty questions, hour-long cell phone interviews
Statewide demographics
+3–4% margin of error.

Top Issues:

1. Economy/Jobs
2. Healthcare
3. Law and Order
4. Conceal-Carry
5. Education
6. Child AI implants

7. Right to Choose
8. Transgender rights
9. Climate Change/the Environment

If election were held today:

Ullman: 55%
Horner: 47%
Leggett: 3%

Jeffery Ullman—Independent: 15% statewide name ID. Tested switching parties; most think he's a Republican. When told he had switched parties, would vote against him at a 3-to-1 ratio. Senator Ullman has a 2–1 favorability rating.

Jack Horner—Democrat: Statewide name ID under the margin of error. 100% of voters came from party loyalty.

US Senator Tyler Leggett—Independent: Statewide name ID is 4%. Of the people who knew of Senator Leggett he has a 3-to-1 favorability. Senator Leggett is weak with men, conservatives, and the religious. He is considered a Northern outsider.

Sitting in Gonzo's conference room, Ty read the survey results as he waited for the meeting. He was soon joined by Carlos and Val. Ty put the survey down on the table and looked up and smiled, saying, "Three percent is not zero. We're not at the bottom. They don't hate us. We can do this."

Val nodded, smiling. "Yep, every twenty-eight days, the campaign can convince more and more voters to support us and we've got time. All it'll take is sixteen million dollars."

They laughed.

Friday, July 1, 7:30 a.m., Leggett campaign strategy meeting, Gonzo Diaz's Montgomery office. Attending: Ty, Val Price, Susie and Gonzo Diaz, Carlos Felix, Tim Tracy and Ed Abbott.

The group was sitting around an oak table in Gonzo's ten-by-twelve-foot conference room. The only objects on the table were three holographic projectors and three conference call speakers/microphones. The room was austere, with sealed concrete flooring and white walls, which projected a serious feeling.

A half-inch-thick floor-to-ceiling glass wall faced the hallway, which led to the reception area and three private offices. Three casement windows, with blackout curtains, faced Commerce Street. The south wall had a six-by-four-foot whiteboard. The north wall had a sixty-inch flatscreen monitor, and under the monitor was an AI hard drive, and a new, Wi-Fi holographic transponder.

Ty kicked the meeting off. "Good morning. Since it's

Friday before a three-day holiday, my goal is to keep this meeting under an hour. Of course, Val, take as long as you feel necessary. Before we get to Val, Ed, where are we with money?"

"We're on track to meet our July and August monetary goals and enter September with a million and half in the bank. In-state fundraising will tap out at eleven million, thanks to the incredible advice of Tim," Ed glanced at Tim and smiled, Tim remained stoic.

"We will remedy the five million shortfall with out-of-state money. The state chairpersons have been selected, and we've scheduled meetings with them. Each chairperson will raise a million dollars. My goal is to have all out-of-state funds in-hand by October first."

"Very good. I want everyone in this campaign to know you and Sabina have done a marvelous job overcoming considerable drama. Thank you."

Ty smiled. Ed looked down at his iPad.

"It's all yours now, Val," Ty said.

Val passed four flash drives around the table. "Those drives contain the full survey and the codes to view upcoming surveys online." He glanced down at his iPad. "Our Democrat opponent is a non-issue; he cannot win unless his party pumps in twenty-five million, which will not happen. Mr. Horner is a rural independent Democrat with outdated ideas; he is unattractive for a national forum.

"We tested whether the Leggett campaign should focus paid media on attacking Mr. Horner. The transference questions exposed the failure of that strategy. Mr. Horner will not have the funds to respond to our attacks and our advertising would fall on deaf ears with no lasting impact. My conclusion is every dollar spent on Mr. Horner would be wasted. It is my opinion Mr. Horner will receive ten percent of the vote regardless of our efforts," Val looked around the room for comments. Seeing none, he continued.

"Which explains why the Democratic Party will focus their efforts on electing Mr. Ullman. Their goal is to gain fifty percent of the Republican vote and ninety percent of the Democrat vote, guaranteeing Mr. Ullman's victory.

"Ullman's persona is his greatest weakness. His cowboy image does not line up with most moderates under the age of fifty, and those voters find that character degrading and a reminder of a racist past."

Val gently tapped his right index finger on the table. "I'm going to disagree with a term in the survey. I do not believe in 'moderates' as a voting bloc. I recently reread *The Ninth Wave* and I agree with the author. They do not exist. We occasionally mention that group in reference to the unknown. By definition, a moderate is an individual who has limited interest and votes for middle ground. That thought is wrong; they do have issues they care strongly about. Reaching them on those issues guarantees their vote. Therefore, moderates only exist for the uninitiated media who believe in their voting impact. For this campaign, there are no moderates, only undiscovered issues."

He glanced around the table, looking for disagreement; seeing none, he continued.

"Mr. Ullman's major weakness is having left his party. That hurts him in two significant ways: First, he has a thirty-year conservative voting record. Second, it makes him an opportunist. Most people find that disingenuous and will vote against him on that issue alone—at a three-to-one ratio."

He glanced at his notes. "Now I'll address our political vulnerabilities. Number one, a Washington DC Black man running in Alabama. Ullman's team will never mention Ty's color, they will just put his face on everything." Val smiled and looked around the room. "And we will do the same. We want every voter to know Ty is Black and has returned home to lead Alabama.

Val smiled, seeming to enjoy himself.

"Ullman's team believes Alabama is full of KKK members and cross-burners, and they will act accordingly in their messaging. The truth is, only a small part of Alabama houses hatred; the majority wants to move on. The change started in nineteen seventy, thanks to the University of Southern California's Sam Cunningham and football.

"Carried today by abundant jobs, home affordability, young people, and hope, Alabama is different from what they think, and their strategy will fail. We can only hope some jerk writes a racist letter or sets something on fire. Guilt and sympathy are worth ten points to us and we need those votes or we're in trouble." Val looked at Ty.

"On that front, I've done some research, and the first slave ship was named the *White Lion*. I can test it in our prospect mail program," Tim said.

"Let's hold off on that. Our immediate task is to raise Senator Leggett's name identity to sixty percent by October first, with three-to-one favorable."

Val looked at Gonzo.

"Your team needs to run feel-good puff advertising, no

negatives until after September fifteenth. Tim, your direct mail campaign should continue to follow local and national issues and raise money, for the time being.

"Our next survey will be July sixteenth and will focus on hyper-local hot button issues that can be exploited by radio, social media, and direct mail. One example of a hyper-local issue is the Gun Chute Bridge and Walkway. Too many trucks, shootings, car accidents, and frustrating daily traffic. Senator Leggett will fix those problems, along with potholes and crappy traffic lights. Elections are won on local issues, and we will run local, in every city and town in Alabama."

He swallowed some Coke and turned a page of his notes.

"The top nine statewide issues are listed and broken down by demographics. The only issue we must absolutely avoid is reparations. The numbers show it is a no-win issue for us. No matter what we propose, it will be attacked and become national media's only talking point. The political attack dogs will lockstep and criticize our proposal relentlessly. To our supporters, it would come across as pandering or worse. We can only hope Ullman says something stupid about the issue, which he might. Regardless, under no circumstances take the bait and respond to any question or comment. Avoid that issue." He looked at his iPad. "That's all I've got."

"Thank you all. There won't be any in-person meetings for the balance of July or August. If something comes up, I'll text," Ty said.

Later that afternoon, Ty called Val. "I don't agree with you on the reparations issue. Too many have suffered under hate, oppression, and violence. Every person on the planet deserves compensation."

"Only one percent had an opinion; Alabama voters are not thinking about it as a local or statewide issue. When asked about it as a federal matter, that changed. The word reparations is polarizing and will never happen. If you want to do something, wait until you're elected. Or you won't get elected," Val responded.

"Val—"

"Ty, win the damn campaign," he interrupted.

12

Wednesday morning, July 6, Carlos called Gonzo from his Montgomery office.

"This is Gonzo."

"Have you finalized the plan for the July and August paid outdoor marketing campaign?"

"Pretty much. I've already bought forty-nine billboards, drive-time radio, and social media. I'll text the short list now."

"I've got it," Carlos said.

He read: Billboards: 2 Birmingham; 1 McCalla Highway; 2 Montgomery; 1 on Highway 65; 1 on Gibbons Drive.

Radio: WJOX 94.5 FM—Sports Talk (Birmingham), WZYP 104.3 FM—Top 40/Pop (Huntsville), WERC 105.5 FM.

"The radio will run for only two weeks, no point wasting money on people out of town. Everything is just a sprinkling. I want to see what works before we buy for the fall. The billboards go live July eighth through August thirty-first. Radio starts July fifth, then restarts when schools reopen." Gonzo glanced at his Apple Watch: he had a text from Susie. It read: Ullman calls Leggett a Northern carpetbagger.

"Did you see what Ullman said today?" Carlos asked.

"Yes, Susie just sent it to me. My bet is it's a test to see if we respond. Back to advertising, after we see the September survey results, we'll adjust the message and restart. Everything right now is name and positive. The theme is 'Hometown hero returns.' On the billboards, he's standing with preachers, Alabama sports heroes, high school coaches and educators. On the radio, same idea. We're matching that outdoor paid campaign with Tim's mail and Gary's free and paid social media."

"What about the churches?"

"I'm doing the religious search now, and we'll be in every church bulletin—after the pastor has endorsed Ty, of course." Gonzo laughed at his own joke. "This two-month advertising campaign will cost four-hundred thousand. It should raise our positives to three-to-one and our statewide name ID to thirty percent."

"Sounds good." Ty said.

"After the September first survey, we'll buy November sixth, backward to September fifteenth. And we must raise the monthly average marketing budget to eight million plus."

"You *are* kidding? Ed will go nuts!" Carlos laughed.

"Too bad for him, I want to win. Lastly, I don't expect Ullman to hit us until early September and only if our name ID is over thirty percent."

"Your budget does not leave the day-to-day campaign much money."

"Ed will have to raise an additional half a million," Gonzo said with a laugh.

"Causing Ed stress makes me happy. However, build a second budget at eight point two-five million average per month."

"Okay." Gonzo glanced again at his Apple Watch. It read: Ullman lines up Hollywood celebrities. "Do we have a date when Simmons's money starts?"

"Only early September," Carlos answered.

"What about Ed's eight million?"

"It's starting to come in; his timeline has it all in by October nineteenth."

"What's our backup if Simmons walks or Ed can't?"

"Ty retires and we look for jobs," Carlos answered.

Carlos called Ed at 5:00 p.m. that afternoon.

Ed answered his cell phone. "You better not ask how much money I've raised today."

"No, that comes later. I just got off the phone with Gonzo, and his two-month ad campaign is four hundred thousand, and—"

"Why are you telling me? Tower has the money and pays bills."

"If I can finish? His budget for the fall is eight-point three million per month."

"What?"

"Yep."

"Wait a minute." Ed held the cell phone up and yelled, "Sabina, Gonzo upped his budget five hundred thousand."

Sabina's right hand and middle finger appeared through the open doorway.

"Sabina's not happy. And you're nuts. That is crazy! We can't raise an extra five hundred thousand. No way!"

"We have no choice. Add some out-of-state events and get us another half million."

Silence

"By the way, how much have you raised today?"

Ed hung up.

"Sabina, we're screwed, let's add one out-of-state high-dollar event."

Silence.

"Okay?" Ed asked.

"I'll think about it," she said.

Ed's monitor popped on. There was a text message from Shirley Knot: *Trial ended. He got 25 years.*

Ed smiled.

"Sabina, forget it. Let's cut out early and go to the Time Zone and play some video games. My treat," he said.

13

On Monday, July 11, at 4:00 p.m., Ty walked through the Montgomery Regional Airport looking for Darrel's shoeshine stand. He had an hour before his weekly flight to Washington. He found Darrel sitting at the stand looking at his phone. "Good morning, Darrel. Got a moment?"

Darrel glanced up with a smile, recognizing the voice. "For you, Senator Leggett, just for you."

Ty sat, and Darrel began to clean Ty's wingtips.

"So, Darrel, what's new?"

"I've seen your billboards over the weekend. You look pretty cool for a native."

Ty laughed.

"I liked them; we need someone who believes in God."

Ty smiled, thinking, *Oh, man.* "Darrel, I've asked Representative Damion to meet with me next week. What do you know about him?"

"Most brothers don't understand him being a Republican and some hate him. Me, he's okay. He come by the

Capitol barbershop once in a while. We talk. His parents be professors at State and he went to Montgomery Academy and Auburn, played a little ball." He looked around and lowered his voice. "You can tell he raised by crackers; he's dry as sand."

"Is he honest?"

"Too honest. Won't cut deals. But he tips well."

Ty smiled.

The following Friday morning, back in Montgomery at the campaign headquarters, Ty was making his daily twenty fundraising calls. Just as he finished with his last call, his headquarters manager, Dave Hillyard, knocked on the door and poked his head into the room.

"Representative Damion is here."

"Show him to the conference room and ask Josh to join us. Also, see if Mr. Damion would like some water or coffee."

Ty tidied up his desk and walked next-door to a twelve-by-seven-foot windowless room.

Damion was sitting at the stained card table dressed in a light-tan business suit, with a blue dress shirt.

Ty's bodyguard, Josh, sat across the table from him.

Ty entered the room and shut the door.

"Thank you for meeting me, Mr. Damion," Ty said.

Damion stood and they shook hands. "Please call me Jeremiah."

"Perfect. Always call me Ty. A quick introduction: Sitting across from you is Josh Washington, my shadow."

Ty paused and smiled. "Josh is a retired detective from the Birmingham PD. I've asked him to join us so he could meet you and know who my friends are and our goal."

The two men smiled at each other.

"Josh's job is to keep me out of trouble. And of course I need that, having been the director of the FBI." Ty raised an eyebrow. "I thought it best to meet here instead of your Capitol office or another public place, so we could be frank with each other. I've heard you think a state office would have been a better fit for me."

"That is true. A brother should never run for high office."

"A couple have made it."

"They got greedy or joined the white boy club."

"It only takes a year for most politicians to pronounce how complicated things are. I can't count how many times I've heard: 'Ty, you just don't understand, it's gray.'"

"Try being the only Black Republican," Jeremiah said.

Ty smiled. "Some get it; the trick is to come in with a bang, do something needed, then leave."

"Sounds good, I've found we're always on our own. Which makes it hard," Damion said with a bitter smile. "How can I help you, Ty?"

"You've seen the campaign stuff. That's part of me, but not the reason I'm running. I left the Bureau because I lost my soul. My father told me, 'If you work in a perfume factory you go home reeking.' What one does for a living rubs off. I watched a decent family destroyed by hate and greed, and all I thought about was doing my job.

"Everyone gets corrupted; we're human. The trick is to move fast. Thurgood believed in the law, as do I. That is the bang. I believe nothing will change for us unless we make amends for the past and lift the future."

"What's your plan?" Jeremiah asked.

"Not to get ahead of myself, win the campaign, and on day one shock the hell out of the club."

Silence.

"Ty, I've lost faith in good intentions. All I can do is trust the person," Jeremiah said. He studied Ty's eyes. "What would you like me to do?"

"Restore your faith and keep an eye on my back."

"That's it?"

"Yes."

Silence.

"Josh, please come by my Capitol office today at five? I have something for you," Jeremiah said.

That afternoon, Ty was driving back to the campaign headquarters after a lunch meeting. His cell phone vibrated; he glanced at the screen: Ed Abbott.

Ty held the phone up and flashed the screen at Josh and smiled.

"Yes, Ed, my calls are done. I reached all five out-of-state billionaires; they said yes to helping and are sending you the dates for us to meet with them."

"Perfect. On another matter, Gonzo screwed the pooch on his budget and we need an additional five hundred K."

"That sounds like a *you* problem."

"Ty, life would be much easier if you would just blackmail the president," Ed said.

Silence.

"That's a no, I take it?"

Silence.

"That's what Sabina figured, so she lined up three events in California. One at the LA Country Club, a one hundred K breakfast hosted by Southern Cal political icon Diane Klinger. The second is in Beverly Hills, a two hundred K lunch, hosted by education and sports entrepreneur Janet Parker. We end the day in Century City, with a two hundred K cocktail reception hosted by oil tycoon Branson Nobel. The events are scheduled for July twenty-seventh, and we take the nine p.m. redeye home out of LAX."

"That's a long day," Ty said.

"Especially since we're flying commercial. You should have kept the jet."

"Not funny, Ed."

"By the way, we got an unsolicited donation of twenty-nine hundred today from a Mrs. Megan Barber in Virginia. Do you know her, and should I ask for a reception?"

"That's very nice of her and yes, I know her, and no reception. Just make sure it complies with FEC and the contribution is from her sole bank account," Ty said.

At four forty-five that same afternoon, after his meeting with the *Montgomery Advisor* editorial board, Ty and Josh drove to the Executive Capitol Building and parked. Josh got out of the car and walked into the office building.

He rode the elevator to the fifth floor and Representative Damion's office. Josh opened the door and, sitting at a used-looking wooden desk, was a middle-aged woman who looked up with an inquiring expression.

He stepped into the room, closed the door, and said, "I'm here to pick up a package for Senator Leggett."

"You work for that fine man?" she asked.

"Yes."

"He hired a brother."

Josh smiled. She glanced down and opened her top desk drawer and removed a sealed number-six blank envelope.

"Here," she said, handing it to him. "Please tell Senator Leggett that there are a lot of us counting on him."

"Will do," Josh said as he turned to leave the room.

"Is he real?" she asked.

"Yes, he'll gives me hope."

Sitting in the car, reading through his emails on his iPhone, Ty did not notice Josh's return until he opened the driver's door.

Josh got in and handed Ty the envelope. He buckled the seatbelt; Ty opened the envelope to find its only content was a mini flash drive. Ty opened the glove box, removed an adapter, plugged it into his phone, and inserted the flash drive. Instantly, an audio file appeared. He tapped play and heard the voice of the president of the United States.

"Governor, we got us a pickle. Neither of us want Leggett back in DC and I understand he's raising money and got a good team running his campaign. I'd like to see if we can work something out," Ralph Rodda said.

"What you got?" Governor Pete Murphy asked.

"I think it might be best if you and I stay out and let the boys in the Senate fight this one out," Rodda said.

"Why's that?"

"Ty's got a lot of friends in the Bureau, and if he's elected, our past ventures could resurface. Hell, it's good for us if Ullman wins."

"Maybe you, but I'm on the hook," Pete said.

"Being on the hook is a good thing. You appointed a black man, and no one expects him to win. Hell—"

"What's your offer?" Pete interrupted.

"I'll get you federal funds to rebuild the Gun Island Chute Bridge and a week hunting Montana Rocky Mountain elk and bighorn sheep, with extra tags," Ralph said.

"This year?"

"Yes."

"I can't stop what's already been promised," Pete said.

"Understood. I know about Simmons. Deal. We spoke, and how his fundraiser is going," Rodda said.

Ty tapped the phone off and looked out the passenger window.

"That's ugly," Josh said.

"Only if they shut down Ed or Simmons."

"What's next?"

"We have two receptions and a dinner. Let's go."

Josh started the car, and Ty called Carlos.

"Yes, Ty?" Carlos answered.

"I want you to go see Ed and tell him he's being watched. Use your law enforcement training to convince him."

"By whom?" Carlos asked.

"The White House and contact your DC lobbyist

friends and find out who's spreading rumors about our fundraising. I want to know how deep the White House is involved."

"What can I tell Ed?"

"Tell him it just got real, and Carlos, I don't want him to know this is coming from me."

"Understood."

At 5:00 a.m., the next morning, Josh and Ty were on their way to Fairhope.

"So, what have we got after the six-thirty breakfast?" Josh asked.

"It's a lot. At eight a.m., Fairhope Chamber; nine-thirty meeting with the Farm Bureau Association in Summerdale; lunch, Alabama Environmental Council in Daphne; two o'clock, logistics APB Terminals in Mobile. Then still in Mobile, we end the day at a six p.m. fundraising reception with Mr. Robert Peterson, Peterson Trucking." Ty put his phone on the car seat.

"Ed's a pain in the ass."

"That's a busy day. We'll get home around ten."

"That's nothing. Would you like to know the cities we'll visit from now until August?" Ty asked.

Ty opened the Excel spreadsheet on his iPad and read:

"Alexander, Athens, Auburn, Birmingham, Carney, Chelsea, Decatur, Eclectic, Homewood, Hover, Linden, Madison, Mountain Brook, Orange Beach, Pelham, Point Clear, Spanish Fort, Trussville, and Vestavia. We average four events a day. And that includes several parades, ribbon cuttings, a 4-H contest, and my favorite, a dance contest judge in Montgomery at the Alley." He put the iPad on the dash. "Then, according to Ed, the world falls off a cliff and we'll have nothing to do until Labor Day. Thank God, this is crazy, and Sabina let me down."

"How?"

"She asked Handmaiden to kill Ed, and it hasn't."

Josh laughed.

July 27, after spending the night at the LAX Hilton Hotel, Ty and Ed were standing in front waiting for the valet to deliver their rental car.

Ed glanced at his Apple Watch: 6:15 a.m.; they had plenty of time to make their 7:00 a.m. breakfast at the Los Angeles Country Club.

The car arrived; Ed tipped the attendant and got into the driver's seat; Ty sat in the front passenger seat. They turned left out of the hotel driveway and drove east on Century Boulevard toward the 405 freeway.

"Tell me more about Mrs. Klinger and who else will be attending the breakfast."

"First, Mrs. Klinger's first name is Diane. She and I are friends. Her father built a great company and her husband, who we will not meet, took it over the top. Diane is fabulous, you'd never know she's rich. Her self-deprecating humor and earthly demeanor is genuine. She's tough, wicked smart, and looks for the best in people. She was born in California, a conservative—which is almost extinct

—and does not carry the baggage of the South or hate of the Northeast."

"Okay, you like her."

"You will, too."

Ty checked his phone for new text messages and emails.

"Go on, there must be more," he said without looking up.

"A quick story about Diane and her husband, Barney. One day Barney and Diane were having a heated discussion about the business while standing outside the office building by the back entrance. Out of the blue, Barney picks her up and carries her across the parking lot and drops her into one of the huge steel trash containers. Diane told me, as she was standing there trying to figure out how to get out, she thought, *I think I like this guy*."

"All right, Ed, I get it. You like her *very* much."

As for the guest list, no one I recognize; she said they are local independent businesspeople, who are almost extinct in California, and we'll raise the hundred K."

They got off the freeway at Wilshire Boulevard and turned east past Westwood and UCLA. They turned left into the LACC driveway. They stopped at the security guard booth.

The uniformed attendant stepped out of the booth with a welcoming expression. "Good morning, Mr. Abbott and Senator Leggett. Welcome to Los Angeles Country Club. Mrs. Klinger will meet you at the main entrance. Please drive to the overhang and a valet will park your car."

The guard pressed the remote control he was holding, and the gate arm lifted.

After a short, two-minute drive along the golf course, they arrived at the main clubhouse entrance. Standing under the white overhang was a petite woman dressed in a cream-colored St. John knit flare dress. Ed drove up to the woman and stopped.

She moved to open the passenger door, but Ty opened it first. "Welcome, Senator Leggett," Diane said.

Ty got out of the car. "It is my pleasure," he said, extending his arm to shake hands.

"Please, I am hoping we become lifelong friends," she said, hugging him. "I'm sorry we're meeting here; it's a little stuffy. However, Ed said your schedule was tight."

They walked into the California ranch-style two-story building. The room they entered was stunning in its California casual comfort. One could not help feeling rich viewing the beige couches, dark-stained cocktail tables, and living room sitting area in the open concept layout. Four sets of French windows opened onto a patio, and beyond it, the golf course and Century City skyline filled the horizon.

"Wow, this is nice. Not many like this," Ty said.

"Just another place for rich men to impress their friends. But the food is very good," Diane said.

Ty smiled.

Ed thought, *Great, I'm hungry.*

"We're on the patio facing the first tee, and it looks like a beautiful morning. Oh, before I forget, please put your cell phone in airplane mode; it's a club rule."

They walked through to the outdoor patio and turned left. Standing and milling about were twenty men and women dressed in business attire.

"Friends, may I present US Senator and former director of the FBI, Tyler Leggett."

The group clapped.

Ed walked to the bar and ordered a diet Coke for himself and a glass of water. Ty and Diane moved around the group making introductions. Ed returned with the glass of water and handed it to Ty.

Diane said, "Let's eat, we all have work ahead."

The group sat and breakfast was served by uniformed waitstaff. After thirty minutes, Diane stood and said, "Trying to keep this under an hour, it is time to introduce Senator Leggett. His accomplishments are too many to list, and you all have his bio. What I found interesting was the FBI's investigations into political corruption and the conviction of several members of Congress, particularly California's former Senator Adam Dodge for bribery."

"About damn time that lying bastard paid the price," someone shouted.

She smiled. "Moving on. In today's news, Nvidia founder Jensen Huang said he wished Congress had done more to regulate AI now that children are being implanted with the educational K chip. Isn't that a little hypocritical? He created the damn thing." Diane smiled and looked at Ty. "Senator Leggett, would you please come forward and say a few words?"

Ty stood and moved to face the seated group. "Thank you for your kind words, Diane. And yes, I will address your questions."

He looked at the guests. "This is my first time in Los Angeles without arresting anyone."

Laughter sprinkled around the tables.

"It's a lot nicer this way." Ty grinned.

More laughter.

It's an honor to be welcomed by Diane and to be down the street from Jackie Robinson's UCLA. Thank you for the invitation." He looked at Diane.

"When I told the president I wanted to run for the US Senate, his first words were 'You're nuts.'"

Light laughter.

"He might be right."

More laughter.

"When I asked the governor of Alabama, who appointed me, his first words were: 'Since you're blackmailing the president, I must.'"

The group laughed.

"Of course that is not true." Ty glanced at Ed. "My decision to run was personal. A friend and his family were destroyed by spies attempting to steal government high-tech secrets. Instead of going after the cause, the victim and his family were blamed." Ty's expression was somber. "I won't let that happen again, and the FBI is not the place to effect change. The place is Congress, and they only know how to react, not be proactive. To put it another way, quoting a song by Otis Redding and using a little poetic license, Congress is sittin' on the dock of the bay, watching time roll away."

A couple of people laughed.

"Cartels will soon use AI to steal everything not nailed down. That technology can't be controlled; it must be stopped, like we did with the atom bomb."

Ty looked back at the faces staring at him, thinking, *Have I gone too far?*

"Government can't legislate against excess; it can only restrain it." Ty looked at Diane. "I hope that answers your question."

She smiled and nodded.

"Alabama has a sad history, and it's a place ready for uplifting change. I learned from an old friend in law school that speeches don't force change, laws force change and it does not happen overnight. I'll give a few examples, which will shock you. In nineteen fifty-four, Brown versus the Board of Education became law. In nineteen sixty-three, George Wallace failed, thanks to President Kennedy. The last school got desegregated in twenty sixteen in Mississippi."

Gasps, and someone said, "You're kidding."

"There is one black Republican in the Alabama state house and I'm the first black man to run for Alabama US Senate. To quote Winston Churchill, 'Government usually gets it right, but only after trying everything else first.'"

Laughter.

"My path is quite simple, really. Get elected, focus on prosperity, safety, and preparing government for quantum computing and stopping AI from being anything more than a tool, like a shovel. Not a weapon of war or manipulating human intervention. I don't believe in the MAD policy of the military or creating an army of machines smarter than us. We have enough weapons of mass destruction."

He looked around the patio. Everyone was intently listening.

"My tenure at the FBI was incredible; the bureau is filled with dedicated, people who want to keep us safe and occasionally pull a major league crook out of circulation." Ty smiled and looked at Diane.

"When I'm elected I will, like the last person selected in the NFL draft, become Mr. Irrelevant. As we know sometimes that person wins a Super Bowl." He smiled and Diane laughed.

"I come from humble means and know firsthand how to start at the bottom. Being Senator One Hundred does not faze me. I have a plan and a long memory." He grinned; people laughed.

"People opened many doors for me, so my door will always be open. Thank you, Diane, and to each and every one of you. Thank you very much for supporting my campaign."

Diane jumped to her feet, walked up to Ty and gave him a warm hug.

After lots of handshaking and words of congratulations and good luck from the departing guests, Ty, Ed, and Diane walked to the front entrance and the waiting car.

Ty turned to say goodbye, but before he could speak, she said, looking into his eyes, "I have met many candidates in my time, and no one, and I mean no one, has impressed me like you have. Senator Leggett, you are genuine. I truly hope you are the first for Alabama." She hugged him goodbye.

As they drove away, Ed glanced at Ty. "I knew you were blackmailing the president."

They left the country club and turned right on Wilshire Boulevard.

"Tell me about Mrs. Parker," Ty asked.

Ed glanced at the dashboard clock: 9:30 a.m. "Before we see Mrs. Parker, we have a ten o'clock meeting with Reverend Steven Neal of the First AME Church of Los Angeles."

"That's not on the schedule," Ty said.

"Carlos added it late last night."

"And why are we meeting with Reverend Neal?" Ty asked, a hint of suspicion in his voice.

"There're three hundred seventy-five AME churches in Alabama. Reverend Neal grew up in Alabama, played professional baseball with the Double-A Biscuits before he started his ministry. His LA church is a major donor to the AME Conference and he's in the process of becoming a bishop."

"Okay. I get it. He's connected, I don't go to church much and we desperately need the black vote. Where are we meeting him?"

"The Coffee Bean, on San Vicente Boulevard. It's about fifteen minutes away."

14

Ed and Ty parked and walked to the front entrance. Lying by the door was a homeless person, dressed in an animal skin parka, Qarlik pants, and a Dodgers baseball cap.

"Only in Cali, an Inuit sleeping on the street," Ed said.

"Sad," Ty said.

They walked into the restaurant.

"What does he look like?" Ty asked.

"I have no idea—a reverend."

"Sometimes you amaze me with your clarity."

Ty looked around the room; they were lucky: only one Black person was sitting at a table, reading a Bible. Ty and Ed approached.

"Reverend Neal?" Ty asked with a smile.

"Call me Steven, Senator Leggett," the reverend said, looking up. He stood and offered his hand.

"It is a pleasure to meet you, Mr. Neal. This is Ed Abbott, my campaign finance director."

"Nice to meet you, Mr. Abbott," he said, offering his

hand. "I understand you're attending a luncheon with Mrs. Parker, and our time is limited," Steven said.

"Unfortunately, we're on a tight schedule, and yes, she is next on our SoCal road trip," Ty said.

"Mrs. Parker is a soulful person; you'll enjoy your time with her."

They sat at his table.

"Well, Senator, how can I be of help?" Steven asked.

Ty leaned back for a moment, looking at Steven's dark eyes and warm face. "I do not want to give you a false impression that I'm a religious person."

"I know, Senator. I spoke with Pastor Leon in Birmingham."

Ty chuckled. "I find it hard to shoot people and act holy."

Steven snickered with a wry smile.

"That is a challenge." He nodded. "However, that's in the past; you don't shoot people anymore. At least, I hope you don't—If I may, Thurgood, whom we admire, understood social justice is rooted in faith. Cynicism is rooted in the language and lies of the devil," Steven said.

"Thurgood was a great man and you're right, he believed in justice and hope," Ty said.

"It takes time to love like a child. And on that note, there's someone you should meet; he's at the St John's AME in Montgomery. Pastor Tim McBride was a Green Beret. He can help you transition away from shooting people."

Ty laughed out loud.

"Thank you. I'll go meet him."

"Senator Leggett—"

"Please call me Ty."

"Ty, why did you leave the FBI, and move to Alabama? Some of us think you're nuts."

Ty laughed. "They're not alone." He smiled. "It was time. I had gotten, as you said, cynical. Truth and law are no longer part of Washington's culture. Everyone I met was a product of self-serving ambition. No truth."

Ty glanced away. "How do I say this; the concept of 'Don't do it,' 'Just stop,' 'It's wrong' are forgotten concepts. I'll give you examples: Do you know we still store smallpox? Why? Because someone else has it; if they release it, we would, too." He raised his voice a little. "We never signed the nuclear bomb treaty. Why? Same damn reason. We send kids to war to settle a score at the same time we work with international murderers." He leaned back and took a short breath. "It's all disingenuous logic."

"You mean like implanting a microchip into a child to make the kid smarter," Steven said.

"You mean the K chip?"

"Yes."

"Exactly, like unfettered AI. A stupid idea," Ty said.

"Are you going to do something about that?"

"First get elected. The rest will fall into place."

Steven nodded. "Why Alabama?"

"It's home, and if anyplace needs hope, it's there."

"True and you really need to see McBride." He smiled. "I'm not saying you're wrong. People want to follow joy and love. So, what's your plan?" Steven asked.

"One step at a time and win."

"How does a Black man win in Alabama with no party?"

"With you and every other sensible person breaking the bounds of conformity," Ty said.

"What do you mean?"

"My parents and most folks joined the Democrat Party and overlooked the crap because Roosevelt got us jobs and money. None of that is relevant today." Ty's voice was soft.

Silence.

"Nothing will move folks forward unless we change. Look at downtown Montgomery as an example. Who the hell would want to visit? I don't think there's a damn flower or bright color in the whole city. Why, why do you think that is?" Ty asked.

"They deserve it."

"They did. You and every preacher should be the first in line to lead the change. We will not move forward until that happens. Did you see the native-looking person lying at the front door?" Ty asked.

"Yes, very sad. They got it worse than we did, reservations and all," Steven said.

"I'm going to do something about that. Getting back to Montgomery, we want every American to visit, so we can tell them a story of perseverance and hope. We can't let those who profit from maintaining the status quo hold us back, and that includes both parties. That's why I am an Independent, and when I get elected, those Washington DC boys will be scared shitless." Ty leaned back and smiled.

"You have more faith than you think, and I'll pray for you," Steven said.

"My mother would always tell me, 'Son, put legs to your prayers.' And Steven, I say to you, it will take you and every member of the AME for us to win. I need legs."

Ed and Ty headed off to Beverly Hills for their luncheon with Mrs. Parker.

En route to her home, Ed glanced over at Ty. "I'd vote for you," he said.

"Thank you. Tell me about Mrs. Parker."

"I've known her for a decade. We were on a nonprofit board together. I hope she considers me a friend. She moved to California from Mississippi when she was a teenager. She married a journeyman baseball player and led the family to tremendous success in real estate; and it was all her. Mr. Parker is very smart, but make no mistake, Janet is the boss, and she is wound a little tight. In her spare time, she created a prominent elementary school in Crenshaw for under-privileged students. Sometimes her past gets ahead of her. She once told me a bank called when her daughter was applying for a car loan and wanted Janet to cosign. She said they were racist for not just giving her daughter the loan. I asked if her daughter had any collateral. Janet said, 'Of course not, she's in college.' I made the mistake of laughing. Man, did I get a dirty look. She told me later she cosigned the loan."

"I think I'm going to like Mrs. Parker."

Ed drove down Roxbury Drive and parked in front of a white two-story 10,000-square-foot Victorian-style home. Like every Beverly Hills property, it was perfectly maintained.

They walked up the stone walkway to the richly painted jet-black front door.

Ty glanced at his wristwatch: Noon. He smiled. *On time,* he thought.

Ed rang the doorbell and thirty seconds later it opened, and holding the handle was fifty-year-old Janet Parker. She was wearing a faded Chrysanthemum St. John knit dress, with black high heels. Her black hair was pulled back and held by a gold and purple Japanese hairpin.

"Hello, Ed and Senator Leggett. Welcome to my home," she said with a beautifully warm smile.

She stood by the door as they came into the house. On their right stood a carpeted white staircase, the light cream walls along the stairs were lined with art: Alma Thomas, Monet, Calder, Gauguin, Faith Ringgold, Miro, Jean Michel Basquiat, and Kara Walker.

They followed Janet through the foyer down a short hallway and turned left into a large formal living room. Twenty couples were milling about, talking. The room went quiet.

"It gives me great pleasure to welcome United States Senator Tyler Leggett," Janet said in her melodic voice.

Ty and Janet moved around the room as she introduced each guest, telling the senator their bio. After twenty minutes, the introductions were finished.

Four people dressed in starched white uniforms came into the room carrying silver hors d'oeuvres trays filled with handcrafted finger food.

Thirty minutes later, Janet said, "My friends, it is almost one o'clock and I promised you we would be back at work by one-thirty, and I'm sure Senator Leggett has other places to be. So, without further ado—" she turned to face Ty—"Senator, would you say a few words?"

"Janet and the Parker family, thank you very much for welcoming me into your incredible home. I grew up in rural Alabama, and I can tell you, this home and Janet's success would have been number one on my field of dreams. I am honored to be here and meet greatness."

He turned and smiled at Janet. She returned the smile.

"This morning, I had a cup of coffee with a Reverend Steven Neal. We had never met, and he said something that made me laugh and it also gave me pause. He said I must be nuts to leave the FBI and run as an Independent. The nuts part he got right."

People laughed.

"What gave him pause was the independent part. He questioned the designation. I thought if he had the question, so will others." He smiled. "I love baseball, and one of my favorite managers was Dusty Baker. Mr. Baker once said they would never use intelligence or tactics when describing him or other Black managers. I believe that is why he won so many games and a World Series. They underestimated him.

"Dusty was right. I moved up the FBI ladder because they did the same to me. If you can't be pigeonholed, you win. I chose to run as an Independent, because the establishment always picks a clone, and the other side knows how to proceed. My announcement of running as an Independent forced them to change the narrative. And that will cost them."

Janet clapped.

"A lifelong Republican changed parties to Independent and shockingly, the Democrat Party is supporting him, and the majority party was forced to support me. Too perfect for words. My opponent, the Hollywood cowboy, as I call him, will lose. Washington, DC, and Alabama will get an Independent, free-thinker, me, and the DC establishment will be just as shocked as the Philadelphia Phillies."

He grinned, Janet clapped and said, "Woohoo!"

"Thank you for joining the team and supporting our historic campaign."

He turned and looked at Janet. "Thank you, Janet."

Thirty minutes later, after many handshakes and comments of "great speech" and "good luck," followed by a warm hug from Janet, Ty and Ed walked back to the car and headed toward Wilshire Boulevard.

Ty glanced at his watch. "We have hours to kill. How about dropping me off at the Federal Building on Veterans, and in the meantime, tell me about Mr. Nobel."

"Lawyer, graduated from Stanford, his family invented oil—"

"What does that mean?" Ty interrupted with a slight laugh.

"His father discovered and drilled billions of barrels of oil in Texas and Oklahoma. Mr. Nobel inherited his father's brains and a lot of his money. He's conservative and is a former debate champion from his days in college."

"Have you worked with him before?"

"No. All I know is he's eccentric. When I spoke to him

about you, he said great, happy to host, and looked forward to meeting us. He said don't worry about the details, he'd take care of the food and booze and, he'd make the max donation. All he asked is that I get the money and people."

"He is smart; you are doing the hard work, and he writes a check," Ty said.

"No surprise there."

Ty glanced at the dashboard clock. "How much longer to the Westwood Federal Building?"

"About five more minutes. Sunset, to Veteran, to Wilshire and we're there."

"Drop me off on Veteran and I'll walk from there."

"Miss the FBI?"

"A little. Great people and full of facts."

"Aw, more blackmail," Ed said with a laugh.

They followed along Veteran past the national cemetery. "It always makes me sad to see so many headstones. I hate war," Ed said.

"Me, too," Ty agreed.

They crossed Wilshire and arrived at the twelve-story, white marble-and-glass Federal Building. Ed pulled over to the curb.

"I'll meet you at Nobel's Century City condo at six p.m.," Ty said.

Ed arrived forty-five minutes early for the six o'clock Nobel reception. He drove along Avenue of the Stars toward Pico, turned left on Central Park Lane, then right at the driveway. He followed it around the fountain and parked at the entrance to the second condo building.

He got out of the car and looked around; he was surprised by the drabness of the gray, seven-story building. *Maybe he's not as rich as I thought.*

The surrounding grounds were beautiful, red and yellow roses, red-and-white tulips, and pink begonias. He walked to the front entrance and was greeted by a uniformed security guard.

"May I help you?" she asked.

"Yes, I'm here to meet Mr. Nobel."

"He's drunk," she said matter-of-factly.

"What! He's hosting a reception in forty-five minutes with United States Senator Tyler Leggett."

She stared at Ed and shrugged.

Ed pulled out his cell phone and called Nobel. No answer.

"You can try knocking on his door. Maybe he'll answer," she suggested.

They walked to the building's elevator.

"Seventh floor, turn left, his name is on the door."

Ed left the elevator, feeling anxious and a little terrified. He walked down the rich, hardwood-covered hallway toward Nobel's condo. He knocked several times, harder with each knock; at the end, he was pounding on the door.

"Shit, what am I going to do?" he worried out loud.

He went back to the main entrance, looking for the security guard.

"Do you know a locksmith I can call?" Ed asked.

"Yes, our tenants, like Mr. Nobel, sometimes lose their keys." She handed Ed her phone after making the call.

"Hello, my name is Ed Abbott, and I work for United States Senator Leggett. We're locked out of Mr. Branson Nobel's apartment and—"

"He drunk?" the voice on the phone interrupted.

"I have no idea; I just need the door opened. Can you get here, now?" Ed asked, his voice filled with panic.

"It'll be time and a half."

"I don't care if it's double time, just be here in ten minutes."

The locksmith appeared just as Ty and ten of the wealthiest business leaders in Los Angeles arrived. To Ed's shock, he was carrying a handmade wooden box full of tools and wearing a denim coverall jumpsuit; there would be no doubt what he did for a living.

Ed looked at Ty, raised his right hand and mouthed, "Wait."

Ed and the locksmith rode the elevator to Nobel's condo. The locksmith stopped at Nobel's door and within thirty seconds opened the door. Ed shoved the door open and raced around the 2,000-square-foot condo yelling, "Mr. Nobel! Mr. Nobel!"

He found the bedroom door and slowly opened it to find his host passed out on the bed. Ed ran into the room and shook him several times, no response.

"Shit," he said. Thinking: *I can't let him leave this room. What if the bastard throws a fit?*

Ed looked around the bedroom, opened the closet, grabbed a handful of ties and tied Nobel's hands and feet together. Finished, he raced into the living room. "Nothing, he ran into the kitchen. "Shit, he didn't do *a thing*!" Ed shouted.

He pulled out his cell phone and called Mrs. Margaret Becken, who lived in the next building.

"This is Margaret."

"Mrs. Becken, this is Ed Abbott. I'm at Nobel's apartment for a fundraiser for Senator Leggett."

"Oh, Ed, I'm sorry, I can't attend—"

"That's not my problem, Mrs. Becken," Ed interrupted, "we are here and Mr. Nobel's asleep in his bed."

"Drunk," she said.

It seems I'm the only one in America who didn't know he's a drunk. "I have William Ahmanson, Tray Watt, ten legislators and fifty other business leaders downstairs waiting to come up. I have no food or booze. Do you know who I can call?"

He could hear her laughing.

Ed took a deep breath.

"I can arrange the libations." She skipped a beat. "Wait, Steve Kenny is here, maybe he can help. Steve, Ed Abbott is on the phone, he's in a pickle."

"Hi, Ed, you're at Nobel's. What's up?"

"He's passed out and I need hot hors d'oeuvres and fast."

He heard Steve laughing.

"I know a place. But Ed these people are different."

"I don't care if they're from Mars."

Steve laughed again.

"They might be. I'll text if there's a problem."

Ed ended the call and looked around Nobel's condo.

"I can't believe there's no bar. Shit. At least it's clean," he said.

He ran to the elevator and walked out of the building

to see Ty talking to twenty or so people on the sidewalk. Ed waved at Ty and the others. "We can go up now."

Ty walked up to Ed, and whispered, "What's going on?"

"You don't want to know," Ed answered.

Twenty minutes later the liquor was delivered along with a bartender. Drinks were served. Ten minutes after that, the catering service arrived.

Oh, my God, they are *from Mars*, Ed thought, as he saw five unisex, velvet and leather-wearing people carrying silver trays with finger food enter the condo. They were wearing purple pants, pink long-sleeved shirts, bright red flip-flops and black painted toenails. Each person had a different hair color, bright green, purple, fire red, light-blue and one had a jet-black spiked Mohawk.

They moved around the room offering food. Ed glanced at Ty; Ty slowly shook his head from side to side.

I'm fuckin' dead, Ed thought.

A man dressed in a custom-made dark-blue suit came up to Ed. "Hello, I'm Dan Pierce, Mr. Nobel's associate. I'm aware of the situation and if you don't mind, I'll stand by Mr. Nobel's bedroom in case he awakens. I think most of the guests have already peeked in and if you don't mind, I'll untie him."

"Thank you," Ed said.

Ty gave his standard pro-business speech. An hour later, after questions and the guests started to leave, Ty approached Ed. "Will you join me on the balcony?" he asked with a cool, inquisitive voice.

They walked out through the sliding patio doors onto the 100-foot-long balcony. Ed noticed how high it was from the street below, and how beautiful the downtown LA city lights were in the distance.

"Interesting evening, Ed," Ty said, with a touch of sarcasm.

Ed placed his right hand on the metal railing that topped the balcony and squeezed. *Here it comes, I'm dead. He's going to throw me off.*

"Ed, I want to thank you; this memory will last me a lifetime. It's the first time I've ever seen a locksmith with a wooden box break into a fundraising event, the host tied to his bed, and been served hors d'oeuvres—good food, I must add—by people who did not look like anyone I've ever seen in DC or Alabama—undoubtedly, they're from another planet." Ty grinned. "I think I can say California's a little different." He shook his head side to side and laughed out loud. "Let's catch our plane."

15
AUGUST

"It's hot, the Senate is closed, Washington is a ghost town, and I have nothing to do for the next two weeks. It seems everyone who can has left Alabama. Is that right?" Ty asked.

"Pretty much. Unless you've got friends in the Hamptons, Maine, or Malibu," Carlos said, leaning back in his black ergonomic Office Depot chair, rubbing his nose.

"Sitting around is not exactly my style. To quote former San Francisco Mayor Willie Brown, 'Do all you can and more.' So, Carlos, what's the more?"

"Ty, we're eighty-five days out from the election and the last sixty-nine are killers. Why not call Ed? Maybe he—"

"I already did; he and Sabina are cleaning up, working halftime and playing video games at the Alley Bar," Ty interrupted.

"Okay, call Tim and go bass fishing. Or the Diazses

and ride in their restored pickup truck around the ranch and drink bourbon."

"Carlos, you're missing the point. What more can we do to win this campaign?"

"Nothing. The press corps has gone fishing or whatever. The cable pundits are on their yachts, and everyone with money is drinking mint juleps and staying cool up north. Go see someone you like and have a laugh."

"I don't know where he is."

"You've got to have more than one friend."

"No. Work always came first, never made the time."

"What happened to your friend, where's he?"

"Saving the world."

"Aw, a dreamer."

"No, John Barber is no dreamer, just a great friend."

"Sounds like you miss him." He cocked his head. "Christ, Ty, you ran the FBI. Where is he?"

"I retired so I wouldn't have to find him."

"I don't understand."

Ty looked out the window for a moment. "I don't think he does, either. Never mind. Maybe you're right; I'll call Tim and go fishing. Thanks for the ideas." Ty stood and turned to leave. "I'll call next week to discuss the September survey with Val."

"Oh, I just remembered," Carlos said, "you asked me to find out how involved the White House, specifically the president, is in shutting off our funding. I can say it in three words: one hundred percent. He gets weekly briefings and meets with the Senate Minority leader regularly. I understand that they feel an Alabama swing could shift the Senate. He is on a mission to screw us."

Saturday, August 27, 7:30 a.m. Ty, Gonzo, Susie, Ed, Carlos and Val gathered around Gonzo's Montgomery conference room table.

Rick Stat, a new campaign intern, entered the room carrying a box of Dunkin' Donuts. He opened the box and put the donuts on a silver tray, with six coffee cups, napkins, and a sixty-eight-ounce Cresimo stainless-steel carafe filled with hot coffee. Finished, he sat in a chair along the back wall facing the group.

"Thank you, Rick. Good morning and welcome to our first campaign team meeting. Tim will not be joining us. His back went out. Ed will not be joining us. He has nothing to offer," Ty said.

"Very funny," Ed said.

Laughter.

"Ed, please give us a quick update on our money position," Ty said.

"We've spent a lot and have five hundred thousand cash in the checking account, thanks to the California adventure."

"California is different," Ty said coolly.

Laughter.

"We have no debt, and those events in California were a godsend." Ed glared at Gonzo. "Your revised budget was the reason we had to go."

"Oh, well," Susie said.

Ed reached into a black leather briefcase on the floor and removed six blue plastic folders and passed them around the table.

"Enclosed in those folders are the revised fundraising plans and timelines. Senator Simmons's eight million is scheduled to commence September eleventh. The last trip to top off the out-of-state five million will be September twelfth in Little Rock, Arkansas, with Mrs. Frank." He looked at Ty. "You will really like her."

Ty smiled. "So far, I like all your friends." Ty looked at Val. "Val, this is your meeting. You're up."

"Good morning," he said, looking around the table.

"So, we will conduct two full surveys, four tracking surveys, and nightly tracking calls."

He got up and went to the white board, wrote:

1st full survey, Wednesday, 9/7, 60 questions.

1st tracking survey, Friday, 9/16, 30 questions.

2nd tracking survey, 9/29, 15 questions.

2nd full survey, 10/13, 100 questions.

Last two tracking surveys: 10/26 and 11/1, 15 questions.

He looked around the table. "The results and analysis for the full surveys will take two days. The results and analysis for the tracking surveys will be ready the next day or early that evening. The nightly tracking calls will ask three questions, and the results will be tabulated and ready by seven a.m. the following morning. Carlos will have an online link to the surveys for dissemination."

Val stopped speaking and looked at Gonzo.

"Gonzo, what can you add about the marketing?" Val asked.

"We have reserved as much paid media advertising as we can afford. Radio, television and social media are partially funded. We bought backward from November seventh to October eighteenth. That's all we could afford. The billboards are paid up for the duration. We are designing the television and outdoor marketing campaigns now. All we need is the strategy, which is yours and Val's prerogative, and money. Our goal is to be on the air by Labor Day," Gonzo said.

"You're up, Carlos," Ty said.

"Depending on the results of the September seventh survey, we will stay positive until Ullman or his surrogates hit us. As we previously discussed, we'll ignore Horner and focus our message on state, hyper-local, and national issues that affect Alabama. Regarding the attacks, we will not respond if it's true or Val tells us to. We have a team of five lawyers ready to respond to any legal or voting rights violations. Susie will inform that team the moment she suspects our media buys are being restricted." Carlos turned to look at Susie. "Do you have anything to add?"

"Not really. We have a good relationship with most of the media outlets and social media advertisers. Our only issues will come from the national press corps and the Hollywood celebrities flown in to attack us." She grinned. "Standard fare. Same bullshit, different state."

Ty smiled.

"On that front, Gonzo, please design a short duration message to marry those attacks to Ullman. Lastly, I suggest we meet every Saturday morning to formulate a weekly game plan," Carlos said.

"Anyone have something to add?" Ty asked.

Silence.

"Thank you for helping me attempt the impossible."

Ty took a sip of coffee. "In eleven days, we go pedal to the metal. The other side will test us, especially me. I'm not long on patience or taking a punch. Having said that, I know you will keep me calm and on message. Please keep in mind, I have your back; we are a team."

"They will use dirty tricks; follow us, set us up. So, please be careful, don't even think about drinking and driving or trusting a new best friend, especially a beautiful, sexy one," Carlos said, looking at Ed.

"I'd take one for the team," Ed said with a grin.

"Forget the sexy one. Not happening," Carlos said.

Gonzo almost spit out his coffee with a laugh.

"We have seventy-seven days until November eighth. A lifetime of lows and highs. I can't say this enough; we are all being watched. Please keep that in mind. Have a great week, relax, and I'll see you next Saturday," Carlos said.

September

Saturday, September 3, 7:30 a.m., campaign team meeting at Gonzo's Montgomery office, in attendance: Ty, Gonzo, Susie, Ed, Carlos, and Val.

"Val, this is your meeting," Ty said.

"Good morning," Val said, looking around the table. "I'm not going to go through the survey in detail. You can do that on your own. The executive summary covers the highlights. We now know what it will take to win and on the flip side, how to lose.

"To win Ty must be safe, likable, and non-threatening. His FBI background helps. We must craft an image of a strong figure protecting us but not exactly coming over for dinner."

Laughter.

"Ullman's team will paint us as dark and evil from carpet-bagging Washington, DC. They will cast Ullman as a hero cowboy, fighting for the environment, education, family values and the little guy." Val looked down at his copy of the survey.

"There is no liberal in the race, and Alabama will not elect one. Ty and Ullman will run right down the middle. If either campaign crosses that line, it's over and that candidate will get slammed. The two issues that work in our favor are law enforcement and federal experience. Our best issue, which I call the hammer, is Ullman changing parties. He has no defense." Val took a sip of coffee. "Our opposition research will comb through his legislative voting record for liberal votes. The game is to bait him into saying something stupid or, for that matter, doing something embarrassing to himself, or better yet, Alabama.

"Lastly, we need one million, one hundred thousand, six hundred forty-five votes to win. That's counting Horner getting one percent of the vote."

Val looked at Ty.

"That sounds so easy," Ty said, sounding sarcastic, "Carlos, you want to add anything?"

"Yes, some very good news. Dave called this morning, Mr. Nobel sent a two-hundred-thousand dollar check to the Independent Expenditure Super PAC Senator Joseph set up," Carlos said.

"I love guilt money," Ed said, laughing.

"Our July FEC report had a double-edge: It showed we raised money and had cash on hand—"

"Unfortunately, Ullman's team reacted and started spending," Susie interrupted.

Ty took a deep breath and smiled.

"Ed, what do you got?"

"All is good. Our out-of-state events are organized and scheduled. You and I will be flying around the county picking up money. Our last million-dollar state is September twelfth in Arkansas. The in-state fundraising is producing expected results. The only thing that seems odd, I'm having a little trouble getting through to Simmons regarding his donation; and I've learned when people don't return calls or texts, it's not good."

"You worried?" Ty asked.

"A little," Ed said with a worried expression. "His first installment is due in two weeks. That's when we'll find out."

"Do you want me to reach out to Roka?" Gonzo asked.

"Wouldn't hurt," Ed said, shrugging.

"Okay. Carlos, how are we doing with the AME churches?" Ty asked.

"Not good," Carlos said.

"What's the problem?" Ty asked.

"We don't have a friend inside helping."

"Okay, I've got an idea," Ty said.

"Dave," Carlos continued, "texted me that we've raised six million since the July FEC report. Discounting overhead and FR cost, we have five point one million in free cash." He looked around the table.

"Nice job, Ed," Ty said.

"Susie, what do you know about Ullman's media spending?" Carlos asked.

"He dropped just under twenty-five million last night for October and November. His television buy was twelve million, radio was six million, and three million on social media ads."

"That it? Is that's all?" Carlos stated, sounding sarcastic.

"No. He paid five hundred thousand to five Alabama social stars and another three million to content actors. That brings his total marketing to twenty-five point five million," Susie said.

"They've left the kitchen sink for later," Ty said.

Uncomfortable soft laughter and smiles worked around the table.

"That's a lot of fun vouchers. Wouldn't it be great to waste that much money? We spend sixteen million and win. They spend fifty or more and lose. They must hate us," Ed said.

"That they do," Val chimed in.

On Wednesday, September seventh, at five-thirty in the morning, Ed showed up at Ty's home. He knocked on the front door.

The door opened. "Josh, you're early. Oh, Ed, it's you. This can't be good," Ty said, standing at the front door, holding a cup of coffee, dressed for the day.

"I can't prove it, but my gut tells me Simmons is

playing games with the money and we're going to get screwed. I didn't sleep last night thinking about this. Every time I talk to his staff, especially that bitch Paddick, I get a different excuse about the money. I'm telling you; they're going to screw us. And I don't buy the crap Roka told Gonzo."

Silence.

"Okay, what's your idea?" Ty asked.

"There is an unspoken rule in fundraising. Legislators will never lie in front of a large group of major local donors."

"Okay, go on."

"With your okay, I'll tell Paul what I think and ask him to call a finance committee meeting at Central for Wednesday the fourteenth. I'll invite Simmons, asking him to give a rah-rah speech," Ed said.

"And?"

"It's probably better you don't know the details."

"Sounds like Simmons will hate you again," Ty said with a wry smile.

That afternoon Ty and Josh were driving to Spanish Fort for a meet-and-greet when Val called Ty's cell.

"The September seventh survey results have been tabulated. We could be in the game," Val said.

"Okay, tell me more," Ty said coolly.

"We're doing much better; Carlos's marketing strategy is working, your name ID is twenty-nine percent, and the positives are three-to-one. We do better in the cities; the bigger the city, the better we do. We're not so good in the rural areas. A little weak with women, and men think you're a city slicker Northerner. Carlos will probably put you on a horse."

Josh laughed.

"Oh, God," Ty said, looking at Josh.

"What're Ullman's numbers?" Ty asked.

"His statewide ID is thirty-five percent, and mind you, he has not spent a dime. He's good in the rural areas and his Western cowboy demeanor does not play well in the cities. Older women like him, younger women think he's cute. His numbers among conservatives are weak; most are uncomfortable he changed parties. That is, as I hoped, his weakest issue among that group. All the other issues break along conservative-liberal lines."

"What about the minority community?"

"Not too good. They follow the party line. Ullman has a ten-point lead," Val said.

"Horner?" Ty asked.

"He doesn't register, statewide."

"Can we beat Ullman?"

"If Simmons's money arrives early enough and Gonzo's team spends it right, we have a shot."

"Bad choice of words," Ty said with a laugh. "Where are we the weakest?"

"A carpet-bagging DC city slicker."

"That's no surprise, and I can't change either. So, what do you suggest?" Ty asked.

"The numbers show law and order is at the top; people want to feel safe, yet they don't want Big Brother looking over their shoulders."

"Has Carlos seen the survey?"

"Yes, I spoke to him an hour ago."

"Okay, is that it?"

"For now."

"See you Saturday morning."

Ty hung up, then called Carlos.

"This is Carlos."

"I just received a thumbnail briefing on the survey from Val. Have you spoken to Gonzo and have any thoughts?"

"We haven't had a lot of time to study it, but one thing is clear: We have to shore you up with men and soften you up for women."

"Oh, God," Ty said.

"Yeah, you're on a horse and kissing babies," Carlos said.

"No," Ty said emphatically.

"You might like it."

"Not a chance."

"I had a wild candidate once; she hated people and hugging. By the end of the campaign, she'd hug a porcupine."

"How'd she do?"

"She lost, but that's another story," Carlos said.

"Good, no hugging."

"Ty, we must warm you up. People like rooting for the underdog, especially a nice one."

"I hate porcupines."

Saturday, September 10, 7:30 a.m., a team meeting at Gonzo's Montgomery office, in attendance: Ty, Gonzo, Ed, Susie, Carlos, Tim, and Val.

"Good morning, we have fifty-two days before the election," Ty said. "Ed, where do we stand with money?"

"Simmons's money is scheduled for deposit next week. We have a finance committee meeting on the fourteenth with Senator Simmons. The three million in-state money will continue to trickle in, with the bulk arriving by October fifteenth. The five million from our out-of-state fundraising will be in hand by the end of next week." Ed looked around the table. "A reminder: Our last out-of-state trip will be September twelfth, Arkansas. All told, we should have fourteen million free cash to spend a week or so from today."

"That should put a smile on Susie and Gonzo's faces," Ty said.

"It does. We can really fight back now," Gonzo said.

"Val, you're up," Ty said.

"Oh, sorry, Val, I almost forgot," Gonzo interrupted; "Ullman hit us this morning: 'Northern carpetbagger, disgraced FBI director,' and Ty's face is all over the ads. It's everywhere."

"They are predictable. I've reviewed the September seventh tracking survey, and the link is open." Val turned his head side to side, looking at his notes. "Ullman's hit does not come as a surprise; we tested that strategy. It will hurt for a couple of days until we hit back." He opened a yellow manila file folder and looked down at his notes.

"The sixth survey showed our name ID continues to climb, we've moved five points to thirty-five percent and our favorable has stayed the same. That, of course, will change now that we're being hit. On a side note, the timing of their attack tells me they're tracking us and our surveys match. We must have hit the magic thirty-five percent ID number on their survey, too. Time to hit Leggett."

Val smiled.

"Nice to be validated, but that's a mistake, too predictable, especially using their best issue. They either want us to panic, fire all guns, wasting money in September, or there's something worse coming." Val looked at Carlos. "What could we have missed?"

"I don't know, ex-wife, shooting bad guys. I don't know, they'll probably just make crap up," Carlos said.

Silence.

Val looked at Ty. "What about John Barber?"

"That's the crap they'll make up."

Val sighed.

"Who's that?" Ed asked.

"My best friend," Ty answered.

"So, what's the problem?"

"He's a government fugitive," Ty said with a deadpan expression.

"Wait a second; is his wife named Megan? The Megan Barber who donated to us?" Ed asked.

"She gave us money," Val said, looking at Ty.

With a shrug, Ty said, "Yep."

"This is exciting! FBI drama!" Ed said, beaming at Ty.

"As you requested, I double-checked her donation; it met all the FEC rules, we should be good," Ed said.

"Okay, we'll just have to wait for the hit," Carlos said.

"The next survey will be September twenty-ninth," Val said. He looked down at his notes. "That's all I got."

"Gonzo?" Ty said.

"The boards are doing well and the little paid media we bought worked." Gonzo looked at Ed. "Trusting your timeline, let's use our free cash now and hit Ullman's voting record, and his non-inclusionary history. When the big money comes in next week, we'll open it up."

"Susie, what do you have?" Ty asked.

"Ullman's team is trying to freeze us out by buying all the electronic and the paid social media space. He dropped another five million yesterday for TV, one million on radio and another million on social. I don't know about the influencers yet. This won't work if *we* move soon. I can fight our way into whatever we want. This buy brings his paid advertising total to thirty-four million," Susie said.

"Starting to sound like real money," Ed said.

"Trusting Ed will meet the budget," Susie said.

"Tim, have you run into Ullman in the mail?" Carlos asked.

"No, they traditionally don't use mail. Not enough commission for the consultants."

"What about their absentee mail program—any sign of it?" Carlos asked.

"No, they probably won't, same reason as direct mail, and we're lucky there's no early voting, which they're very good at. They'll focus on Election-Day voter turnout, as we will. I'll contact Maxwell Air Force Base to learn how they plan to coordinate their absentees with the Sec of State," Tim said.

Silence.

"We're making good progress. As long as our fundraising stays on track and Simmons doesn't jump ship, we'll meet our nine million September goal and elevate this underdog campaign into first. Great job, everybody. I'll see you all next Saturday, thank you. Have a restful Sunday," Ty said.

16

Ed and Ty arrived at Montgomery Airport at two in the afternoon for their three o'clock flight to Little Rock. Ed was driving Ty's truck. They parked and walked into the quiet airport.

"Ed, you look like you need a shoeshine. I have a friend who can fix you up," Ty said.

They passed through security and just before the food courtyard was a wooden shoeshine stand next to the north wall, and there was Darrel next to the wooden box working on a shoe.

"Hello, Darrel," Ty said.

Darrel glanced at Ty and then Ed. "Hello, Senator Leggett. Who's your little buddy?"

"This is Ed Abbott, a friend and campaign associate."

"Nice to meet you, Mr. Abbott. You're lucky to have Senator Leggett as a friend. Like a shine, Senator?"

"Just Ed, and my shoes are still perfect from last time," Ty said.

Ed sat on the shoeshine chair and Darrel rolled up his pant cuffs and started to polish Ed's black wingtips. Ty stood watching.

"Ed, Darrel is also a friend and if you ever need to know what's going on in Montgomery, you come here or the barbershop next to the Capitol," Ty said.

"That's the truth," Darrel said proudly. "Where you goin' today, Senator?"

"We have a three o'clock flight to Little Rock."

"Bad history there, like here," Darrel said.

"It's much better now, football and all. They put on ties and took off the sheets," Ty said.

"Yes sir, yes sir. It's better here."

Darrel looked at Ed and tapped his leg. All done, son.

"Hand him twenty-five, Ed," Ty said.

"I thought you were buying," Ed said, shocked.

Ty just looked at Ed.

Ed shook his head, mumbling to himself, as he reached into his wallet and grabbed a twenty.

"More," Ty said.

Ed looked at Ty, with an *Oh my God* expression and pulled out another twenty-dollar bill and paid Darrel.

"Thank you, Darrel. Ed, we've got to go," Ty said.

They walked toward the gate, passing a Coffee Bean stand.

"Let's get a hot cup," Ty said.

"I suppose it's on me," Ed said.

"Yep. You're a quick study." Ty grinned.

Finished, they walked to the gate. Ty went to the ticket counter to check on their seating. Ed stood by the windows and read emails.

Their boarding section was called for the hour-and-half flight to Little Rock, Arkansas. As they walked down the gangway toward the plane, Ed said, "That ticket agent was good-looking."

"Yep, a nice person, and she thinks I'm hot," Ty said matter-of-factly.

Ed rolled his eyes. "For assisted living," Ed quipped.

They sat in the front row, and ten minutes later the plane took off.

After forty-five minutes of reading emails and news reports, Ty glanced at Ed and said, "Okay, tell me about Mrs. Frank."

"I met her ten years ago at an event I managed for Food for Kids. She was standing by the back gate away from the crowd, smoking a cigarette. She looked stunning, in a bright red St. John knit dress. I walked over to introduce myself and we became instant friends.

"Mrs. Frank is one of a kind. She was raised in Little Rock, graduated from UCLA Law School—That reminds me, her father sent her to an exclusive New England finishing school when she was a teenager; they sent her home a month later." Ed grinned. "The story goes that the headmaster was yelling at Elizabeth for sneaking out. The argument culminated in a right cross to the jaw. When her father picked Elizabeth up at the airport, and they were driving to the ranch, he said, 'I don't think that fancy school took too well.'"

Ty laughed.

"After law school, she went to work for Bank of America. She did well, but too many men were telling her what to do. She left, bounced around for a while in Santa

Monica, then she met and married a man who owned a small retail steel business. It only took five years before she turned it into a national business. The monster success came when she got the specs changed on the steel the prisons used. That simple change allowed her to sell her steel for thirty percent less. She cornered the market, and for the next thirty years the company supplied most of the prisons in America with steel."

Ed stopped when the flight attendant handed him and Ty bottles of water.

"Elizabeth is a fixer; she sees a problem or discovers drama; she races in and puts everything in its proper place."

"Her husband?" Ty asked.

"Ten years older, good guy, strong in his own way. But he knows when to lay low and let Elizabeth take control. An example: When her father shot and killed his care worker."

"What?" Ty exclaimed.

"With a shotgun. Elizabeth arrived in Arkansas the next day with a Chicago lawyer." Ed looked at Ty. "You know the kind. And cleaned up the house. She told me it was a real mess." Ed cringed his face. "The end result: Her dad did not spend a second in jail, or court, for that matter." Ed looked at Ty. "So don't piss her off." Ed laughed. "She's a workaholic, with a massive heart. She saw some kid at LAX crying, she talked to him, found his parents and a year later adopted him. She has a couple children of her own; they're not the same but both smart. The original is always better."

"She's quite different from Diane," Ty said.

"Yes, both are wonderful. I'd tell you more, but I just got a text from Sabina, and I have to respond," Ed said.

Thirty minutes later the plane landed in Little Rock. While they were standing in the aisle waiting for the cabin door to open, Ty asked, "Why is Mrs. Frank doing this?"

"Besides loving me, she hates the president, and I told her you were blackmailing him." Ed laughed.

Ty just looked at him.

They followed the signs to the street and, to Ed's surprise, Elizabeth was standing at the curb dressed in blue jeans, a white silk blouse and white sandals. She looked stunning.

"Ed, very nice to see you, and you must be Senator Leggett. Ed has told me so much about you and the president."

Paul Snider stood at the doorway at Central Restaurant in the second-floor reception room, welcoming his friends and fellow Leggett for US Senate finance committee members at five p.m. on Wednesday, September 14.

"Welcome, welcome. Thank you for coming on such short notice. Please get yourself a stiff drink, and Executive Chef McCarry has cooked up some unbelievable hors d'oeuvres," he said enthusiastically.

"I would not have missed this for the world," one friend said as he passed by Paul.

Paul grinned.

Ed and Ty were already in the room, shaking hands

and sharing political gossip. Senator Simmons arrived at five-fifteen.

"Welcome, Senator; thank you for joining us," Paul said, while shaking Simmons's hand. "Senator Leggett is here. Please get yourself a quick bite and a drink. We'll start at five-thirty."

Simmons went up to Ty and Ed; he said, "This is remarkable; you have almost every major Alabamian here. I'm impressed," he said, looking around the room.

"Thank you for joining us. Everyone is looking forward to your political insights and thoughts on the twenty-forty legislative agenda," Ty said.

"Thanks again for inviting me, and I'll do my best to motivate your team," Simmons replied.

Ty smiled.

Ed walked up to Paul Snider. "You ready? We start in twenty minutes."

"Yes, sir. Does Simmons have a clue?" Paul asked.

"No."

"I hope you're right, Ed; this could get ugly, fun but ugly," Paul said with a smile.

"How many of the finance team know?"

"All of them."

Oh, God, Ed thought.

Twenty minutes later, Ty stepped up on the riser and switched on the microphone. "Ladies and gentlemen, it's time to begin," Ty said. "Thank you for attending this finance committee reception to hear from Majority Leader John Simmons. Paul, would you do the honor of introducing the leader?"

"That would be my pleasure. John, would you please come up front?"

Simmons stepped up on the four-foot-square riser next to Paul and the microphone. Paul stepped off the riser and moved to the side of the room. Then Simmons spoke for five minutes about the direction he and the Senate members wanted to take the legislature in 2040.

"With that said, my number one priority is to work with you all, to elect Ty to the United States Senate. His campaign is making history every day. My DC friends regularly call and say how impressed they are with Ty and how they hear good things about the campaign. They, like me, are convinced Ty will return as a six-year incumbent United States Senator."

"You betcha!" a person shouted out.

"To quote former California politician Jessie Unruh, 'Money is the mother's milk of politics.' Unfortunately, that's true and why Paul and Ty have worked so hard building this incredible team. For my part, my finance team has offered to support your and Ty's campaign."

Ty turned and whispered into Ed's ear, "You're right; he's walking it back."

"Ty is going to win, and we'll be in his corner." He grinned and looked around the room. "Having said that, let's open it up to questions," John said.

Paul Snider stepped toward the center of the room and said in a semi-loud voice, "You and your team offered to donate eight million, so where's our fucking money?"

Simmons almost gave himself whiplash turning his head to stare at Ed.

"That's right—where's the money?" another voice shouted out.

"You made a commitment. You a man of your word?" a woman shouted.

"Whoa, whoa. My team has some reservations, and I'm doing the best to bring them along," John said.

"Bullshit," another person shouted.

John remained calm, he looked at Ty, hoping he would get bailed out. Ty did not move or offer any sign of encouragement. He just smiled and continued to watch the room.

John looked at Paul. "I will fulfill my commitment, and the eight million will be raised and deposited into the campaign account by September sixteenth, but on one condition. Your finance team takes the extra step by raising an additional three hundred thousand by tomorrow afternoon," John said.

"All those in favor of accepting Senator Simmons's challenge, say aye," Paul said.

The room echoed with everyone shouting, "Aye."

Ed quickly left the room and raced home.

Ty walked up to John and shook his hand. "Thank you, John, that was the best rah-rah speech I've ever heard," he said, grinning.

"It was fun," John said as a sarcastic smile crossed his lips. He looked past Ty and scanned the room. "Where's Ed? I'd like to thank him."

At nine o'clock the next morning, Ty received a text

message from State Representative Jeremiah Damion: Tell Ed to stay out of the Capitol. Simmons wants his ass.

Ty laughed out loud.

A moment later Ty received a text from Ed: *Paul just called, he asked me to pick up $300K.*

Perfect.

Friday morning, September 16, Ty called Ed.

"Hello, Ty," Ed answered.

"Ed, thank you for fighting so hard for me."

"You're welcome. We're doing our best."

"Please pass along my gratitude to Sabina."

"Of course."

"Ed, please add Atmore, Alabama, to my schedule and make it the last stop of the day. Reserve the Pleasant Grove Baptist Church through Pastor Leon Woods and also coordinate a group meeting at the church for that same day and time. I would like to have the following indigenous tribes' chiefs attend: the Alibamu, Cherokee, Chickasaw, Choctaw, Creek, Hitchiti, Koasati, Natchez, Swanee, Tuskegee, and Yuchi. I believe you can coordinate all that through the Poarch-Creek Band Indigenous Tribe."

"Ty, Atmore is the most rural, forgotten place in Alabama. We won't raise a dime."

"I know."

"Why, then?"

"I have a plan."

"Okay, I'll put it together."

Ty disconnected the call and made a second one to Reverend Steven Neal in Los Angeles.

"Hello, Ty," Steven answered.

"How are you?"

"Depending on this call, I'm great. How can I help?"

"We just got our second survey back today, and our nightly tracking calls matched our findings."

"I feel doom coming."

Ty laughed. "We're doing well. There is one challenge. The numbers showed we're not getting the Black vote; it's at five percent with the majority going to Ullman. Have you picked that up from your AME friends?"

"Yes, the AME, DC leadership and Alabama Council have sent a directive that no money or campaign support can go to Horner or you. Ullman is the candidate," Steven said.

"How does that make you feel?" Ty asked.

"Exactly like you and most Black folks. A pawn."

"What do you suggest we do?"

"I don't know. We're not good at standing up unless someone else is in front."

"Okay; how do I get out front and give them cover?"

"With power and money."

"That's Washington and they don't help anyone but themselves and we're not them," Ty said.

"No one believes it will change. Years ago, BLM tried; same old happened; all we got was statues moved and streets renamed."

"What will it take?" Ty asked.

"I don't know, when white guys go crazy, they kill; that

scares the hell out of everyone. When we go crazy, we burn down the neighborhood."

"I have faith, and you seem to be losing yours."

"It seems only old ladies have faith; everyone else goes fishing."

"Steven, I can't effect change unless I'm elected." Ty paused. Thinking, *a cowboy and Indian, and the Inuit in Westwood.*

"I will be in Atmore, Alabama, soon."

"Atmore. What could possibly be there?" Steven asked, sounding surprised.

"Something that will restore our faith. Will you please meet me there? And I need you to bring the leadership of the Alabama AME to Atmore with you."

"That's going to cost a lot."

"I'll pick up your air and charter a bus out of Birmingham through Montgomery and back. Tell them there'll be plenty of food and drink on the bus."

Silence.

"Steven, can I depend on you?"

"Atmore!"

"Please. You and the AME leadership."

"What are you doing?" Steven asked.

"Because of you and a homeless Inuit in LA, it dawned on me while flying back to Alabama. I might be number one hundred in the Senate, but there are ninety-nine others I can persuade to legislate justice. Steven, we have a path to make a difference in our country."

Saturday, September 17, 7:30 a.m., Ty, Gonzo, Susie, Carlos, Ed, and Val met again.

Ty arrived five minutes early and walked down the short hallway to the conference room. He saw two feet, heels down, toes up, sticking out of one of the office rooms farther down the hall. Ty hurried to look. Gary, Gonzo's social media writer, was lying on the floor.

"Gary, you all right?" Ty asked.

"Yes, writer's block. I'm terrified it'll happen, so every time I feel stress, I lie down."

"Does it work?" Ty asked, with an incredulous look on his face, trying not to laugh.

"Not all the time," he said, getting to his feet.

"Okay, whatever works," Ty said.

He turned and went into the conference room and waited for everyone to arrive.

Rick Stats was last to enter. He placed the hot Krispy Kreme donuts and coffee on the table and sat against the back wall.

"Rick, would you like to join us at the table?" Ty asked.

Rick jumped to his feet and quickly sat.

"Good morning, we have forty-six days before the election. Val, you're up first."

"The September sixteen survey results have been tabulated; the online link is open. In the all-important head-to-head, we have moved from five percent versus Ullman to twenty percent. Ullman has dropped to thirty-five percent. Horner has fallen to twenty percent. The undecideds have climbed to twenty-five percent. Ullman is weak with the under-forty demographic and liberals will vomit when they learn how he's voted for the past twenty years.

"I suggest we keep the billboards positive for the next five days. On October ninth, we change them to displaying Ullman in cowboy regalia. On October sixteenth, we plan to run a full-court attack campaign on Ullman changing parties."

Val leaned to his left in his chair and looked at Carlos. "It's time to shift our message in mail and social to attack for the next ten days. We'll send the link this afternoon listing the hyper-local issues and Ullman's liberal votes. Please use those issues. On the social side, be careful; our numbers show most purveyors of social media are young and all about feelings. They dislike anything that appears disrespectful."

He looked down at his iPad.

"Tim, on the mail side, hit as hard as you want, mail is perfect for that; that age group loves fear and going after the bad guy."

Val again checked his notes.

"The next survey will be September twenty-ninth. That's all I got."

"Ed, how are we doing with money?" Ty asked.

"Keeping our nose above water, overhead is covered, and we have one hundred thousand in the bank. Simmons's second installment of seven hundred thousand is scheduled to arrive on October first. The final installment of six hundred thousand is due October ten. That will fulfill his eight million commitment—yippee ki-yay," Ed said with a laugh.

"Yes. Thanks to you and Paul. Yippee ki-yay, we're in the game," Ty said.

"To top everything off, Sabina is planning a major

October twenty-fifth rally and fundraiser. The goal is to raise three hundred thousand net. It will cover our remaining campaign expenses. The rally will not generate income, and the cost will be covered by the fundraiser. Sabina's goal for the rally is a thousand people. We'll have a band, games for children, and you get to give a rousing get-out-and-vote speech," Ed said.

"Where are we doing this?" Ty asked.

"Noon, at the Riverwalk Amphitheater on High Red Bluff. The fundraiser starts at four p.m. and will be hosted by the Alley Bar, and we'll use the alley for seating. It'll be a great way to end the campaign," Ed said.

Ty laughed. "All your favorite places and walking distance to your home. Man, you're funny," Ty said.

Everyone grinned and nodded.

Carlos spoke up. "I just ran the numbers: With Ed's three hundred thousand, combined with the miscellaneous donations, we can spend all of Simmons's money on voter contact and end the campaign with no debt."

"Great," Ty said.

"On another front, I received a conference call at my office last night from a Professor Royer and a woman, whose first name was Min. I didn't get her last name. They said they were friends and asked if they could write an AI program to help our phone program," Val said.

Before responding, Ty thought about John Barber talking about Royer's excitement over quantum computing at the Nevada Genetic Answer facility and how Min, the five-foot-tall mathematic genius, said she loved cowboys and line dancing. Two incredible people.

"What did you tell them?" Ty asked.

"I'd talk to you," Val said.

"Please tell them absolutely yes. They'll create cutting-edge AI. Just like an electric drill vs a handheld screwdriver. If they want to speak to me, schedule a phone appointment of their choosing."

Carlos left the room to make the call.

"What do you have, Susie?" Ty asked.

"Our media times are placed and locked down. All I'm waiting for is Gonzo to finish creating the ads and we're off. I've learned that Ullman's team is organizing their free media campaign and the Hollywood slime parade. The circus will roll into Alabama on Tuesday, October eleventh, to spread their 'We hate racist, misogynistic, gay-lynching, dirty cop Ty Leggett.'" She looked at Ty. "Different idiots, same crap. They would have resurrected Jane Fonda, but she's entombed at the Seoul Hanoi Hilton. They're bringing a former FBI bureau chief; I don't know who." She stopped speaking and again looked at Ty.

"Keep going," he said.

"The shitshow lands in Birmingham around eleven a.m. They bus to a rally and concert at the National Memorial for Peace and Justice around three p.m. Then they fly back to California for dinner in Malibu."

"If I'd not registered as an Independent, that would have been us. They're just trying to help their team," Ty said.

"I would not like being on their team," Susie said.

"I think we can turn this in our favor. Their message has nothing uplifting, just name-calling. And having cowboy Ullman standing alongside them hating Alabama. We can make him look like a fool," Gonzo said.

"If you boil it down, they're coming into our home and telling us we're ugly. How rude," Ed said.

"You've nailed it. That's it! We've developed the final ad campaign about Ullman's leaving his party. It's titled 'The Cookie' ad. The theme is betrayal," Gonzo, said feeling excited.

"We can expand it to his betrayal of Alabama and time that concept to the Birmingham and Montgomery show. Susie, we want every news outlet for October nineteenth through the twenty-first. We'll saturate the news," Gonzo said.

Carlos entered the room and looked at Ty. "They don't need to speak to you and are onboard with the AI program. We'll have it by tomorrow morning," Carlos said.

"Great. Val, you were saying?" Ty said.

"I like the counterattack idea," Val said. "I'll test the idea in our September twenty-ninth survey."

"This will work," Carlos said.

17

Sunday, 9:00 a.m., Ty received his three-day itinerary from Sabina. It read:

Monday, September 26:

8:00 a.m.: Maxwell Air Force Base press availability to discuss the importance of Maxwell Air Force Base and suggest increasing funding.

10:00 a.m.: Troy University students.

11:30 a.m.: Jackson Hospital.

12:30 p.m.: Light lunch, Steiner-Lobman Building, real estate developers.

2:00 p.m.: Campaign HQ, fundraising calls.

5:00 p.m.: Riverwalk Stadium Biscuits ownership meeting. 7:00 p.m.: Alabama Women in Politics Annual Dinner; SURVIVE THE PURPLE HAIR HOTTIES.

Tuesday, September 27:

7:00am: Tuskegee Airmen Museum breakfast meeting, press event.

10:00 am: Auburn Rotary meeting.

11:30 am: Mrs. Blakes's fundraising coffee.

1:00 p.m.: Auburn University president/department heads, students for rally (should be riotous fun).

2:30 p.m.: Fundraising calls.

4:00 p.m.: Columbus Chamber mixer.

6:30 p.m.: Birmingham Kelly family fundraising dinner.

Wednesday, September 28:

7:00 a.m.: Mobile Chamber breakfast.

8:30 a.m.: Port of Mobile Trade Association.

10:00 a.m.: Meet Mr. Mais at his Mobile office.

11:30 a.m.: Grand Hotel, Fairhope luncheon.

2:30 p.m.: Atmore Pleasant Grove Church, AME and indigenous tribes.

P.S. I asked Handmaiden again to kill Ed. She said NO!

Ty and Josh walked out of the Grand Hotel, Wednesday, September 28, and stood at the entrance waiting for their car.

Josh said, "This is a nice place. While you were in the meeting, I walked around. There're two massive swimming pools, bikes, a Trent Jones golf course across the street, fishing. I had dinner by the pool, took a Jacuzzi and slept like a teenager. Man, I wish I were rich; this place has everything."

"When we win, we can always hold a three-day symposium here," Ty said.

"Right now, you're my favorite candidate."

Ty laughed out loud.

They got into the car. Josh set the GPS for the Atmore Pleasant Grove Church.

"How long?" Ty asked.

"About an hour. It's fifty-one miles."

Ty sent a text message to Reverend Neal: *We good?*

The reply: *On way, be there in an hour. Nice bus, too much food.*

Ty smiled and texted Pastor Woods: *On the way, should arrive in an hour.*

The reply: *Ready.*

Ty made fundraising calls while he waited. After forty-five minutes, he put the phone on the dash and looked around.

"Wow, I'll bet this area has not changed in a hundred years. It's all agri, no houses, just raw land with a cracked single-lane road loaded with potholes. Man, it feels like poverty was born here."

"I'm glad I've got my gun."

"It's not that bad. My parents grew up in an area like this," Ty said.

"Can't be too safe." Josh glanced at the GPS screen. "We're almost there, three miles." He pointed to a street sign: *County Road 45, Atmore 15 mi.*

They saw a steeple ahead on their left. Josh slowed down as they drove alongside the grass lawn facing the road. Josh almost stopped the car. They looked at the white one-story Gothic church building on the left and the monument sign that read "Pleasant Grove Baptist Church, Saturday Night Football," facing the road.

"God and football. You've gotta love it," Josh said.

"And look, there's a cop car in the driveway. I just got a chill."

"Humph," Ty said.

Josh turned left into an uneven, cracked and beaten, concrete driveway. He parked next to the police car.

Ty got out and looked at the person sitting in the car.

A woman got out of the car, smiled at Ty. She was wearing a sheriff's uniform, flak jacket and duty belt with a handgun.

"Senator Leggett?" she asked.

"Yes."

"I'm Deputy Janet Jonsson."

"What brings you here, deputy?" Ty asked.

"A Mr. Abbott called our office and asked us to offer help if needed."

Ty turned and looked at Josh, and said, "God love Ed." He turned back to Jonsson. "Well, thank you. I don't think we'll need any help, but if you would like to join us, that's fine."

She smiled. "I'd like that," she said with a thick Southern drawl. "Not often a United States Senator comes to these parts."

"Come along," Ty said.

She glanced at Josh. "Is he a campaign aide?"

"No, his name is Josh; he's security and a friend. Josh is a retired Montgomery police detective."

"That's exciting," she said with a lovely smile.

"That's a Beretta APX you're wearing?"

"Yes."

"Nice gun," Josh said with a warm expression.

"I'll go into the church and look for Pastor Woods while you two compare bullets," Ty said with a laugh.

Ty walked up to the glass French doors and pushed on the handle. The doors were locked. He walked back toward the driveway and followed the path around the church to the side door; it was also locked. *This isn't good,* he thought. He continued down the walkway to a tiny thirty-by-ten-foot tin-roofed home.

He knocked on the front door, and was greeted by a short man, dressed in a white, long-sleeved shirt and black slacks. "You Senator Leggett?" he asked.

"Yes, and are you Pastor Leon Woods?"

"A miracle. I thought someone was playing a joke on me. And here you stand. Brother Leggett, welcome to Pleasant Grove Baptist Church."

He put a broad grin on his face. They shook hands.

Just then a sightseeing bus, followed by a Mercedes-Benz E-sprinter van turned into the driveway and stopped.

"Pastor Woods. Would you please open the recreation hall?" Ty asked.

"We don't have one; we use the church for our multi-purpose events. It's set per your request for twenty-six, including me. I just learned that six tribal leaders could not make it. I didn't really expect you to show up, so I didn't change anything since this morning."

"Perfect. Let's go."

Ty and Pastor Woods walked to the French doors and Woods opened the doors, pressing the rubber doorstop with his right foot to keep the doors open.

Ty walked to the bus and van.

Finished with the door, Woods turned to see the bus

and to his utter shock saw twelve men who looked and were dressed just like him standing in the parking lot and another five men dressed in casual business attire exit the van and join the group standing by the bus.

Ty spotted Reverend Neal and walked to his group. "Wonderful, thank you for doing this," he said.

Steven introduced the eleven ministers, and Ty shook hands with each introduction.

A man dressed in casual clothing approached Ty and introduced himself. "I'm Chief Roskin, Cherokee Nation."

Four other men dressed similarly to the chief joined the now assembled group. Chief Roskin introduced the other men to Ty and the ministers.

Ty shook each man's hand, as did the ministers.

An e-Ford 2500 pickup truck drove into the parking lot and parked next to the van. The group watched as a thin, professionally dressed woman got out of the car.

Choctaw Chief Ben smiled. "I'm glad she came."

The woman walked up to the group.

"Hello, Joanie," Cherokee Chief Roskin said.

She smiled and looked at Ty. "Senator, I'm Joanie Bright, Tribal Chair, and CEO of the Poarch Band Creek Indigenous Tribe."

They shook hands.

"She's the first," Shawnee Chief Bear said with a proud expression. "The first woman to attain such an honor."

Ty cocked his head. "First?"

"Yes, they're very proud of me. I'm the first female to chair and manage the Poarch Indigenous Tribe."

"Since the tribe was recognized by the federal government in nineteen eighty-four?" Ty asked.

"No, going back to the eighteen thirty Trail of Tears, probably earlier."

"Congratulations, that's a great honor," Ty said with a beaming smile. "I am very happy you're here."

"Stephanie and I are cohosts," Pastor Woods said.

"Thank you again for doing this. Let's get started," Ty said, and the group turned and followed Pastor Woods into the church.

Josh and Deputy Jonsson did not enter the building; they stayed outside and sat on the steps under the overhang roof.

When Pastor Woods opened the door, a cool waft of air passed by. The church was austere in its furnishing and liturgical décor, but the forty-by-sixty-foot room presented a feeling of being lovingly maintained. The pews were made of pine and freshly varnished to a glass shine. The sanctuary was raised and matched the church's modest surroundings.

Two ten-by-four-foot worktables were joined together and covered with a white tablecloth. Four plastic pitchers filled with water and twenty empty glasses were on the tables. Nineteen fold-up metal chairs surrounded the table; one chair was at the head of the tables with its back to the sanctuary.

"Please sit where you like. Senator, you're at the head," Pastor Woods said.

The twelve AME pastors, including Steven Neal, sat together to Ty's left with Pastor Woods closest to him, and the five tribal leaders sat to his right, with Joanie Bright closest to Ty.

"Thank you, all of you, for coming all this way to meet

me, and Pastor Woods. Thank you for opening your church to us," Ty said.

He took a moment to look at each person around the table. "I chose this location because of the historical significance of the Poarch Band Creek Indigenous Tribe Reservation and its proximity to this church. I have a simple question for all of you: Has a gathering of Alabama religious leaders and indigenous tribal leaders ever happened?"

Silence, as the group looked around the table at each other.

Ty looked at Pastor Woods. "Why not, Leon?"

"I have no idea," he said.

"Chief Roskin?" Ty asked.

No response.

"There is no formal reason why not. I just know it has never happened before," Joanie said.

"That's surprising —" Ty said.

"Not to me," Chief Roskin interrupted angrily. "And I'll tell you why. We fought back. We didn't just cry and bitch."

Reverend Jackson of Huntsville Methodist shouted, "*What!* Who do you think you're talking to, *slave owner*?"

Chief Roskin shouted right back, "So were you! Slavery wasn't invented in America. And we didn't join the US Cavalry Buffalo Soldiers and hunt you down. 'The only good Indian is a dead Indian,' right, Reverend?"

Reverend Jacobs of the Baptist Shiloh Missionary jumped in. "Don't play that game with us. There's the Tulsa massacre, Tuskegee syphilis, KKK lynchings. Those events mean anything to you?"

The two men stared at each other.

"We chose a different path, a path of nonviolence," Pastor Neal said.

"How did that work out?" Chief Roskin fired back.

"Not now, Chief," Joanie said.

"Why not? They *never* stood up, never offered help. We're alone; we've always been alone," Roskin said, almost shouting.

"Did we see you in 1860 when the KKK was lynching and burning churches? No! Did you step up after the nineteen twenty-one Tulsa massacre? No. Did you step up in nineteen thirty-two when we were injected with syphilis? No," Reverend Jackson said, in a deep Southern drawl, looking at Roskin.

"Don't talk to us about syphilis. They gave *us* smallpox." Chief Roskin sneered at Jackson.

Ty watched the faces around the table grow angry, and he thought, *It's working.*

"It's never-ending for us; hate is always lurking," Jacobs said.

"Poor you, 'I'm not loved.' At least you're alive. Can you say *genocide*, Reverend?" Chief Roskin snarled.

That ripped it. Shouting commenced from both sides of the table. The pain of the past filled the room with sound.

Suddenly there was a loud bang when Pastor Woods slammed his Bible on the table. "I will not have hate in my church!" he shouted, popping to his feet, glaring at everyone.

Silence replaced hate.

He sat down.

"This is why I wanted us to meet; the same dog that bit all of you, bit us," Ty said. "In sixteen hundred and seven, the *Susan Constant* landed in Jamestown carrying pilgrims and the fate of native people was sealed. Twelve years later, in sixteen-nineteen, the *White Lion* landed at Point Comfort carrying the first slaves," Ty said, looking at Chief Roskin.

"The Europeans who did this to all of us are dead; only the residue of that wicked time remains. We, us," he stopped and looked at each person at the table, "must reconcile the past, bring closure to that pain, unite and direct our efforts toward forgiveness."

"How?" Joanie asked in a soft voice. "We have nothing to offer. Only Ponca Chief Standing Bear had an impact and that was a hundred and sixty years ago. We did not have a Martin Luther King or a President Lincoln; all we had was Andrew Jackson and the Bureau of Indian Affairs. We've never received an Emancipation Proclamation or a march to freedom," she said. Her voice faded into a whisper as she lost control of her emotions.

"Why did you ask us here, Senator?" Neal asked quietly.

"Because I have an idea, and it involves all of us."

"You dragged us all the way here to talk politics?" Roskin asked. He started to stand. "The only reason I came, Senator, Joseph said you were a decent man."

"Is this about your campaign?" Neal asked.

"No, it's about what I'm going to do after I win."

Chickasaw Chief Calbent touched Roskin on the arm. "Please sit."

"I've seen how hate moves the world and love moves a

moment. A person can hold a newborn and cry with joy and a moment later walk outside, join a mob, and kill another human being. Hate is the enemy, not us, or each other; we are the victims," Ty said.

Contemplative silence filled the room.

"What's your idea, Senator?" Pastor Neal asked politely.

"Trust and faith. In January, I will announce legislation for the federal government to atone for its actions against us. It was President Andrew Jackson who violated the Indian treaties. It was a political compromise that allowed slavery to continue, and after we were freed, it was President Andrew Johnson who did all he could to stop Reconstruction and fostered hate by allowing black codes." Ty looked around the table.

"On that day I'll need every AME leader and tribal chief there to witness the unveiling and celebrate its creation and—" he looked around the table again—"its belated arrival."

"Witness? Witness what? What are you going to do?" Roskin asked.

"I learned long ago that some details are best kept under wraps. 'A reliable comrade obliges trust and faith that the law can atone for injustice,'" Ty quoted from the *Federalist Papers*.

"Senator, we've heard thousands of platitudes and every time we've been betrayed," Joanie said.

"I understand that betrayal is not uncommon. Pastor Neal trusts me, as you should. I will not fail if I am elected," Ty said.

Ty reached into his coat pocket and removed a folded

piece of paper. He opened it and said, "I found a poem; I have not met the author. It reads:

"Death is hot; memory frozen.
Hope conceived, stillborn, stolen.
Hate shadows atonement, concealed.
Pray, anonymity and prosperity be.
Colors free, past anchors me.
The *Susan Constant* lands, seeds planted.
The White Lion drifts along,
Seeking comfort to embark.
The *White Lion* sails on; hope disembarks.
The *White Lion* sails on and on until frozen dawn,
Searching for hope and anonymity to set us free."
Silence.

Saturday, September 24, 7:30 a.m. Ty, Gonzo, Susie, Ed, Carlos, and Val at Gonzo's Montgomery office.

"Good morning, we have thirty-eight days until the election. Ed, where are we now with money?" Ty asked.

"The FEC report is due on October fifteen, and our secret of success will be out. They'll see we have money and no debt, and that will not make them happy." He looked around the table. "Normally a good October FEC would help raise money in DC. PACs and lobbyists would start to hedge their bets. That won't happen for us unless Senator Joseph makes lots of calls." Ed glanced at his iPad. "Some great news, Simmons's seven hundred thousand was deposited this morning. Our in-state fundraisers are covering day-to-day overhead and outreach." Finished, Ed nodded at Ty.

"How is Tim doing on the mail program, Carlos?" Ty asked.

"We have a hundred thousand small donors to date, with an average of twelve dollars per donor. The program will pay for itself and put money into the campaign. It's doing fine."

"Good. Val, you're up," Ty said.

"Our nightly calls were productive. Our messaging is working. On the head-to-head, we are at twenty-five percent and Ullman is at forty. Horner has dropped to fifteen percent of the vote. But we have a major problem with men."

"What, why?" Gonzo asked.

"Men do not perceive Ty as an outdoorsman and we're getting clobbered. We've seen that before, but not with someone as manly as Ty," Val said with a laugh.

"Not funny," Ty said.

"Gonzo, we need a short ad campaign, with Ty on a horse—"

"A horse? You're kidding, I've never ridden a horse," Ty interrupted.

"You don't have to ride, just sit, and let Gonzo's people take lots of pictures."

"No cowboy hat," Ty said.

Val laughed. "We are picking up solid majority votes, but we are still not receiving the Black vote. We should; our messaging is on target. I'm at a loss."

"I had a good meeting with the Alabama AME leadership. I trust things will change," Ty said.

"I heard from Josh there was a lot of yelling," Carlos said.

"Clearing of the air," Ty said.

"Should we change the messaging?" Gonzo asked.

"No, keep it the same," Val said.

"Okay, then, we're on track. Our comparison ads start this week, and we should see significant progress. My only worry is Horner; he's fading faster than I thought," Val said. "Our next survey is October thirteenth; we'll know then what's working or not. That's it for me," he said.

"Gonzo, are we ready for the October nineteen Hollywood Road Show?" Carlos asked.

"Yes, we have three days of paid television and social coverage. We have created some very funny TikToks, Snaps, and X movies with Influencer visuals. We'll cover all the news time slots with television ads and, I believe, Ullman will regret the road show." Gonzo smiled.

"What about the boards?" Carlos asked.

"They all roll over on the eighteenth," Gonzo said.

"It'll be interesting to see how Ullman's team reacts to our response to the road show," Susie said.

"I'll bet they'll hit us with everything they have," Val said.

Two days later, Ty and Josh were driving to Tuscaloosa for a noon fundraiser when they got a conference call from Carlos and Val.

"What's up?" Ty asked, feeling concerned.

"We're in the phase of dirty tricks and surprise crap. Tell me about John Barber," Carlos said.

"That's a long story. He's my best friend. We worked together on a special project, named Genetic Answer, for the president. It ended badly with the death of two sick drug dealers."

"How long ago?" Carlos asked.

"Over a year," Ty said.

"I heard something about this from a DC lobbyist; she said this story is emanating from the White House. I suppose this is the crap you referred to at the September ten meeting?" Carlos asked.

"Yes," Ty said.

"So, tell me more," Carlos asked.

"John discovered a cure for a specific ailment that would have been earth-shaking. The Barber family was violently attacked by two spies who wanted to sell it to a foreign drug company. John killed one; I killed the other. John has gone into hiding to protect his discovery. That's all there is."

"Have you seen Barber since?"

"Like I said, no."

"What about his family?"

"Not for a year."

Silence.

"This is good stuff: murder, a fugitive, a campaign donation from the wife. It's got all the makings of a great October surprise, if not a sci-fi thriller," Carlos said.

"I was just doing my job. And the bad guys died."

"The White House and security folks are all over this?"

"Yes."

"Any ideas on a counter to the White House?"

"Not until we win."

"They'll drop this on us the last two weeks of the campaign."

"Why not at the Hollywood Road Show?"

"Too early. They'll want this to be a last-minute gotcha and let the national media chew us up." Val thought for a moment. "Right now, I do not know how to handle it. Maybe we just call it a dirty trick, play the race card."

"I don't think that will work, sounds 'poor me.' And I hate the idea."

"Okay, we come out shooting, no pun intended," Val said with a grin.

"I like that," Ty said, laughing.

"Why did you keep Mrs. Barber's donation?" Val asked.

"That family is the best part of my life."

Silence.

"Sorry, I was thinking. The fugitive part, who cares? The donation is the problem. They'll say it's hush-up money. Is Mrs. Barber sophisticated? Can she handle hordes of screaming reporters at her door?"

"Yes, she can handle the pressure. She's an MD and tough. If given a heads-up, she'll do fine," Ty said.

"Okay, what's her first name?" Carlos asked.

"Megan."

"You have her cell number?"

"Yes."

"Text it to me and I'll talk to her tonight."

"No. Val, you call her."

"Why me?"

"You're not a cop and if they use this issue, I want you by my side."

"You know they'll go after her first."

"Yes. When you speak to her, give some background on our relationship and explain this attack is coming from the White House. We will respond, not her, and that will end it," Ty said.

Saturday, October 1, 7:30 a.m., campaign team meeting.

"Good morning. We have thirty-nine days before the election. You know how we start: Ed, where do we stand with money?" Ty asked.

"Senator Simmons's pledge has been fulfilled. We are on budget and have enough money to pay for our marketing campaign and expenses. All is good," Ed said.

"Thank you, Gonzo, you're up," Ty said.

"The ad for the Hollywood Road Show rally is scripted. We'll have a camera crew at their first stop in Birmingham. They'll send me the footage of Ullman on the stage bashing Alabama. I'll edit it and Susie will place the ads for midday news and social media. Should be straightforward and fast. Depending on what we learn from Val, 'The Cookie' ad will drop October fifteen, and our billboard campaign will reflect that message."

"Susie, we good?" Ty asked.

"Yes, this is when it gets exciting, and I get to scream at media people!" she said with a full grin on her face.

"Val?" Ty said.

"Good morning. My first thought before I get into the numbers is to reinforce the strategy regarding the potential attack on the Barber contribution. Let's keep it to a one-day story. The national media will only prolong the attack if we make a mistake." He looked around the table.

"My guess is the story will break Monday, October thirty-first. I can already see their Halloween references. Ty will be in DC on the twenty-ninth and, if nothing happens, he'll be back to Alabama on Wednesday. If it breaks while he is in Washington, he will make an impromptu press statement from his Capitol office. He will state that Megan Barber is one of his closest friends and he cannot discuss any ongoing FBI investigations. This is a last-minute dirty trick." He looked at the team. "The campaign will not respond. If cornered, repeat that it's just a dirty trick by a desperate Jeffery Ullman.

"Okay, onward. The results from our nightly tracking calls show the horse worked; men moved, and women liked how he looked in blue jeans and a blue work shirt and cowboy hat. Nice job, Gonzo," Val said.

"Way to go, Ty, hook-'em-horns," Susie said.

"So embarrassing," Ty said.

"We are gaining on Ullman. How much won't be clear until the October thirteenth survey. Horner continues to drop, down to four percent of the vote. The Black vote is continuing to climb in our direction. Again, I won't know anything definitive until the thirteenth. I feel we are about to make our move. That's all I've got," Val said.

"There is a lot before us; we will face some outrageous challenges. Please keep doing the little things and everything else to get our message out. The next three weeks will determine our fate," Carlos said.

On October eleventh, a private E-Bombardier Global 8500 jet traveling from Burbank, California, landed at Birmingham-Shuttlesworth International Airport. The plane taxied to a preselected location, facing the assembled media horde.

The gangway rolled up to the plane, the cabin door opened and out walked twenty of California's hottest actors and political activists, all smiling and waving to the assembled television cameras and media sycophants.

Jeffery Ullman walked up to the gangway to greet his newest best friends. The look on his face revealed he was living his finest moment; he had made the big time. Jeffery stood facing the gangway, dressed in new, unwashed blue jeans, brass belt buckle, custom snakeskin Western boots, a plaid, flannel, long-sleeved work shirt, topped off with a handmade fur cowboy hat.

After hugs, introductions, and waves to the television cameras, Ullman approached the assembled gaggle of press, and said, "Today puts Alabama on the map. This could be the greatest day in Alabama history."

Next to speak was Oscar winner and political activist Windy Hammer Dolly, who set the theme for the day when she said, "We are here today to part the Red Sea and free Alabama of its racist past and lead this backward state into the twenty-second century!"

Jeffery smiled and was so enthralled with the attention he did not hear what Windy said.

Susie was watching the event on television at her Montgomery office with Gonzo. "We are going to nail that stupid man. How dare they?"

The message, all day, was just more of the same. Alabama was filled with backward hicks and racists, and Ty Leggett was a dirty cop who used his badge to kill innocent people and resigned from the FBI in disgrace.

The message became even more emotional when the Hollywood crowd arrived at the National Memorial for Peace and Justice in Montgomery, and one actress fell to her knees, sobbing and wailing at the Memorial Wall.

"How can anyone live in such an evil place?" she cried.

After the group finished their walk through the memorial park, they assembled on the grandstand, with a country western band in the background. Each person took turns at the microphone bashing Ty and Alabama. Ullman stood up front, smiling, drunk on the adulation; oblivious to what was really happening to him.

At 6:00 p.m., that evening, the Hollywood troupe assembled one last time at Dannelly Field for their flight back to Los Angeles. When the last actor finished speaking to the media, a reporter handed him a photograph of Senator Leggett, saying, "I thought you'd like to have this," she said.

"He's Black!" the actor spit out, with utter shock on his face.

That evening on the national news the first five minutes was spent on how wonderful it was Hollywood's finest had flown from Los Angeles to Alabama to celebrate their activism and turn the tide on America's racism. There was little mention of Senator Jeffery Ullman until the commercial breaks, and the "Ty for US Senate" commercials aired. The best commercial showed Windy waving her middle finger as she stepped into the Global E-8500 jet, shouting, "This is for Alabama." The following smash cut was of Ullman banging his cowboy hat against his leg and dancing on stage with Windy.

"Now *that* is priceless," Susie said with a smile after watching the commercial.

Saturday, October 15, 7:30 a.m., campaign team meeting at Gonzo's Montgomery office. In attendance: Ed, Carlos, Val, Susie, Gonzo and Ty.

"Hi, all. I hope you all are as happy as I am this wonderful autumn morning. There are twenty-five days left before the election, and Jeffery Ullman looked bad," Ty said.

Everyone was grinning.

"Ed, how we doing?" Ty asked.

"Very well. The last two nights we've seen a significant uptick at our online contribution page." He looked at his phone. "Actually, a five-hundred-percent increase and the average amount donated doubled to fifty dollars. It appears our donors were not happy with Ullman's performance Tuesday," Ed said, grinning.

"And he deserves it," Susie said.

"Continuing our money upswing, I heard last night through the DC grapevine, Senator Joseph's Independent

Expenditure PAC will start spending media money next week, and three of the large national special interest PACs have joined that IE, along with several DC lobby firms covering their bets. Our budget is looking good. Carlos might have a little extra to spend. Look out, though. Ullman money is flowing." Ed smiled, looked at Ty and continued: "On a Debbie Downer note, the RNC will not donate a dime. The president, behind the scenes, is all in for Ullman and pressuring everyone to donate. There's no doubt our governor is out, and the incumbent Republican Alabama US Senator is also out and will not help."

"I never expected their help. We came into this campaign a foolish underdog. Now we're making waves. Still an underdog fighting Fox News political pundits and DC insiders." Ty looked around the table. "That's okay, we have us in this room and the Alabama voters. I like our chances. Gonzo, what about your social media campaign?"

"Somewhat of a mixed bag. Some college students loved the anti-Alabama rhetoric and flooded our platform with crazy allegations. What was heartwarming, there was significant blowback from UA Birmingham and Auburn students. They did not buy into Hammer Dolly's 'I hate Alabama' message. The best post came from Auburn that read: Hammer Dolly takes it in the hills," Gonzo said.

Val was next. "Susie, you did a great job, and the numbers show it. The October thirteenth survey showed we've made significant gains. In the head-to-head, we have moved to thirty percent, and Ullman remained at thirty-five percent. Horner has dropped to three percent, and the undecided rose to thirty-two percent, which is high. Having said that, we tested the undecideds, and they were uncomfortable with outsiders and Ullman bashing Alabama. We won the day, and what should have been a big hit, wasn't. Nice job."

Val clapped his hands, with the team joining in.

"We've made significant progress in the Black community; we're up fifteen percent from our low of five percent Ullman is still strong in that segment. The October twenty-six survey should show that Ullman was really hurt by the Hollywood rally. That will force his team to change their marketing strategy, and their October surprise is fully on the table." Val looked at Ty.

"Ullman's team has made several mistakes: First, being predictable; second, Hollywood; and lastly, taking the Black vote for granted. If we keep making gains there and 'The Cookie' ad reinforces his lack of character, we will be in the game. That's all I've got," Val finished.

Gonzo looked at Ed. "Can you come by the office later this afternoon? I'd like to show you the first cut of 'The Cookie' ad," Gonzo asked.

Ed nodded.

"Okay, Josh and I are off to meet Jonny Rain and Maggie Murdock in Abbeville for dinner tonight. Together, they could eliminate Alabama's debt," Ty said jokingly. "Let's have another great week. Thank you for your hard work. Nice job, Susie."

18

Later that day, after lunch, Ed drove to Gonzo's office. He parked on the street and walked into the one-story building. He walked down two short hallways, passed the conference room and then Susie's office, where he saw her sitting at her desk.

"Hey, what's up?" Ed asked.

"Just working. How are you?" she asked.

"Perfect."

"Sabina hasn't quit?"

"Nope, not until I quit first."

"She likes being the boss."

"Very funny. She only tells me what to do in the morning," Ed said and laughed.

Susie also laughed.

"Are you going to join us for the viewing of 'The Cookie' ad?"

"No, one of our television stations is screwing around with our placements, and I've got to call them in five minutes. Gonzo's expecting you; just go on into the viewing room, and I'll tell him you're here."

"Perfect. By the way, would you and Gonzo like to join me and Sabina for a drink tonight after work at the Alley Bar? It's trivia night."

"Sounds like fun. What time?"

"Seven, and Sabina is wicked good."

Ed left her office and went down the short hallway to the viewing room on his left. He sat on the couch that faced the far wall.

Carlos came into the room. "Thank you for coming by," he said.

"My pleasure. I'm looking forward to seeing the cookie ad."

Gonzo picked up a remote from a side table and pointed it at the far wall. The viewing screen began to unfold from a slit in the ceiling. Ed watched as a five-by-five-foot soft glass digital projection screen slid toward the floor.

Gonzo picked up a voice-activated remote control. "Play Leggett for US Senate cookie ad," he said.

"That's new," Ed said.

"Just got it Monday, not cheap. It's for 3D images. The screen is amazing; it's infused with three hundred microbots per inch and nine hundred pixels per inch. We do have the holographic table projector; but most people use the flat 3D Wi-Fi monitor at home. And to be honest, I don't like the look of holographic table programming. It's great for sports and nature. But for what we're doing, this is better. Ready?" Gonzo asked.

The lights turned off and multicolored diagonal, red, blue, and green color bars appeared on the screen. Suddenly, a mature, heavy-set woman, maybe seventy-five years old, appeared, sitting on the edge of a tan-colored ottoman. Her hair was bobbed and a gray-blue color. She was leaning forward toward the camera, wearing a pastel muumuu.

A very thin man, not healthy-looking, about eighty years old, sat behind her, on the edge of a gray couch. He was holding a homemade chocolate chip cookie in his right hand.

"Jeffery Ullman, you should be ashamed of yourself," the woman yelled, wagging her right index finger at the camera. "How dare you abandon your values to win public office? You should be ashamed of yourself. Jeffery Ullman, you should be ashamed of yourself."

The old man in the background was shaking, his mouth gaping.

The screen went dark. Gonzo switched on the lights. "What do you think?" he asked.

"Gonzo! We're getting killed by men and you have a blue-haired woman pointing her finger and yelling at Ullman with a decrepit man sitting behind her." Ed laughed. "The best I can say about him is he wasn't drooling. It's horrible!"

"You don't know what you're talking about. Fuck you, Ed Abbott," he said, and stormed out of the room.

Ed left the room and walked back down the hallway. He poked his head into Susie's office.

"Well, what did you think?" she asked.

"Trivia isn't going to work tonight."

At six p.m., that evening, Ed received a text: *Gonzo changed the ad. See you at 7.*

Friday, October 22, 7:30 a.m., Leggett team meeting in Gonzo's Montgomery conference room. In attendance: Ty, Carlos, Ed, Susie, Gonzo and Val.

"Good morning," Ty said to the assembled team. "We have nineteen days until the election. Carlos, how are we doing with our voter outreach?" Ty asked.

He picked up his iPad and read. "We have hired drivers to deliver voters to the polls and people to conduct exit polling."

"I'm curious, why would we spend the money on exit polling? We can't affect or change what's happening. So why do it?" Ty asked.

"So, we know what's going on, just in case the electronic voting machines produce different results than our exit polling. Then our lawyers would have something to work with—that's really the only reason," Carlos said.

"A waste of money, but I understand," Ty said.

"We have six lawyers on retainer and a team of Reason Foundation lawyers on call. We have ranked and are focusing our walking campaign into the twenty-two-hundred precincts. Those precincts are ranked in order of potential Leggett votes, voting history turnout and demographics."

Carlos looked around the table.

"The new AI program that Professor Royer and Professor Min cowrote is incredible. We're testing it on voter outreach calls and it's a wow. There's no way one can tell it's an artificial creation. There is no delay when the call is answered. A normal sounding voice introduces itself, if someone hangs up, it calls them right back and asks, 'Why did you hang up? I'm just trying to help' and restarts the conversation. The program knows where the voter shops, eats, favorite sports teams, education. Most amazing is the family data. It knows where everyone lives and when they were last together."

Carlos shook his head.

"It knows their wealth and even who they're cheating with. To top it off, the AI voice matches the voter's accent and inflection. If the person wants to switch to a Facetime, no problem. I'm telling you, it's scary good. With it we can call almost everyone in Alabama in one night. No more scripts, paying phone bank callers, and tabulating responses. All we need is one person to monitor the control center and turn the system on or off." Carlos looked down at his notes.

"Now that I understand how good this thing is, we'll use it to call our identified voters starting seven days from the election, reminding them to vote. For the voters who don't have a phone, which is a very small number, we'll send a volunteer to visit. It's an amazing tool; wow! This program will change campaigns forever." Carlos looked around the table with a big grin on his face.

"Back to old-school: the absentee ballots are starting to return to the counties' election offices." He glanced at his notes. "Last item. We are putting the finishing touches on our Get Out the Vote campaign. The AME churches are providing most of our volunteers," Carlos finished.

Ty smiled. "Sounds good. Carlos, thank you."

Gonzo, how's the media?" Ty asked.

"The revised cookie ad is up and running. And from the screaming we've heard from the Ullman campaign, it's working. Our outdoor media, social media, radio and mail have converted to that message. My hope is we will have touched each voter seven times by Election Day," Gonzo said.

"Susie?" Ty asked.

"I'm done unless you decide to run some last-minute ads," she said.

"I am getting excited. Val, what do you have to say?" Ty asked.

"We are gaining." He smiled. "Our nightly tracking phone calls—the pestering never stops—show we are within ten points and climbing, and by the October twenty-six survey, we should be within five points. There is one caveat: The Barber hit in late October. Depending on how that turns out, I believe we will be within the margin of error, plus or minus three points by the October thirty-first survey. The last nine days of the campaign will be very exciting."

"Ed, what have you got? Ty asked.

"The October twenty-fifth rally and fundraiser are going well. We're raising money and on track for a thousand people attending the rally and we should have a couple hundred donors at the restaurant."

"Nice job, Ed." Ty smiled, and looked around the table. "The end is almost here. I'm excited and exhausted. Thank you for getting me this far," he said looking around the table, feeling sentimental.

Tuesday, October 25, 8:00 a.m., Sabina and Ed are at the Montgomery office working on the final details for the rally.

"You ready to go?" Ed called out from his office.

"Where?" Sabina said.

"The Riverwalk."

"Ed, nothing has changed since we were there last night. Please stop being such a crazy person."

"I want to be there when they arrive to set up."

"We have an hour and it's a five-minute walk. Please take a chill pill or something. This is our last event. Please don't make me want to kill you."

"Have you heard it might hit ninety-nine today?" Ed said.

"That's perfect for the rally, hot, dry and a grass field facing the Alabama River."

"What if there isn't a breeze from the cooling the bluff?"

"Oh, God, Ed. Then the Silos Red Bluff bar will make lots of money selling beer. Now stop, everything is all set. We've farmed out all of the setup and catering. Stop it. We're supposed to have fun today. Don't screw it up," she said, pointing her index finger at him. "If you really need to do something, go get the balloons and wash your disgusting SUV. Remember you're taking Ty to the airport at five tomorrow morning for his DC flight."

"Okay, I'll get the balloons. We should double-check with Mario."

"If you call Mario one more time, he'll join Handmaiden in killing you. Mario still hasn't forgiven us for the May seventeenth opening dinner."

"What? I don't understand," Ed said.

"Which part of you bugging the crap out of him and me don't you understand?"

"Okay, I'll get the damn balloons and wash my truck."

That same morning at 9:00 a.m., Ty received a text from Sabina:

Following note sent to entire Leggett database. — Friendly reminder: Ty Leggett for US Senate, Red Bluff Rally, today at 2:00 p.m., Montgomery, Red Bluff Park. Mass family picnic, band, and celebration. Casual attire. Don't miss it! Great way to meet friends and carry Senator Leggett to victory on November 8!

A second text read:

Your itinerary for above referenced event via email.

Ty found the email with the subject line "Events Itinerary"; it read:

2:00 p.m.: Arrive Renaissance Hotel; meet Sabina main entrance. Walk to Riverwalk Park.

St. Paul and the Broken Bones are performing.

4:30 p.m.: You will be introduced by Senator Simmons.

5:00 p.m.: Event ends.

At conclusion, exit amphitheater, stage right. Josh will be waiting in golf cart. He will drive south through the back gate over railroad tracks to Coosa Street and Central Restaurant.

7:30 p.m.: Central event (casual) You address guests, rah-rah, let's go! Speech. Thank everyone you see. Especially Paul, finance committee, Mario, Central staff and Senator Simmons.

8:00 p.m.: Event ends after your comments. Josh will drive you home.

Following morning, 5:00 a.m.: Ed arrives at your home to take you to Montgomery Airport and your 6:30 a.m. United flight to DC.

Later that morning, finished with his fundraising calls, Ed glanced at his cell phone: 10:00 a.m.

"Off to Dynamite Ballons. See you at the rally," he said to Sabina as he walked down the stairs to his car.

Ed got into his new 2039 e-Ford Bronco and drove to Tallapoosa Street, turned left, and merged onto Columbus Street. Thirty minutes later he arrived at Dynamite Magic & Balloons. He turned into the driveway, and standing before him were ten people holding five hundred red, white, and blue helium balloons.

"Oh my God, that's a lot of balloons!" he exclaimed.

He opened the back hatch, unlocked the doors and rolled down his window. A sudden rush of hot air pressed against his face. "Man, it's hot," he said out loud. He glanced at the dash thermometer gauge: 95° F. "It's only ten-forty."

A lady holding ten red balloons came up to him.

"Ed Abbott?"

"Yes." He glanced again at all the balloons." There's no way they'll all fit."

"No problem. You might find it hard to see, but we can do it," she said.

After stuffing the car with balloons, she closed the back hatch. Ed waved goodbye. He had to push balloons out of the way so he could see out the front windshield. He drove back to Montgomery toward the A#1 carwash. There were four cars in front of him as he waited his turn. He had to switch the air conditioner off, afraid the car would overheat. When he got to the front, an attendant waved him in. Ed rolled up his window and waited a moment as the tire guide pushed him into the washing machine.

The moment the cold water hit the car; he felt the air pressure change. To his sudden horror, a loud pop preceded a machine gun of sound as the balloons popped.

"Shit, shit! This can't be happening!" he screamed, as he rolled down the driver's side window.

White globs of soap shot through the window.

"Fuck, fuck, fuck!" he screamed, as soap filled his left ear and covered his head.

He closed the window and waited for the horror show to end. He pulled up to the exit and waited for the attendant to wave him forward. The young man stood in front of Ed's SUV and stared at Ed. After a moment he waved for Ed to move forward. When the driver's side window was next him, he put up his hand and said, "Stop."

Ed rolled down his window.

"Sir, are you okay?" he asked.

"I'm fine," Ed said with the highest-pitched voice of his life.

The young man burst out laughing.

Twenty minutes later, Ed was driving down Tallapoosa Street, and as fate would have it, he stopped at the intersection of Coosa and Commerce Street, and crossing the street in front of him were Ty and Sabina. They walked up to Ed and looked at him with expressions of dismay.

Ed rolled down his window, and Sabina asked, "What happened to you and where are the balloons?"

"I hate you," he said.

October 26: The Hit:

"Breaking news: NBC has learned, through credible, anonymous sources within the Justice Department that United States Senator Tyler Leggett is under investigation for the double murder of government scientist, Gloria Gysin, and her brother, Peter Gysin. The murders took place last year while Senator Leggett was serving as Director of the FBI.

"It is believed Senator Leggett and Doctor John Barber conspired to cover up the Gysin murders. It was also revealed that Megan Barber, Doctor Barber's wife, donated thousands of dollars to Senator Leggett's special election campaign. Sources tell us Mrs. Barber's donation is under investigation by the Federal Election Commission for violating federal campaign law.

"It's been suggested by our sources within the Justice Department that Mrs. Barber's contribution was hush money to protect her fugitive husband. Doctor John Barber is wanted for the murder of Peter Gysin and stealing government secrets. He has been placed on the FBI's most-wanted list since his disappearance last year. We have asked Mrs. Barber for a statement. She has declined to comment.

"It's believed Senator Leggett resigned from the Bureau to thwart its murder investigation of Doctor Barber. OAN reached out to the FBI for comment and was told they will not comment on internal matters. Lawyers within the Justice Department are telling us indictments are imminent. It is believed these revelations will force Senator Leggett to withdraw from his special election campaign and will eventually lead to his resignation from the US Senate." A photograph of Ty filled the television screen.

"We can now report that former FBI Director and special election candidate, Tyler Leggett, will make a statement from his Washington, DC, Senate office at three p.m. today."

Susie, Sabina, Ed, Gonzo, and Carlos were at the Montgomery Alley Bar, watching Fox News. They switched on two other televisions, and the same story was airing.

"Even though we were prepared, this is awful," Susie said.

Suddenly a breaking news headline scrolled across the bottom of all three television screens: Fox News is reporting two women have come forward accusing Senator Leggett of sexual harassment. One of the victims is alleging rape.

Sabina gasped, "Oh, my God."

Ty was in his DC office in the Hart Building, watching Fox. He turned the television off and looked across his desk at Val and his campaign attorney, Nicole Dennison.

"I'd say that's the kitchen sink."

"The new wrinkle is the two women. Any truth?" Nicole asked.

"No, of course not," Ty said calmly.

"The statement we have about the Barbers remains the same," Nicole said. "When you're asked about the two women, tell the truth: It's not true; it's a dirty campaign stunt. Turn around and return to your office. This is a no-win scenario. Keep your cool and do not say anything, no matter what jumps out at you. One of the women might show up and scream terrible things. Do not respond. Just read your statement."

"Ty, you know why rich candidates can't buy elections and lose?" Val asked.

"No."

"When they're lied about, they don't have friends who come to their defense and they must buy their way out of trouble—which hardly ever works. You have a lifetime of friends who will fight for you, and the truth is on your side."

"Thank you," Ty said.

"Remember, Val and I will stand behind you with our backs against the door. Val will have his hand on the handle. When you're finished, turn to your right and Val will open the door, I'll prevent anyone from following," Nicole said.

At three p.m., Ty Leggett opened his office door and stepped out into a hallway packed with media people. There were ten television cameras lined against the hallway rail facing Ty's office doorway. At least fifty men and women were packed next to each other on each side of his door, all of them holding up their cell phones, pressing toward him. A tactic to hold him from getting away.

The door closed behind him. Ty took a moment before speaking to look at the mass of people and television cameras facing him. He turned his head slowly from side to side, feeling disgust as he recognized many of the reporters glaring at him.

"I have a statement regarding the false accusations dumped on me and my campaign today. John and Megan Barber are my closest friends. What Mr. Barber and I did to save his family's life is public record. I left the Bureau to run for the United States Senate with the support of President Rodda and the governor of Alabama. Today's events are another example of filthy politics. The same tricks are foisted on candidates every election cycle. The factless accusations and campaign tactics of personal destruction are disgusting. Everything CBS, ABC, MSNOW, and Fox News have reported are false. I will repeat, every accusation is false."

He looked around and along the hallway again, his disgust apparent.

"I was honored to serve as the director of the FBI, and I'm honored the governor of Alabama appointed me to the United States Senate. I look forward to winning the special election and serving Alabama and the American people in the United States Senate—"

Suddenly there were high-pitched screams coming from the center of the press gaggle. "He raped me, that man raped me!" a woman screamed. "He *raped* me," she wailed. She dropped to the floor, wailing.

All eyes and television cameras were focused on Ty's face. He displayed no emotion and looked calm.

"Regardless of how loudly one yells or how loudly they scream a charge, it does not make it true. I stand by my statement: The charges leveled against me are fictitious and false."

Ty turned to his right, Val opened the door and he walked back into his office with Val close behind. Nicole pressed herself against the door and glared at the assembled throng. Even with the door closed, Ty could hear the screaming of questions from the press corps.

His staff was huddled together by the reception desk watching him, and to a person, they looked terrified.

Ty smiled. "We're good, don't worry; they will not win."

Nicole came into the office. "They've left, it's over."

With that said, Ty, Val, and Nicole moved into his private office.

Moments later, there was a gentle knock-on Ty's private office door. Val answered, he opened the door just enough to look out, standing in front of him was Ty's chief of staff, Carol Mary.

"Ms. Laurie McDuffy is here. She worked at GA as Dr. Barber's personal assistant. She would like to speak to the senator," Carol said in a whispering voice.

Val glanced past Carol and saw an attractive middle-aged woman, dressed in business attire, standing by the reception desk. "This is not a good—"

"No, stop," Ty interrupted, as he moved past Val and walked out into the outer room.

"Hello, Laurie. This is a welcome surprise. How are you?" he asked.

"I felt I had to do something. What they are doing to you is horrible," she said, trying to hold back her emotions.

"Yes, it is," Ty said, nodding.

"After what happened at GA, I moved back here and retired and when I saw the news, I just wanted you to know a lot of us are praying for you—and don't believe a thing they're saying."

"Thank you very much, that truly helps." Ty stepped closer and they hugged.

She turned and left the office.

As the media and reporters dispersed and walked down the hallway out of the Hart Building, a United Press reporter was walking alongside a *Washington Times* reporter. She asked the *Times* reporter, "What do you think?"

"That was one of the most impressive displays of composure I have ever witnessed. I hope he runs for president," she said.

Back in Alabama at the Alley bar, Susie took a large gulp of her mint julep. She and Sabina stood and did a happy dance together around the bar. Gonzo looked at Ed, "That went better than I hoped. Saturday we'll learn how much it hurt." Gonzo said.

Suddenly the television flashed a breaking news headline, NBC switched coverage to an impromptu press conference at the FBI Washington DC headquarters. Fox and MSNOW also switched to live coverage.

"Good afternoon, I have a statement to make. My name is Robert Wright. I am the director of the FBI. Standing behind me is the entire administrative staff of the Bureau's executive offices. We are here to state there is no investigation of former Director Leggett in process. Most of us standing before you have worked under Director Leggett for decades, and he is one of the finest men to ever serve in public office. We will address the allegations of sexual misconduct and if we determine there is any validity to those claims, we will fully prosecute under the law. Having said that, if we determine that those allegations were coerced and or part of a political strategy, we will do everything within our power to exact justice."

He and his staff left the pressroom without further words.

A news alert scrolled under the talking heads on CNN. It read: The FEC does not intend to investigate Mrs. Megan Barber's donation to Senator Tyler Leggett for United States Senate.

Saturday, October 29, 7:30 a.m.

Campaign team meeting in Gonzo's Montgomery conference room. In attendance: Ty, Val, Carlos, Susie, Gonzo and Ed.

"Good morning. We have ten days until the election. Thank you for sticking with me through the recent crap. That was one hell of a week. There's no need for you to report, Ed; the rally and fundraiser were outstanding, and we all appreciate you washing your truck."

They all laughed out loud. Ed put a smirk on his face and said, "Very funny."

"Val, how are we doing?" Ty asked.

"The October twenty-sixth survey results have been tabulated. I'll address the events of earlier this week first. We took a bad hit and dropped ten points overall, but that mostly happened among the undecideds. Those who like us held steady, but Ullman's vote got stronger against us. I used Royer and Min's AI program to run a quick tracking survey Thursday and Friday nights. The trend is very encouraging: We will be back to pre-hit numbers by Sunday night."

"Thank God," Susie said, with a giant smile. "Those bastards."

Ed clenched his fists, and said, "Yes!"

Gonzo and Carlos clapped their hands.

"Nice job, everyone. Val, please continue," Ty said.

"The undecideds are trending our way at a sixty–forty rate. By the election, my prediction is the undecided vote will rest somewhere around eight percent and who knows if they'll turn out and vote. Horner is locked at three percent of the vote and will not move. That puts us and

Ullman within the margin of error of plus-or-minus three percentage points. At forty-six percent of the vote. Everything is predicated on the hit we took this week fading, and our trend line returning to normal, which I believe it will. Let's keep pounding our message and focus the AI calls on finding those undecided voters and getting them to the polls."

"Some things never change; it always comes to getting out the vote, and our secret AI weapon will revolutionize that effort," Carlos said.

"We've got this," Susie said.

"From your lips to God's ear," Ed said.

"Our final survey will be Tuesday, November first," Val said.

"Unless there's an emergency, this will be our last Saturday meeting. Thank you all, this has been one hell of an adventure and I'm tired," Ty said.

19

Ed climbed the stairs to his Montgomery office at 8:00 a.m., Tuesday, November 1, seven days from the election, entered, and called out, "Sabina? You here?"

"No, leave me alone. We have nothing to do, we're done. Carlos, Susie and Ty have work, we're done," she answered.

Ed walked to her desk. "Yep, we're done. Just accounting and cleanup. How about after lunch we call it a day and go play video games?"

"Sounds wonderful. Susie might join us. She just has a couple ads to double-check; it's too late to buy new ads. Only Ty, Carlos and maybe Gonzo have work on Election Day. Ty will run around Alabama asking for votes until he's exhausted. Carlos will try to put out fires and triple-check the Election Day organization and Gonzo will just fill the time planning a vacation to Cuba. After the Time Zone and video, let's go shopping for Thanksgiving decorations."

"My apartment is filled with stuff. No room for Thanksgiving. Anyway, I'm going to my parents for Thanksgiving. I hate this limbo time before the election; it's a slow death," Ed said.

"You think we're going to lose?" Sabina asked.

"I don't know, we're behind and I hate not being in control."

"We did our best, Ed. This was our fifth campaign together, and probably our best work," she said.

"Only if we win. Effort doesn't feed the cat."

"You are such a Debbie Downer. Stop. These last days will be filled with hope and fear. Don't make it worse."

"As we know, the end of every campaign is terrible."

"Yes, win or lose, the day after the election it always feels like someone has died," Sabina said.

"Me? There you go again. Ms. Supreme Debbie Downer."

"It's your fault. You put me there. Do you know when Val will have the data from the last tracking survey?" she asked.

"Sometime after six tonight."

"I received one of our AI calls last night. Wow, is it real sounding. I tried to stump it, but no way. I asked it to switch to FaceTime, and boom, I was talking to someone who looked my age and could have been at college with me. I could not tell it wasn't a person."

"I also got one. Thank God, it won't put us out of business; AI can't take you out to lunch."

Ed walked into his office and began to delete icons and organize his desktop.

At 11:30, Sabina came into Ed's office holding a #6

stamped envelope; she waved it. "The postwoman just delivered this. It's addressed to Ty. Should I open it?"

"Of course," Ed said.

"I've never seen this before."

"What?" Ed asked.

"A printed Social Security check. I thought they were all auto-deposited."

"Let me see."

She handed the check to Ed. "Look at this, five hundred dollars, and there's a note. It says: 'Senator Leggett, this is all I have. I hope you win and do the right things.' Wow," he said, looking up at Sabina, "I do, too. Now let's go play video games."

Two hours later, Sabina, Susie and Ed were at the Alley Bar having lunch.

"Best hamburger in Alabama," Ed said.

"I like the wine on tap," Susie said with a laugh.

"You two going shopping?" Ed asked.

"Yes, you want to join us?" Susie asked.

"No, thank you. I'm going back to the office."

"Come on, Ed," Sabina said.

"No, I can't leave yet."

Back in his office, Ed cleaned up the back offices, vacuumed, and took the trash to the outside trash bins. Finished, he returned to his office, opened his laptop and started to play Solitaire.

Time passed very quickly. He glanced out the window

and saw it was dark out; he looked at his phone: 5:00 p.m. He called Val.

"Hi, Ed. What's up?"

"Well, how are we doing?" Ed asked.

"I should not tell you this. I have not reached Ty."

"Tell me what?" Ed asked with emotion in his voice.

"It's over. We're going to lose."

"What?"

"The hit hurt more than I thought; the independents broke to Ullman."

"We have time. What can we do?"

"Ed, it's over. They are not going to move."

"Val, I just received a woman's social security check for Ty. We are not quitting. There must be a way."

"Ed—"

"No, you stop. We are not quitting. There must be a way. Will you meet at Gonzo's office tonight at seven?"

"It won't help."

"Please."

"Okay," Val said, sounding disheartened.

At 7:00 p.m., Ed walked into Gonzo's conference room. Carlos, Gonzo, Susie and Val were sitting around the table. Ed sat next to Carlos, with his back to the window.

"Thank you all for coming. Val, would you go over the survey?" Ed asked.

"There is not much to say. We held every vote category and lost ground with independents. We are at our max with every demographic. There is no upside potential with those groups. The head-to-head is Ullman fifty-one percent, Leggett forty-six percent, and Horner three percent," Val said.

"What about attacking Ullman's vote with a different message?" Gonzo asked.

"Won't work. We've tried crime, drugs, jobs, disloyalty and betrayal. The Republicans came home to Ullman, and the Independents believed the DC hit. We are seven days out. We don't have time and even if we did, I do not know how to change it," Val said.

"There's got to be something. I'm not going to lose," Ed said.

Silence.

"What about Horner?" Ed asked.

"Ed, attacking him will not work."

"I know. What would happen if he picked up votes?" Ed asked.

"It's one for one," Val said with a matter-of-fact tone.

"What do you mean?" Susie asked.

"Every vote Horner gets comes from Ullman," Val responded.

Silence.

"Carlos, have you met Horner?" Ed asked.

"Yes."

"Do you have his cell?"

"Yes."

Carlos handed Ed his cell, Ed looked up Horner's number. Ed pulled his cell out of his back pocket and plugged in Horner's number.

"What are you doing?" Gonzo asked.

"I'm going to call Horner and ask if we can help him."

Susie and Gonzo left the room and stood in the hallway watching through the doorway. "Ed, our campaign can't do that; it's illegal," Val said.

"I did not say Leggett. I said 'us,'" Ed replied. Ed pressed call.

"Horner here."

"Mr. Horner, my name is Ed Abbott, and I work for Senator Leggett. I think you're getting screwed, and I want to know if I can help you?" Ed asked.

"You're damn right I'm getting screwed, and yes, you can help."

Carlos grabbed Ed's cell. "Mr. Horner, this is Carlos Felix. Can you meet at my office tomorrow morning at nine? I have some things to give you."

"Yes."

"I'll text my address to you when I have everything together," Carlos said.

Carlos hung up and looked at Gonzo and Susie, "We can only do this by mail. Social is out—Ullman's team would see it. Mail is the only thing that will work. And we only have one day to pull this off or the mail will arrive after the election. What's the best issue, Val," Carlos asked.

"'I'm a Democrat and the other two are not, and Ullman is a prolife fraud,'" Val said.

"How much will this cost?" Ed asked Gonzo.

"Twenty-five thousand. If we don't have to buy the list," Gonzo said.

"I'll get the twenty-five K, and deliver it to your office tomorrow morning," Ed said looking at Carlos.

"Who is going to call Tim? Carlos asked.

“Forget it, Tim will never write a prochoice democrat piece,” Ed said.

“I’ll call Wayne Thompson, he’ll do it,” Carlos said.

Ed left and went to his office to make calls.

With Ed gone, Gonzo walked over to Susie and whispered into her ear.

“Carlos, go to the back of our building; the trash needs emptying,” Gonzo said.

Carlos went outside and stood by the big metal green trash bin; Susie arrived and tossed a flash drive at the bin; it hit the side and fell to the ground. Carlos picked it up. A yellow sticky note was attached it read: *Three hundred thousand high-propensity Democrat voters, complete address mailing list. US Post Office-ready.*

Back in his office, Ed called Brent Bonner of Outdoor Television at his DC home. “Trent, this is Ed Abbott. Sorry to call you so late. For Leggett to win, the Democrat candidate needs help getting his message out, and I need you to make a donation to Horner for US Senate, to help pay for that mailing.”

“You’re helping a Democrat so your Independent candidate can win?” Brent asked.

“Yes.”

“You’re sure this is legal?”

“Yes.”

“Okay. I’ll Zelle the donation into Horner’s account in the morning. Get me the instructions and campaign info.”

“Thanks, Trent.”

Ed called Paul, Sikh leader Mr. Bains, Mrs. Becken at her Century City condo, Mr. Noble, and ten other contributors telling them all the same story. All said yes.

Finished, Ed called Carlos. "I've raised twenty-one-K. It will be in Horner's account by ten tomorrow morning. I need his campaign Zelle account info and campaign ID numbers and the treasurer's name. Send me that stuff tonight and I want to meet Horner at your office tomorrow at nine to thank him for letting us help. Who's going to write the Horner mail piece."

"Wayne Thompson," Carlos said.

"Wayne said yes? He's a Christian conservative. How's he going to write a pro-choice, mail piece?"

"Yep, he's all that and when I explained what we're doing, he said absolutely; the voters need to hear the truth."

Ed walked into Carlos's Montgomery office the next morning and standing by Carlos's desk was a man dressed in stained blue jeans, dirty cowboy boots, and a blue, long-sleeved work shirt. He looked scruffy, with a short beard and salt-and-pepper hair.

"Mr. Horner, this is Ed Abbott," Carlos said.

"Great, where's the money?" he asked.

"I need your campaign Zelle number," Ed said.

"Here." Horner handed Ed a business card.

"Thank you," Ed said. He left the room and sent a text with the email address and cell phone number to the group supporting Horner. Finished, he went back to his office.

Ed called Carlos November 2. "Did we make it?"

"Yes, God bless the post office for making a mistake. Horner did not have enough money to pay the bulk rate. They sent it out anyway. Lucky us!"

"You think this will work?"

"Hail Mary. Who knows."

Tuesday, November 8, 2039
Alabama United States Senate Special Election.

Jeffery Ullman—Independent
Tyler Leggett—Incumbent—independent
Jack Horner—Democrat.

Josh delivered Ty to the Montgomery polling place at 7:00 a.m. Ty was dressed in a white, long-sleeved shirt, tan Armani slacks, and black Paloma Venetian loafers and carrying a Bobby Jones dark-blue sport coat.

Val met him at the curb. "Man, do you look good."

"I wanted to look my best. This could be the last time anyone sees me."

"Did you say your Hail Marys?"

"A hundred times."

Ty looked toward the polling station; the walkway to the entrance was lined with television cameras and reporters holding their cell phones at the ready.

"Wow, this is quite a show," Ty said.

"We'll know what Ullman's camp believes by the first question. Let's go," Val said.

Ty smiled and walked toward the assembled gauntlet.

"Senator Leggett! Senator Leggett!" a reporter screamed. Ty stopped and looked at her. "Do you think your campaign will overcome the five-point deficit you're facing, and will you return to Washington after the election?"

"Good morning," he said with a warm smile. "I am very excited about today. We ran a tremendous campaign for the United States Senate, and we united thousands of organizations and people around one thought: To lead Alabama to greater prosperity."

"Senator," another reporter screamed, "if you lose today, what are your plans?"

He put a grin on his face. "We're not going to lose. David will defeat Goliath, and Alabama will make history today."

He continued along the walkway into the polling station to the sounds of yelling voices. After he finished voting, he left the building to discover it was empty of people and television cameras.

He came up to Val with a laugh. "Where'd they all go?"

"Ullman announced he'd vote at seven forty-five and off they ran."

"Games to the end." Ty shook his head. "Now what do we do?"

"It could be a long day. Let's get something to eat, go back to your place, watch a movie, take a nap, and when the polls close, go over to Central and watch the results." Val said.

"There's nothing else for us to do?"

"The AI calls are getting people to the polls; the campaign staff is doing the GOTV. Carlos has people at every polling station with exit questions, and a team is at the Alabama secretary of state's office hoping to hear the vote tally before it goes public. It's in the voters' hands. Ty, we're done."

"What do you think?" Ty asked with a concerned look.

"We lose with dignity," Val said.

"Really?"

"No. We're going to shock the hell out of them," Val said.

Josh, Val and Ty arrived at Ty's place just in time to turn on the television and watched Jeffery Ullman arrive at his polling station. He drove up in a black stretch limousine. It parked for five minutes, without any sign or movement.

"Can you feel the tension building?" Val sneered, with a laugh.

The car door swung open and out stepped Jeffery Ullman to the sound of screaming and cheering fans, chanting his last name, "Ullman, Ullman, Ullman!"

Jeffery was wearing his cowboy uniform: new, unwashed blue jeans, silver belt buckle, custom snakeskin Western boots, a plaid flannel long-sleeved work shirt and his fur cowboy hat on his head.

He walked past the throng of supporters, grinning and

matching high-fives. He strutted directly to the Fox News camera.

The reporter was prepared and placed the handheld microphone just under Jeffery's chin. "Senator, when you win tonight, what are you going to do on your first day in Washington?"

Jeffery put a pensive look on this face. "Well, young lady, my daddy taught me never to count your chickens before they laid."

"The polls have you winning by five points. Has your team prepared you for that landslide victory? Will that momentum lift you into a Senate leadership position?" she asked, unaware it was all about seniority.

"I have spoken to both leaders of the Senate, and they will welcome me with open arms," he said.

Ty said, "Screen off," and the television went dark. "There's only so much I can take. Who wants breakfast? I make a mean omelet."

Two hours later, after watching *Dirty Harry*, Val said, "It's almost time to drive to Birmingham to see the campaign staff and thank them."

"Okay. Any chance a TV camera will be there?" Ty asked.

"I doubt it, they've written us off. But we've got to try, and the team up there deserves a visit," Val said.

They got into the car. Josh was driving, Ty was in the passenger seat and Val was in the back, sitting behind Ty.

"You ready for an hour and a half of Motown?" Ty asked.

"Only if you start with Aretha's 'I Say a Little Prayer'

and follow that with Otis's 'Sittin' on the Dock of the Bay,'" Josh said.

They arrived at the Birmingham headquarters at noon. The small, two-room storefront was filled with young people and seniors making telephone calls.

Ty walked in and the room went silent, then they started to cheer. Ty smiled and looked at Josh. "That makes me feel good."

Ty stepped forward and waited a moment for the room to quiet down. "I'm here to say thank you for trying so hard to make a difference in Alabama. And all of you are invited to attend tonight's victory—" Cheers erupted. Ty laughed at the great feeling in his chest. "If you need a ride to the Central Restaurant celebration tonight, call Carlos and he'll arrange it. I want each one of you to know when we win tonight, it's your victory."

Cheers and clapping.

"Thank you, and I look forward to seeing everyone tonight," Ty said as he turned and left for the car.

He, Val and Josh got into the car.

"What next?" Ty asked.

"Back to the Montgomery headquarters after stopping at every small town on the way. Then we go to Gonzo's office for a final update; your place to change, then at six forty-five off to Central," Val said.

"Okay, who wants to listen to a little country?" Ty asked.

"Only if you start with 'Different Man' by Kane Brown and Shelton," Josh said.

As they passed Clanton, Alabama, Val called Carlos.

"Hey, Val, what's up?" Carlos asked.

"That's my question to you."

"Just the same old and some new dirty tricks. We stopped a bus full of people going from one polling station to another to vote. No big deal. We're all good," Carlos said.

"Ty wants to skip the election night briefing at Gonzo's, so let's meet at Central at six forty-five. We have a private room set up to watch the election."

"I won't get there until the polls close and the returns are coming in. But I'll be there regardless," Carlos said.

Election night, at Central Restaurant. The polls are still open, and Ty, Val, Carlos, Susie, Sabina, Gonzo, Tim, Gary and Ed were in the private room. Rick States was studying his laptop screen, with channel WSFA 12 on the television in the background.

Mario entered the room and walked up to Ty. "Senator, a Pastor Neal and about twenty other people would like to join you. May I send them up?"

"Absolutely," Ty said.

Five minutes later, Steven and his fellow AME pastors walked into the room, along with the tribal leaders, including Stephanie Bright.

They greeted Ty, who shook everyone's hand, saying, "I am honored that you have graced me by attending this celebration."

"We would not have missed this. It's not often one gets to witness the birth of greatness," Chickasaw Chief Calbent said.

Ty smiled. "Thank you for those kind words and all you have done for me." Ty's face showed the emotion he felt for the first time.

"The polls just closed—here we go," Val said.

"Okay, my friends, let's go downstairs and join our other friends," Ty said.

Everyone joined Ty and went down to the main dining room. The restaurant was half filled and pensive. The room buzzed with excitement when Ty entered. Groups of people came up to him and wished him luck. To his surprise, State Senator Peterson came up.

"Ty, you ran a tremendous campaign, regardless of the outcome. You overcame every obstacle and attack they threw at you. From the White House, US Senate, to Alabama powerbrokers, you and your team stood tall," he said.

"Thank you for being a stand-up man," Ty said, shaking Senator Peterson's hand.

They were joined by Senator Simmons. "Ty, I just stopped by to wish you luck and I'm sure you'll pull out a win," he said with an unsure smile.

"Thank you, John, for everything you did to finance this campaign, I will never forget your unwavering support. Thank you."

Simmons smiled and left the restaurant.

8:00 p.m.: The first results started trickling in; CNN too close to call.

8:30 p.m.: ABC, too close to call.

9:00 p.m.: FOX National broadcast team announced, "There appears to be a significant development in the Alabama United States Senate special election. A major upset seems to be in the making. Incumbent United States Senator Tyler Leggett, who was appointed earlier this year by the Alabama governor to fill the remaining term of Senate seat vacated by the death of Senator Tubber. Fox News is reporting this race is still too close to call; however, with ten percent of the vote counted, Senator Leggett is leading his closest challenger, State Senator Jeffery Ullman by nineteen points. This is a shocking turnaround. Just last week, State Senator Ullman was leading the race by six percentage points. And it was believed the terrible accusations levied at Senator Leggett had derailed his campaign." She looked at her cohost with an expression of surprise.

Ty and Ed stopped as did almost everyone at Central Restaurant.

"This election has the making of a historic turnaround. Let's go live to Montgomery, Alabama, and Senator Ullman's victory party at the Renaissance Hotel," she said.

The TV cameras lights suddenly filled the Alabama ballroom showing a stunned crowd in the background.

The reporter stepped up to Ullman, holding a microphone and asked, "Senator Ullman, can you explain your opponent's sudden rise?"

"These early returns are coming in from the most rural areas in the state. Senator Leggett is strong there. We expect a significant change when the votes from Birmingham and the other big cities are counted," Ullman said.

Standing next to Ullman was a nondescript man dressed in blue jeans and a long-sleeved white shirt. Ed recognized him. "That guy next to Ullman? That's Paul Anctil, his campaign consultant."

In the background Senator Simmons passed behind Ullman.

Ty smiled and thought, *Covering his bets.*

Carlos and Gonzo joined Ed, Ty and Val to watch.

The camera was still recording when Paul Anctil turned to face Ullman. "How's Horner getting his votes?" he asked with a shocked look on his face.

Ty turned to Ed. "Oh my God, it worked. Val told me what you did," he said with a broad grin on his face.

The celebration was on:

Final vote: Leggett 52%, Ullman 33%, Horner 15%.

Josh arrived at Ty's Montgomery home at 5:00 a.m., Wednesday, November 9, to take him to the airport and his 6:30 a.m. flight to Washington, DC.

He parked in the driveway and texted Ty he'd arrived. Five minutes later, Ty walked out, put his luggage in the trunk and got into the car.

"Good morning," Ty said.

"Good morning to you. What's the plan, Senator?"

"Why so formal?" Ty asked.

"Well ..."

"Well, nothing. It's Ty now and forever."

"Okay." He smiled. "What's the plan?"

"Thank my DC staff, see Senator Joseph and most importantly, thank my friends at the Bureau; they saved us. And lastly, meet with the president."

"Why do you want to meet him? He tried to screw you?"

"That wasn't personal. And I want to tell him something important."

"How long will you be in DC?"

"I don't know. I hope to join Megan Barber and her daughters for Thanksgiving. The lease on the Montgomery house expires on December fifteen, which happens to be the last day of Senate business. I have my DC condo, of course. I want to go someplace warm and quiet to relax, though ... which might be difficult since I hope to introduce some legislation in January."

Silence.

"Josh, it's been less than a year, but it feels like a lifetime. At times I felt it would never end, and now that it's over, I feel lost and sad, like a friend has died." He shook his head slowly from side to side.

"I thought I'd never say this or even think it; I've come to love Alabama and the people in it, and when this is all done, I'll move to Fairhope, fish and disappear."

"That sounds like a good plan." Josh smiled. "I've enjoyed my time with you, and I wish you the best of luck in that horrible place."

"Thank you. I feel the same. I hope you and Miss Jonsson make a great life together in Atmore."

"Atmore, why Atmore?"

"She loves being a cop, and Atmore is her home. I'd like to thank her for taking you off my hands. Text me her contact information."

Josh laughed.

"Girl does make the rules."

"As she should."

They arrived at the airport. Ty got out, as did Josh.

"Aren't we a little early for your flight?"

"I want to thank Darrel."

Josh smiled and nodded.

They shook hands goodbye.

At nine-thirty that morning, Ty walked into his Hart office to the sudden cheers and clapping by his staff.

"Thank you all very much. The last time I was here it was doubtful I'd return as a senator. Thank you for standing with me," Ty said, grinning; he shook everyone's hand.

He walked into his private office and sat behind the desk, leaned back, smiled, thinking, *I did it.* A warm sense of relief and accomplishment filled his chest.

He picked up his cell phone and called the president's Chief of Staff, Eric Berg.

"Hello, Senator," Eric said.

"How you are doing, Eric?"

"Not anywhere near as good as you. Congratulations. What a marvelous campaign! I look forward to hearing how you pulled it off."

"How about next week? A drink at the Circa at Foggy Bottom?"

"Great, we'll coordinate next week. How can I help you?"

"I'd like to see the president tonight."

"That'll be tight. Let me look. I've got six-fifteen to six-thirty. But I don't know—"

"I'll be on time," Ty interrupted.

At 5:00 p.m. that same evening, Ty left his office and walked over to the Russel Building and Senator Joseph's office.

"He in?" Ty asked the receptionist.

She pressed the intercom and picked up the telephone. "Senator Leggett is here, and he would like to see you," she said.

Momentary silence.

"Please go in, and Senator, congratulations. Everyone in this office was rooting for you," she said with a bright smile.

"Thank you."

Senator Joseph was standing in front of his desk when Ty came into the room. He put a full smile on his face and stepped forward to shake Ty's hand.

"Wow, wow. What a victory. You're now a legend."

Ty laughed. "Legend or not, thank you for standing with me and everything you did; your friendship means everything. *Thank you,*" Ty said, feeling overcome by emotion.

"My pleasure. You deserved to be first. Are you going to the floor tomorrow? There're a lot of new best friends who can't wait to slap your back and profess their faith," Joseph said, almost giggling.

"You said that last year."

"I know this place."

"I'm sorry to ask for a favor."

"What are you thinking?" Joseph asked.

"I have the number one hundred parking spot, which says everything about my legislative prospects. I won't live long enough to effect positive change. So, I must rely on you to join my crusade and help provoke a conversation. As chairman of the Commerce, Science and Transportation committee, can you get me a seat on your committee?"

"I'll see what I can do, if possible, yes. Why do you want to be on that committee?"

"I want to submit legislation to make future development and testing of AI implants the same as nuclear weapons— forbidden."

"That genie is loose; it's needed. But wow, that'll be a massive fight," Joseph said.

"So was atomic testing," Ty said.

Silence.

"Joseph, there's no gray on that issue. We remain human or we don't. There's no halfway. As the joke punchline reads, 'I'm a little bit pregnant.' No, it's all or nothing. There's no benefit or cure that justifies the loss of our humanity."

"You're not exactly starting small."

"The next two are just as important."

"Do I need to sit?"

"No," Ty said with a laugh. "I've got a meeting with the president and can't stay much longer. I want to announce the other two efforts in January, and I hope you'll join me in crafting a successful strategy."

"Okay, go on," Joseph said, sounding cautious.

"The first is simple, every US African American presently over retirement age will, retroactively, receive the maximum social security benefits. A counterbalance to lost economic opportunity."

"Okay. That's a wow," Joseph said.

"Next, every Indigenous American tribe will be gifted all BLM land owned by the federal government and the Bureau of Indian Affairs will manage the transition, then be dissolved."

"That one might be difficult." He laughed. "You know how this place hates shrinking government."

Ty laughed.

"Jesus, Ty, talk about coming in with a bang." He grinned. Then with a thoughtful look. "You're one and done, aren't you?"

"You in?" Ty asked.

Silence.

"You get the black caucus to agree a hundred percent in writing ... I'm in," Joseph said.

"I can do that," Ty said.

"Okay you pull that off, I'll set up and join you at a meeting with Sue Le Levier. She chairs the Committee of Indian Affairs and sits on the Energy and Natural Resources Committee."

"Thank you." Ty reached out his hand, and they shook on the deal.

"Ty, you're going to need more than the Black Caucus. You'll need a lot of outside help for this to work."

"That's covered. The AME and the leaders of the Indigenous tribes will all be here in January. That's a guarantee. This has been a long time coming," Ty said with a strong, confident voice.

"Thank you again." Ty said in a soft voice, as he focused on Joseph's eyes.

Joseph smiled.

Ty glanced at his watch.

"I've got to go. I can't be late for the president," he said with a wry smile.

"You going to tell him about—?"

"No." Ty interrupted with a mischievous smile and happy eyes. "There's something else he needs to know, and afterward, I believe he'll be my best friend for life."

At 6:10 p.m., Ty walked into the Oval Office reception room. Mrs. Oland was sitting at her desk; she glanced at her desk clock. "Senator Tyler Leggett, this is impressive! You're on time," she said with a twinkle in her eye. "I am very glad to see you. Congratulations on your victory. Wow." She was beaming.

A moment later a green light flashed on her desk intercom phone. "Senator Leggett, you can go in; he's ready."

Ty opened the door, took a quick breath, and smelled the President's Clive Christian No. 1 perfume. Ty smiled and thought, *If I could only afford it.*

He stepped into the Oval Office, feeling happy. In twenty years of visiting the Oval, this was the first time he did not feel pressure, and he had a sense of coming home.

Standing in front of his desk, facing the door was the

President of the United States Ralph Rodda in all his glory. He was wearing a dark-blue, hand-brushed wool suit jacket and slacks, an "optical white" dress shirt with a Brioni ruby silk tie.

"Ty Leggett, *Senator* Ty Leggett, congratulations. You did it—I could not be prouder. I thought you were nuts. But you did it. Wow, wonderful. You beat them all. Our prayers were answered; you are now in the club." He almost raced toward Ty, reaching out his right hand; Ty grasped it and they shook.

Ty smiled, enjoying the presentation. "Thank you. I had lots of help."

"This is wonderful. I told everyone around this place to do all they could to bring you back home. I am so happy to see you. How can I help? Anything, you deserve it. Just ask."

"Mr. President, first, thank you for seeing me on such short notice, and for everything you did for my campaign."

"Ty, it was nothing. You deserved this victory, and I am honored to have helped. It wasn't much but it was all I could do," Rodda said, grinning.

Ty smiled, thinking, *The Chute Bridge and hunting trip was special.*

"The last time I was here in the Oval Office, I told you, upon my appointment, I would pick up the crap on my desk and go to Alabama?"

"Yes sir. Yes sir, I remember every word; it was great to hear," Rodda said, beaming, almost bouncing on his toes. "You are a man of your word; a great man and you're going to make Alabama proud, and America is fortunate to have you in the Senate."

Ty stood, watching, absorbing each word, enjoying the moment, feeling happy he'd made it back to Washington.

"Yes, Mr. President, I believe we'll have a tremendous working relationship."

"Yes sir, I believe we will, and I hope, once you get organized, you'll reconsider your party affiliation."

"That is something to consider."

"I hope you do. I hope you do. I'd love to be on the same team."

"Mr. President, there is something you must know."

"Tell me, tell me more wonderful news," he said, grinning, lifting his heels, twitching his eyebrows.

Ty hesitated, thinking, *Ed Abbott.*

"The crap on my desk."

"Yes, yes."

"Was your file," he said with a deadpan expression.

Ralph gasped, his jaw dropped, and his eyes popped open.

"Good night, Mr. President." Ty turned and left the White House with a grin.

ALSO BY JAMES BARRETT GRUBBS

John Barber: A Tale of Two Times

John Barber: San Francisco

No Safe Border

ABOUT THE AUTHOR

James Barrett Grubbs has lived in Long Beach California with the love of his life for the past twenty-five years. They have three grown children.

Mr. Grubbs competed internationally in the 470-Snipe sailing classes. He qualified for the Olympic trials and won several Olympic class regattas. He skippered and won his first national championship at nineteen and his last at forty-nine.

Mr. Grubbs has a United States Patent and has written four novels.

https://jamesbarrettbrubbs.com

www.ingramcontent.com/pod-product-compliance
Lightning Source LLC
Chambersburg PA
CBHW020555310726
48979CB00008B/1227/J

* 9 7 9 8 9 8 9 3 0 2 2 7 7 *